Liz

F. G. _xoxo_

KEAGAN

THIS IS OUR LIFE SERIES
F.G. ADAMS

Aaliyah xo

Cover Design:
LJ Anderson with Mayhem Cover Creations

Photography:
Reggie Deanching with RplusMphoto

Model:
Alfie Gordillo

Interior Design & Editing:
Daryl Banner

Dedicated to all the families

who are searching for a loved one who is lost.

Adult or child, the pain is the same.

CONTENTS

PROLOGUE

Ominous black clouds loom over the horizon. The sky is darker than normal for this time of the afternoon. I survey the surrounding cliffs and open space through the standard issue binoculars in front of me. A lightning bolt streaks across the rolling clouds and thunder erupts somewhere close by. In the distance the mountain peaks grant an eerie painting between the landscape of assorted trees, plants, and clouds.

The uncommonness of the weather isn't easing the already tense group.

The entire team is on alert. When a loud crash of thunder echoes through the terrain, not one body shifts or twitches, all remaining frozen in their spot, etched into the scenery and only visible by the whites of their eyes.

We are scoping out another terrorist threat, a secluded hideout somewhere inside the enormous mountain before us. We need to locate an entry point and collect as much intel as possible without being detected. A ghost mission. In and out.

An uneasiness washes over me and we continue on the trail before us. Sweat drips from my jaw like a leaky faucet as I make my way. The path is thick with underbrush and low floating tree limbs that part for the caravan of ten soldiers. The embankment up ahead shields so many blind spots. Dread filters into my psyche. We will have to climb it, and the vulnerable position is not welcomed by anyone.

I hold my left fist up, halting our progress, and search the perimeter once again. By all outward appearances, nothing has been disturbed. The moss on the rocks show no imprints. Years of fallen debris accumulates at the bottom of the giant peak, so we make our way upward, hugging the shadows offered by the foliage. I signal forward progress.

We've been trekking on foot from the drop zone for almost eighteen hours, only stopping for a few minutes to refuel, rehydrate, and rest. Body fatigue isn't even a part of my thoughts at the moment. I'm focused on each footstep and the sounds around us. A bird chirps and the cadence of insects calm me, signs from nature alerting me of no disturbance.

When we reach the embankment I look at Ollie and Lukas flanking me. Lukas lifts his finger to his nose and Ollie's "go" signal is an uplifted hand to his earlobe. Good. Neither one suspects any danger. We are good to go.

I signal to Carlito and Jimbo to go before us. Both are avid rock climbers. They can scale the side of any natural rock formation with an uncanny talent at knowing what path to use with no previous knowledge of the site, securing a pathway on smooth rock for us to follow. They make their way toward the front of our group and start finding the footholds in the smooth rock for us to climb. The first point is covered by a spider's web and easily deflected.

We've climbed two-thirds of the way when Jimbo falters as he reaches for his next hold. Earth tumbles to the ground below. Everyone goes utterly still, listening to the disruption of rock and dirt falling below. After several heartpounding moments of hanging off the side of the ledge, we begin again. Proceeding up to the small landing, only a couple yards away. One foothold to the next.

I grip the hand that's being offered and help pull myself up. Looking down at the valley we've left behind two football fields below, I marvel at the beauty of this dismal place. Why so much pain and suffering is concentrated into this small area, I'll never know. Maybe it's been cursed since the beginning of time.

Moving forward to the front of the procession, I stop midway when a faraway noise enters our sphere. Fucking hell! From up above, a tail of smoke follows in slow motion as the bazooka's ammunition descends. The soldiers' bodies implode in front of me. Limbs fly. A booted leg lands in front of me minus the rest of the soldier. I react slowly. Shock lingers.

Another bomb explodes and I'm thrown from my stoic position. I land face down with a heavy weight on my back. I can't move. The breath is knocked from my lungs. I'm immobile. A warm moisture drips on my face. I heave and try to extend my arms, lifting, then sagging once to the ground.

I'm not sure how much later I wake. The heaviness from earlier is still on my back. I can't move. I struggle with the weight trying to move back and forth, up and down. What's holding me down? The weight suffocates my already fatigued body.

I find my footing and with one final push, I jarr the weight bearing down on me and roll sideways. Gasping for air, I roll forward and land on my knees and elbows. Praying to God for strength, I extend my elbows and push into a sitting position and take in my surroundings.

"*Oh God!*"

Jimbo's severed head is lying to the right of me, one of his eyeballs bulging from the socket. The rest of him is laying where I was only moments before. He saved my life. I stumble to my feet, silently screaming from the horror surrounding me.

Lukas is sprawled out on his stomach feet away from me. I rush to his side. His breathing is slow when I roll him onto his back. His eyes are closed. I shake him and his eyes slowly open.

"Don't leave me here, Luc!"

"Not going anywhere, man," he mumbles, licking his lips. "I've got to steal your angel from home you keep talking about all the time."

"You're delirious, dude. I never said she was mine."

"Yes. You did. Every day now for, damn ... I don't know how many years."

Startled as a hand grabs my shoulder, I rotate with my beretta drawn and aim it at the new target.

"Ollie, man, shit. Don't sneak up on a brother like that."

"I've been yelling at your ass for the last five minutes. Probably what woke little man, here," he says, grimacing as he moves to Luc's other side.

"You're bleeding really bad, Luc."

He looks lower and sighs.

"You're losing a lot of blood and we don't know how long it will be before help arrives. We've got to tourniquet your leg or we could lose you," I pant.

"You might lose your leg," Ollie says, pulling his belt from around his waist.

"I'll still have my pretty face for the ladies, so y'all don't stand a chance," Lukas halfway jokes.

"Always the ladies' man," Ollie chides.

"Yep. I'll be six feet under before I give that title up."

"Or the right woman will find you and you'll be a goner."

"Never gonna happen. I'm a free roaming bull." He laughs and his eyes glass over in pain.

"One. Two. Three."

I tighten the belt. The piercing sound of his cries echo in my mind, shattering my calm façade.

"I've canvassed the area. No one else made it. I was thrown back behind the rock ledge. The blast knocked the air from my lungs, but I'm good to go,

Keagan. We need to make it back down and to our rendezvous with the helo. You look rough, too. Where's the blood coming from?"

"I'm fine. Worry about Luc."

A twig snaps nearby and Ollie's gaze rivets to a nearby opening. Two masked soldiers appear and walk closer to the three of us. My gun is by my side but I'm too late again. One man aims and fires off a shot. The impact from the bullet throws Ollie backwards and he doesn't move.

"Fucktards, don't come any closer," I threaten, aiming the gun at them.

Laughing at my comment, the larger, bulkier of the two separates. "Who's going to stop us? You?"

I'm momentarily shocked. He's altering his voice. *Why*?

"I will if that's what I have to do."

"You're in no position to threaten us. You should have stayed in your homeland. Never left."

I find my bearings and reply, "And you shouldn't have killed innocent Americans."

"They deserved what happened. My god blessed the sacrifice. As he blesses yours."

"You are one mental asshole. Ain't never gonna happen. I'll make sure you die."

"Such a tough one, laying on the ground bleeding. Trying to protect your fallen comrades," he chuckles.

"Enough!" shouts the other man standing with his gun drawn. "I don't have time to listen to your bullshit rhetoric. Why are you here?"

I remain silent, knowing that if my men are alert, they will follow my lead. Pain immediately follows as a bullet enters my gut.

"Why are you here?"

I fall forward and cover Lukas's body. He's already wounded.

Another bullet collides with my back and I wince from the excruciating pain.

"Why are you here?"

Click. Click. Click. Click. The guns power off, finding a mark over and over. I pray Ollie and Lukas are not hit, again.

I've almost lost consciousness as a hand grips my hair and retches my head backwards.

"You will die. Just as the others they've sent. No one can stop me. Know who sent you to your maker. I am Mustaff, and your country will bow down to me and all that is mine ..."

"NOOOOOOOOOOOOO!" I scream.

Sweat is pouring off my temples, rolling down my jawline to my neck.

"Keagan! Man! Keagan!"

Someone is shaking me. The darkness surrounding me begins to lift. I'm thrashing under a strong hold. Am I tied down, now? I squint to open my eyes, cracking them slowly until I've adjusted to the light streaming in.

I lie motionless when I see Ollie and Lukas

standing on each side of me, restraining me by holding my shoulders and arms down.

"You awake now?" Ollie asks.

"Fuck. You wouldn't wake up, Keagan," Lukas exhales.

I shake my head, unable to answer. I'm embarrassed and mad because I have no control over the nightmares plaguing me. Turning, I look towards the window and see the light begin to overpower the darkness. I hate the night; that's when the nightmares return and I have to remember.

"Yeah. I'm good."

I close my eyes and breath. The pain radiating from my back is a staunch reminder of what happened exactly one year, three months, five days ago. I won't ever be able to forget. The memories haunt me and the pain reminds me. I'll never be normal again.

CHAPTER 1
KEAGAN

The first day I met Jocelyn Blackwood was my first day of high school as a senior and I didn't know a soul. My parents served in the military and we moved so many times, I lost count. We moved to Lakeview, Florida that summer when my pop received new orders. That was me, a military brat, all my life.

I walked into the first class and was greeted by stares. New kid on the block. I didn't stop until I reached the back corner and slid into the chair. Glancing around, my stare returned to the door when a group of kids made their way in and took their seats in the chairs next to me.

"Hey dude, you new to the area?" the biggest one of the group of guys asked.

I shrug. "My family moved here in July."

"What's your name?" he inquired.

"Keagan."

He smiled and saluted me. "I'm Bo, and that's David. He's a transplant, too. I've lived here all my life and David moved here last spring. This place is cliquish and if you weren't born here, it's hard to make friends. So stick with us and we'll show you the ropes."

We were interrupted when the door opened and laughing echoed in the room. I looked up and saw her. She was taller than the girl walking beside her, but you could see the similarities. They are related.

She's *aingeal*—an angel. And I wanted to know who she was.

"That's the Blackwood sisters. They're off-limits, so don't even waste your time. Totally out of your league, dude," Bo commented when he noticed me staring.

David nods and added, "Their family owns most of the town. Her pop has a big ranch near Pond Creek. Couple of guys got busted out there a few weeks back and he tackled 'em and called the cops. They were trying to sneak in and meet with Fallyn. She's the shorter one."

I continued to stare. "Who's the other one? What's her name?"

"Jocelyn. She's really shy and doesn't talk to anybody but her sister. She comes to school, cheers, and goes home. That's about it."

"Why's that?"

"Not sure. She keeps to herself."

Our conversation ended when the bell rang. The teacher stood and began the lesson. I wanted to know more about the *aingeal* named Jocelyn. That was the day I met her and it changed my life forever.

A week later, I was standing in line waiting to get my shoes at the local bowling alley. My brother Wade talked me into bringing him on that day. I hadn't stopped thinking of Jocelyn Blackwood. She consumed my thoughts too much. I glanced around the alley, looking for something to take my mind off of her. The music was blaring as the lights flicked different colors to the beat.

I had hoped by coming here we'd meet some new friends and a few girls to help take my mind off of her. I was probably the youngest in my grade. Most guys had been driving for two years and I had just got my license in the spring. My momma said I'd be a late bloomer, but at the time, I was a seventeen-year-old with raging hormones and all I could think about was, well, girls, girls, girls.

That's when I saw her standing there through the cut-out window in the wall handing out shoes.

The timid slip of a girl had sandy blonde naturally curly hair that sat just above her shoulders. Her hair was hanging loosely in her face, but I got a glimpse of the most beautiful pair of emerald green eyes. I couldn't breathe. *M'aingeal*. My Angel.

My brother nudged me forward, but all I could do was stare.

That's when I heard her say, "What size?"

The sound of her voice did funny things to my insides. My brother bumped me again, slightly laughing, when he gave her his shoes and size.

When I finally mobilized myself, I reached the counter with my shoes in hand and brushed against her fingers for a brief moment. The electricity bolted from her into me and I instantly wanted to touch her again. She smiled at me as if she knew what I was thinking. She was the cutest little thing I'd ever laid eyes on.

She asked again, "What size?"

I then mustered up the courage to speak in a quick breath, "Ten and a half."

She disappeared behind the counter and came back a few moments later with my bowling shoes. I didn't want to leave, but seeing as there were more people waiting, I left the counter. As I walked away, I mumbled to myself, "I'm going to marry that girl one day." She's *M'aingeal*.

During midterm exams, I was amazed at the performance Jocelyn gave Mr. Manfurd, our Spanish teacher. I didn't even have to say a word; she took care of everything. And the best part of all, her pop would not find out, which seemed like a big deal to her, always. And this girl had me wrapped around her finger, even if we're just friends. I smiled my biggest smile. She was amazing. Everything about her was simply fantastic. I wished she could see herself the way I did.

After leaving Mr. Manfurd's class, I had a moment to talk to Jocelyn. "Thanks, Jo," I said. *Wow that was deep, Keagan!*

Since the night we went out to Vino's and got to know each other, I became her not-boyfriend. She'd tried to set me up with several of her friends, never even considering the little messages I'd been hinting to her here and there. That's alright. I was a patient guy; I could wait, and I knew she'd be worth it.

Although, it's not just her I had to contend with. There was Mr. Blackwood, since she couldn't date yet. I had a few conversations with him in Farm Ed. He was a tough nut to crack, but I liked puzzles, so I'd figure him out.

Jocelyn stopped in her tracks and peered up at me with those gorgeous green eyes. It's like she could see right into my soul. I wonder what she saw.

"I'm glad I could help us both out. We did not need the trouble, Keagan. After all, you were trying to help me. I couldn't let you take the fall for something that was mostly my fault! I appreciate you and your friendship too much, Keagan. High school wouldn't be the same without you."

I watched as her lips formed the words. I heard her voice, but I couldn't reply. Those pouty lips needed to be licked and sucked. Damn, I needed to get laid. I mustered up my control and told her what I thought she'd want to hear: "Ditto, Jo. I feel the same."

We continued down the noisy hallway, weaving in and out of the hordes of high schoolers on their way to class. I followed tightly beside Jocelyn so I didn't lose her in the crowd. I enjoyed our talks and time together. The relationship we had commissioned was uncomplicated and effortless.

We shared two classes: Art and Spanish. They became my favorite classes of the day, aside from lunch, when I got to see her too. We'd sit and talk with all our friends. I actually got to spend a little more one-on-one time with her without much distraction.

"Thanks for walking with me, Keagan. I'll catch you later. Hey, don't forget to say hello to your pop for me," Jo called over her shoulder as she entered the door of her next class.

Jocelyn had met my parents at the homecoming game. They adored her. She really took to my pop like a bee to honey. But what's not to like, really? He's an awesome pop, even if he is mine. He served his country, took care of what belongs to him, and I'm better for it. I respected the hell out of my pop. She said that I reminded her of him.

I remember that night they met. Jo was cheering and when the game ended, my pop walked right up to her and introduced himself.

Reaching out his hands and pressing Jo's between his, my pop said, "Hey there, pretty girl. You must be Jocelyn Blackwood. Buddy Fontneau. We've heard so much about you, Boo. And some of it didn't do you justice at all." Looking my way and then back at her, he said, "Keagan, you didn't say she was a ravin' beauty."

Jo blushed and smiled so hard, I thought her cheeks would freeze in place. That's my pop. He's smooth with the ladies and his Southern Cajun charm doesn't hurt, either. I hoped to become half the man he was one day.

Refocusing, I strolled down the emptying hallway to my next class. English was never my favorite subject. I walked into the room and found my seat. I nodded my hellos to the guys and eyed a few girls who gave me those fuck-me eyes. One in particular caught my attention: Darcy. She was easy on the eyes and easy every other way, too. I'd had her a few times. Been there done that. Yet with every single person I fucked, I found myself comparing them to Jocelyn, and we'd never even held hands.

She fascinated me. I was intrigued by how beautiful inside and out Jo was: very humble, meek, but at the same time tenacious. I liked everything about her. She'd dug her claws in without knowing and I just didn't care if they ever came out. She always kept me at arm's reach. I understood why, but this was high school, a time to play the field, have fun, and sample as much as possible. And that's what I did. Maybe one day, I could have a taste of Jocelyn Blackwood. Then again, maybe not. Either way, just being around her filled my life with the sun and warmth she offered everyone she touched. Jo was unlike the other girls that littered the halls of this school. She was my best friend, and it was enough for me.

After Christmas break, everything went to shit. Jocelyn began to slide deeper and deeper into a hole of her own making when her sister Fallyn left school and her life. I'd tried over and over to garner her attention again—the girl I knew, just one more time—but it didn't happen. Jo still wouldn't even acknowledge me. She'd been walking around school for a few months in a daze. Her movements were robotic. Her light had vanished and along with it was the girl I fell hard for. She'd go to class, do her work, and then leave. She even quit the cheer team, something she loved to do. It was day in, day out. I thought we were friends, but she'd shut me down every attempt I made to talk to her.

The last time I'd tried, I searched her out at lunchtime. She was sitting under the tree tucked into a corner of the courtyard, the spot she'd taken up since Fallyn disappeared. She'd be picking at her lunch and staring aimlessly into the sky. I often wondered, was she looking for the sun again? Trying to find a way to get it back? No, that would've been too simple. Jo looked so lost, abandoned. I wanted to help, take her in my arms and let her know she'd never be alone, tell her she still had a friend in me. Whatever she needed me to be, I'd be it. Fuck, *I* felt lost.

I approached from the front, so she saw me coming. "Hey, Jo. How's it going, Boo?" Not too deep; just conversation. I waited to see if she responded.

She turned her head and looked up at me with glassy, empty eyes—her new everyday look.

"Hi, Keagan. Good, thanks."

She turned her head back towards the sky, ignoring my attempt at a conversation.

I pushed forward in a jovial, nonthreatening tone. This was a start. "So, I'm in the mood for some of Vino's pizza. Pepperoni, jalapeño, and Canadian bacon. What do say? Want to go with me tonight? It's Friday, so we could even catch a movie if you want to. I heard some of our friends talking about going to see that new movie *Beetlejuice*." I chuckle. "It's rated to be epic in the funny department. A good laugh would do us all some good. What do you say, Jo?"

"*Beetlejuice*, yes. I've seen the previews. Very funny," Jo commented back in a mechanical manner, then mumbled something I couldn't discern as she turned away again. This time, she was lost to me.

My mood turned from bad to worse in the sixty seconds it took me to walk across the yard to the door that day. But I couldn't watch it. I couldn't stand by and watch her fall to pieces anymore, pieces I wanted to put back together.

The worst part was, she wouldn't let me help her.

I tried to connect with her a few more times before I left. I went by her house, but she never came out of her bedroom. I called right before I left for basic training. Nothing. I even went as far as sending her letters and tried to call her a time or two, but I never got a response.

Fuck me. I walked away that day. I didn't want to, but it was too hard to sit and watch her fall apart like that and I couldn't do shit to fix it. She pushed me away and I had to let her go.

CHAPTER 2
Jocelyn

The first day I met Keagan Fontneau was my first day of high school as a sophomore. I was really nervous, but just like always, Fallyn was showing me what I needed to know and didn't leave my side except to go to her classes. We had the last class of the day together—Art—and were on our way there.

"How's your first day going? You haven't had any problems, have you? You'd tell me if someone picked on you, right?" Fallyn interrogated me as we walked to class.

"No. I haven't spoken to anyone today at all."

"Why the hell not, Jo? You don't have to blend in here. You can make friends. I'll protect you."

"Just don't want to."

"Okay, sis. We're almost done and then I've got practice. How 'bout you?"

"Not today, but I think I'll wait for you in the gym. That way, we can leave together."

"You know, you're looking really good in those boots, JoJo. I can't believe you actually wore 'em to school."

"Why the heck not? They totally rock this skirt, and you know I love my pink snakeskin boots."

"That's the prob, sis. It's the 1980's, for God's sake! I'm wearing jeans and converses and you've got your boots. We are *so* opposites in clothing."

We both started giggling as we walked into the classroom. Everybody stopped and stared at us. I know Fallyn always liked the attention, but I preferred not to be seen. I wanted to remain in the background. It's been an instinctive action since I can remember. I've been able to keep *him* from attacking me if he didn't see me. There's been many times that Fallyn hadn't been home and I've been in his path.

"Where do you wanna sit?" I looked back at her and she was grinning.

"Follow me."

"Why do I feel like you're about to embarrass me?"

"No clue, Jo," Fallyn replied and weaved in and out of the desks until she stopped in front of a guy I'd never seen around here before. She put her backpack down on the desk and slid into the chair. I followed suit and sat down beside her, wondering why in the world she chose to sit so far back in the room.

"Don't look now, but you've got an admirer," she whispered when Mrs. Campbell began calling attendance.

"Huh? What're you talking about, Fallyn?"

"Someone couldn't take their eyes off you as we were walking around looking for a seat. I'm just trying to help my little virgin sister get a date," she added with a smirk.

"Fallyn! Good grief. Don't do me any favors. Please!" I begged.

We had to quiet when Mrs. Campbell's stern glare turned our way. When the bell rang and class was over, I made for the exit only to be stopped by Fallyn when she grabbed my arm and looped hers with mine, slowing my progress.

"What's the rush? Aren't you curious?"

"No. Not at all. I want to leave."

"Come on, sis. Live a little."

I was stuck. She wouldn't let this go until I gave in, so I had to nod in agreement, and she eagerly stopped us and waited for their group to catch up.

"What's up?" Bo asked as he hugged Fallyn.

"Hi, Bo. How's life been treating you lately? Who's your new friend?" Fallyn asked him with a smile.

"Keagan. Sorry man, didn't get your last name."

"Keagan Fontneau," the boy answered. "Just moved here from Texas. Nice to meet y'all," he said with a heavy southern twang, smiling at me.

I didn't say anything and lowered my eyes.

"Hmmm. You don't say," she muttered, glancing back and forth between me and Keagan. "Well, okie dokie. Nice meeting you, Keagan. Sorry we can't stay and chat, but I've got practice. Let's go, Jo."

I looked up and he was staring at me with a stony expression on his face. He had the most beautiful blue eyes I'd ever seen. I was jerked from the moment as Fallyn pulled me away and into the hall.

What in the world was that? I never look at guys, and I'm positive he's totally not interested in me. No one ever is. That was the first day I'd ever laid eyes on Keagan Fontneau. It was also the beginning of a long friendship. One that inadvertently transformed my life forevermore.

Throughout the course of the first half of the school year, Keagan and I became best friends. We hung out as much as possible, in and out of school. I'd even snuck out with Fallyn to meet up with him a time or two. I was walking on the edge and it was exciting. A path I'd never traveled before.

One I wouldn't ever follow again.

It was Christmas Day. We'd just arrived home from my grandma's annual party. It was the first night Keagan called me his angel and the night everything went terribly wrong in my world. When we got home, I noticed Fallyn was nowhere to be found and neither was Dad. Not good. My momma called us into the kitchen and asked us to sit down. She was at the table feeding Grayson. Not understanding what was going on, Sage and I took our seats at the table as momma motioned for us to take a cookie from the platter in front of us. Little Grayson was in his highchair blabbing in baby talk. He'd gotten pieces of cookie all over his face. I smiled and cooed at him, garnering a toothless grin in return. I heard Momma clear her throat as if she'd been crying.

"Girls, your Aunt Polly Jean has asked for y'all to come spend a few days with her during the holiday break," Momma began. "She'll be here in an hour to pick you up. Aren't you excited? You'll have so much fun with your cousins! You need to go pack and be ready."

I could tell Momma was putting on an act. We can always spot it. She was nervous and my anxiety hiked up another level.

"Where's Fallyn?" There was concern in my voice because I hadn't seen her and she was upset about something earlier.

"She's in town at your grandmother's," Momma replied, and I was even more concerned than I was before. "Now finish your cookies and go pack. Love you, girls." She gathered up Grayson and walked into the bathroom to give him a bath and get him ready for bed.

Sage and I shared a look between each other and finished up our refreshments, then went to go and pack, because what choice did we have?

Fallyn was gone and she wasn't coming back. While we were shuttled out of the picture, all hell broke loose in Lakeview. We came back home from Aunt Polly Jean's just in time for winter break to be over and back to school—all without Fallyn. She was living with David and they were expecting a baby. What the heck happened? I never saw that coming.

She told me everything, always. That was our pact. Now she was gone and I was alone.

My dad had been on a tirade for the last few months. We were all walking around on eggshells. It was only a matter of time before he focused in on me. Being the oldest sibling in the household now, it would be my job to keep the heat off of Sage and Grayson, my job to protect them. I wasn't as suave as Fallyn and I'd captured his attention more lately than ever. He would get mad at everyone and everything without provocation or mishap. His pride was hurt, and for a man like our dad, that was a very bad thing.

One night, I went into the kitchen to get a drink of water before bed, tiptoeing quietly through the house as to not make a sound or be detected. Dad was sitting at the large kitchen table, staring off into nothingness. That should have been my first clue to turn around and exit as quietly as possible. I'd thought I could get in and get out without him noticing me, but an ice cube dropped onto the floor, causing him to look my way.

"What are you doing in here, Jocelyn? You should be in bed. You have school in the morning. You won't make me late again."

"Yes, sir. I apologize. I was just getting a drink before I went to bed. I'm sorry for making a mess. I'll be up on time, I promise."

He approached me with disdain. What did I do?

As he drew close to me, he said, "Are you sorry?

Really? I didn't realize you were a *sorry* person. You're sorry. I guess you will be if you don't get out of this kitchen right NOW!" He spouted venom and bellowed angrily at me.

I dropped the plastic cup into the sink, making a clinking sound as it crashed on the bottom of the stainless steel bowl. I hightailed it out of the kitchen as quickly as possible, praying all the way that he wouldn't follow me. When I got to my bed, I hurriedly scooped the covers to the side, sinking in, and then pulled the covers back up over my head. I lay silently for hours, or minutes, in and out of fitful sleep.

Why did you leave us, Fallyn? Please come back. We need you. I need you. The silent prayer didn't pass my lips, afraid of being heard by him. Finally, I drifted off to sleep. I dreamed of happier days with Fallyn, me, and Sage … just to be woken again by the terrible nightmare of my sister leaving me forever.

When morning came, my alarm clock rang loudly beside my head. I reached out to push the snooze and gain a few more minutes of sleep, but that's when I heard him. He was already up and started on his rantings. Unfortunately, my momma was the one garnering his unwanted attention.

I said another silent prayer to the angels that my momma would be okay for one more day. Then, I slid out of my bed in stealth mode and made it to the bathroom undiscovered. I turned on the shower and tried to wash away the never-ending nightmare that was part of my life. I got ready for another day at school. Alone, without my sister.

Keagan popped into my mind as I washed my hair. A genuine smile burst from my thoughts. It lingered on my lips through conditioning my hair and shaving my legs. But as the water started to turn cold, so did my mind. Maybe today would be better. How? I couldn't see the light at the end of the tunnel. So, I promised myself: *One day at a time, Jo. One day at a time.*

The tendrils of pain are vast and far-reaching. Living daily in the struggles of the shadows caused a torment that seemed to be endless. Everyday meaningless tasks such as driving to school, to and fro, unfurl the prick of misery my heart suffered. This is my life now. Smiling took effort, something I just didn't have the strength to do at the time. I lost my sister months ago, my best friend in the whole world, yet the pain was still ever present.

Everything rolled downhill for me. I couldn't eat right, sleep well, or carry on a normal conversation with anyone. I decided to quit cheering. Things that meant the world to me just didn't matter anymore. It was like she died instead of moved out to live with her baby daddy. I missed her so much and I kept thinking if it could happen to Fallyn, it could happen to me. So it was best to keep to myself. Study hard, nose to the grindstone, and get the heck out of there as soon as possible. That's what I lived for during my last few years at home.

My momma and Grandma seemed most concerned. I didn't reassure them, because the truth was, I felt lost enough that I just didn't care. Maybe things would change in the future. In the here and now, I chose the darkness. If Fallyn had to be away from her family, then I would suffer right along with her, like she's always been there for me.

A month later, I received a phone call.

"Hello?"

"Hey, sweet girl. How are you doing today?"

Grandma's graceful, soothing voice echoed through the line, filling me with all the love she freely gives to the ones she loves. That included me.

"I'm doing okay. Thanks for asking, Grandma. Today's not so bad. How are you?"

"Good, good. You worry me, y'know? You can't keep going on like this, Jocelyn. It's time to pick yourself up, wipe off the dust, and start again. You come from a long line of strong women. Accept it. Your sister wouldn't want you to do this to yourself. You know that, right? It's a crying shame that you are so sad all the time. We need our sunshine back, sweet girl."

I heard what she was saying, but I just wasn't there yet. "I know, Grandma. I'm just not ready to stop mourning. Please understand. I'll be okay. I just need a little more time."

"Alright, sugar. Well, I might just have something that'll put you back on the right track. I just got a call from a certain someone. And I wanted to give you a message." She paused to make sure I was listening.

I perked up. "Yes, ma'am. Come on, do tell. Please."

I anxiously waited to hear what she had to say. *A message from a certain someone?* It had to be Fallyn. Please let it be Fallyn.

Her voice turned softer, saddened, and in pain she said, "She misses you and Sage, sweet girl. Terribly. Baby is growing up fast and she said to make sure and tell you 'everything is going to be alright'."

I gasped and tears spilled down my face. It was our code. Our cipher to each other when things weren't right in our world. It was a comforting phrase we've used when all hope seemed out of reach.

"Thank you, Grandma. Thank you so much." In between sobs, I echoed, "Everything is going to be alright."

"That is correct, sweet girl. Perk up! I love you, Jocelyn."

"I love you too."

After I hung up with Grandma, I sought out Sage to share the news. Knocking on her door, I heard her respond, "Come in."

"Hey, baby sister. May I come in for a few minutes?" I relinquished a smile and her face instantly lit up.

"Sure. What's up, Buttercup?"

I giggled at her comment. She's using the nickname I gave her long ago. Sage has such a way with words. She tunnels her pain through comedy and always speaks what's on her mind. At the same time, Sage is a force to be reckoned with; she's going to make the Blackwood name extremely proud one day.

"I've got some news I wanted to share with you."

I shut the door behind me because we didn't need any unwanted guests or eavesdroppers.

"Really? Spill it, JoJo."

"I just got off the phone with Grandma."

"And …?" The anticipation was thick in the air as pools of water rush into our eyes.

"Everything is going to be alright, Buttercup. She's good, Harper's good. They are doing just fine, according to Grandma."

Relief stormed its way into both of us as we huddled together in a warm, sisterly embrace. I didn't realize I'd been holding my breath for months, waiting for any kind of news about Fallyn and little Harper. Sage continued to cry as I ran my fingers through her long dark hair, singing *The Little Mermaid*'s "Part of Your World" softly to her, soothing Sage and alleviating a small amount of my own discomfort for a brief time.

Shortly after, I was studying my history books. The rumble of a motorcycle drew my attention. The sound imparted a sense of relief, staunching the sting out of my most recent bout of numbness. My body was stiff and my eyes ached from the crying. It didn't help that I'd rubbed them over and over as I tried to study for my final exams the next week. My mood was a little better, thanks to the phone call with Grandma.

The familiar chimes of the doorbell played loudly throughout the house, a song of Bach's "Minuet in G Major", which had me pausing to listen for who had come to visit.

The motorcycle. Oh, no. It was Keagan. My consciousness poked her head up, sending a spike of adrenaline coursing through my body.

Momma came to my door and rapped lightly.

"Jo, honey. Keagan is here to see you. Can you come out?"

Momma sounded skittish and distressed. Another round of guilt enveloped me, but I answered.

"Yes, ma'am. I'll be right there."

I paused and stared into the mirror, my lungs inflated at the sight. My hair was in ringlet tangles, mussed up on one side. My green eyes were dull and comatose from the stress of my present situation. My appearance was appalling and I pondered on why anyone, especially Keagan, would take interest in me. I hurriedly tried to run a brush through it with no avail, giving up because the brushing was causing me unwanted pain, so I opened the door to go see Keagan.

Minutes passed as I watched Keagan from the

darkened hallway. He hadn't noticed me yet and I was pleased. I enjoyed him from my unobstructed view and he was breathtaking. Why hadn't I noticed this before? His hair was cut shorter on top, more of a buzz cut, which accentuated his jaw line and revealed his flawless perfection. I couldn't see his eyes from this angle, but I imagined they were a stormy blue, the color they'd been lately when he tried to talk to me. His eyes were the window to his soul, confessing his mood, wants, and desires.

My feet were anchored to the hardwood floors, not daring to budge in my position forward or backwards. I felt trapped in emotions that were unsafe, unacceptable, and scared me to death. He didn't need this pathetic rendition of Jocelyn Blackwood. I would only bring him further down into my depths of depravity, and he's too perfect for that. I had to let him go. I hope one day I could reach out to him again, thank him for his friendship. Not today, though. On this day, I would surrender to the self-torture I was willingly inflicting upon myself.

My decision was made. Before he saw me, I moved quietly back into the shadows of the hall, back to my cave of loneliness, my hiding place. Momma could take care of sending him away. I was too vulnerable at that point in time. My resolve would crumble if I talked to him. It is what it is. It was what it was, protecting Keagan and myself from the affliction of getting too close to another person or loving that person had to be.

I couldn't take the chance of being crushed like that ever. Lesson learned from Fallyn leaving me and the pain that came with it—her pain she's enduring on a daily basis. I did Keagan a huge favor by letting him go, because consequently, in the end, everyone leaves.

CHAPTER 3
KEAGAN

Why the hell am I here again and how the hell do I get myself into these situations? I've asked myself those questions at least a hundred times in the last hour. I gaze around the seedy bar. The smells of sweat, smoke, and booze permeate the air. The dim lit bar is a hole in the wall, floors covered in peanut shells and wrappers. I've been staking out my suspect for the last week—another undercover mission for Trident Securities. This time, the stakes are high and failure is not an option, especially with the people involved with the Cabricci Family.

Paul "Gunner" Tavers is known to drop in and party with the owner of this fine establishment, along with half the club from Phantom Prophets MC. I blend well with the patrons. Today, my polished bald head covered with a skull cap, trimmed goatee, and leathers fit in with the crowd of bikers sitting across from me at a table. I look like I belong here. Who would have thought? Little Keagan Fontneau would hit a growth spurt at twenty and not stop.

So much has changed in my life since I graduated

high school. I joined the Army and soon after was knee-deep in shit I never anticipated happening. War is brutal and ugly. It can rip your soul to shreds and leave an empty man walking. The things I have seen or done in the name of serving my country make my skin crawl. Every life I took is burned into my memory. I wake up some nights in a cold sweat seeing faceless victims dead. I'm a decorated veteran now, honorably discharged after serving my country for eight long years. Battle weary, scarred inside and out. I often reflect on the day I signed my life away, how my pop felt and his words that I've carried with me through it all.

It was Monday and my pop and I were meeting with an Army recruiter after school to decide my future. I'd known serving my country was inevitable, being from a military family. Choosing the Army as my branch of service was a shock to my parents at first. They were warming up to the idea of me being a ground pounder. But I didn't think I would have doubts about enlisting. Those doubts all stemmed from a green-eyed beauty who didn't even care if I existed anymore. I knew what was expected of me and I would do it. I wished I had more time to help Jo come back to the land of the living.

The door chimed, announcing entrance as we entered the recruiter's office in a strip mall on the outskirts of Lakeview. My senses were inundated with smells of Pine-Sol and shoe polish. I smiled because it reminded me of home. The room was set up in straight lines and hard angles, from the lone desk to the stately American Eagle and flag pictures hung on the walls. Crisp, clean, and organized.

"Hello," a deep voice from the corner of the room addressed me and my pop. My gaze landed on a mammoth of a man dressed in an Army Service Uniform with muscles that seemed to be busting out of his shirt. He could literally squash me like a bug. For a brief moment, I was intimidated. Then I took a closer look to realize I was going to be just like him.

Growing up, my pop was my hero, a man I strived to be like, a man I looked up to. Still do. He taught me to love the family, respect women, recognize authority, and instilled the need in me to serve my country. The decision to go into the Army and not the Air Force was a tough choice. However, maw and pop always said I had to follow my heart and listen to my gut. That's why we went to the Army recruiting office.

My pop, who is a substantial fella too, reached out to shake the other massive man's hand, and the electricity in the air crackled as if two giant gorillas were vying for alpha. Powerful. I read his name tag during the standoff: Sergeant Aims.

"Hi, Buddy Fontneau, former Pararescue, Air Force."

An understanding passed across the sergeant's features, "Nice to meet you sir, Sergeant Aims."

He turned to me, holding out his hand.

"Keagan Fontneau, sir. Good to meet you. I have an appointment to discuss my Army career." Sergeant Aims' handshake was strong and firm when we clasped. He nodded and let go, as if he was satisfied with the grip I imparted.

"I've been waiting for you to come in today, Keagan. Your ASVAB scores are impressive. Let's sit and we'll talk about your options."

Sergeant Aims gestured to the chairs parked in front of his desk.

"If you don't mind me asking, Keagan, why the Army and not the Air Force?"

I laughed, glanced at my pop and his newfound scowl when it came to this subject. "Honestly, sir, I want to be in the special forces like my pop was. But a Green Beret. Maybe it's the green and the luck of the Irish. It calls to me."

Pop half-laughed at my comment. The Irish is from my mother's side.

"However, I know I want to serve my country and I feel a strong pull to the Army to do it."

"Well said. Alright then, let's look at your scores and talk shop." Sergeant Aims began to explain the options of my future.

We finished up a few hours later. I'd signed the dotted line. I was to leave for boot camp in two months, which was two weeks after graduation. The career path I chose was to be a military police officer.

My ASVAB test scores determined I was a suitable recruit to be an MP. Had to wait a few years to step into the role of Green Beret. It was all good. I'd learn a whole lot to prepare me for special forces.

"Thank you, sir," I said, shaking the sergeant's hand again.

"Thank you, Keagan. I'm sure you're going to do great things in the Army. Mr. Fontneau," he added, gripping Pop's hand as well. "I'll see you in two months, Keagan, when you head out to MEPS in Montgomery. That's where you process and ship out. Remember, if you have any more questions, give me a call. Welcome to the fold, son."

Sergeant Aims saluted and turned away as we walked out the door.

Pop was quiet as we drove home. I knew he was thinking about the shit storm I'm stepping into and how he couldn't stop it. I hoped he was proud.

"Pop, what's on your mind?" I used the question he'd asked me thousands of times over my life.

"Ah, shit, son. Just thinkin'," he sighed. I saw the hard lines creasing on his forehead while he permitted a half smile.

"I hear ya," I replied, nodding my head. It was short, but my mind was reeling from the changes coming, a turnabout that wouldn't involve my best friend Jo. My only qualm with leaving so soon was I wouldn't have time to help her through the rough patch she'd landed in. She had her family though; I

hoped it would be enough.

The silence ended and pop spoke up. "Things are shifting for you, son. Life's about to get really fucking tough, Boo. You're gonna wish at times you could roll over and die. And then other times you'll be so damn excited that you got to be part of something so important. You're prepared. You've wanted this for a long time. No doubt you can do this, K."

"I know." Another short response, but it was the truth. There were no reservations; I would succeed.

"Thanks, Pop."

When my team was hit during an ambush, only three out of ten soldiers survived. Try living with that. I was their leader and I hold myself responsible for each death. It's a miracle I'm walking. I've got scars on my body from the bullets' entry points. The motherfuckers who tried to kill me are still out there breathing. One day, I will find Budahar and Mustaff and have my revenge. I've learned the scars you can't see are the hardest to heal.

The bartender saunters my way with a smile on her face. "Another one, sugar?"

I nod yes and she pours a shot of whiskey and sits it in front of me.

"Anything else you need, you just let me know. My shift ends in a couple of hours." She winks and leans closer to my ear displaying her plump breasts at my eye level. "I'll wipe that frown off your face and replace it with a satisfied smile, baby."

I don't respond, but the look I give her relays my thoughts: back the fuck off, now.

She stares a moment longer, stunned, then backs away.

"Your loss," she mumbles and makes her way down the bar to another waiting customer.

Closing time draws near. I'm just thinking about how tired I am of nursing watered-down whiskey when the door opens and in walks my perp. Busted! My adrenaline spikes. I love the rush of danger when uncertainty of the outcome depends solely on your quick wit and response. I eye him as he walks up to the bar. He leans over, grabs the back of the bartender's head, and molests her mouth with his tongue. When their display of raunchiness ends, he orders a beer and sits down on the stool next to me.

He's so young to be involved with these dumb fucks. I'm shocked. He looks like your average preppy college grad. He's wearing loafers, blue jeans, and a cardigan? I feel like I've been transplanted to a different place. I glance around, checking. No. Still in the same shitty bar.

"Hey, man," he says. "You're new. Haven't seen you around these parts before."

I nod, lift my glass and take a sip.

"Silent brooding type, are ya?" He turns. "Cookie, where's Razer? Need to talk to him."

"Gunner, he done left 'bout an hour ago on a run.

Won't be back 'til Wednesday night."

"Shit, I need a place to crash then. I was planning to head down south to the club's safe house and needed to borrow some wheels. Looks like your place will have to do 'til then, bitch."

I've about had all I can take of this asshole. He's seriously grating on my nerves. I shift to rise from the barstool, grabbing my gun stashed in my shoulder holster, and make to walk out. At the last second, I pivot round, release the grip, and nod, slowly caressing the whiskers of my goatee and acting as if I'm pondering whether to help this fool.

"Hey, bro. I'm headed to Miami on some business that requires a cage for transfer. If you wanna hitch a ride. Staying at the local rent-a-room and plan to split at the crack of dawn." I relax my stance more, crossing my arms across my chest. "Name's Crash."

I can tell I've caught him off-guard because he pauses and stares. "Not going that far, brother, but if you're offering, man, I'm a goner. Hightailin' it outta here. Got some smokies on my ass and I ain't wantin' to wait 'til they catch up with me."

Stupid fucktard. After all these years of trailing scum of the earth, I'm caught off-guard time and time again by how they react the same way. Some things never change. Human stupidity surfaces when preservation kicks in, and admission of the idiots spew forth. Case and point: Did he really just admit that shit in a room full of people?

"We can head out now. Just need to grab my shit and I'm smoke."

"Meet ya out front in a few," Gunner yells on his way down the hall. "Gotta hit the john before we leave."

The room is eerily silent as I slowly make my way from the bar to the exit. Two of the bikers from the table I had been watching earlier stand between me and the door. Their intimidating stance almost has me chuckling, but I blanket my expressions, not giving my true feelings away. They don't know me from Adam, so I'll let it pass … for now.

The larger dumbass of the two stares menacingly my way trying to intimidate me. His left eye twitches as he sizes me up, and I know I've pissed him off when he sees the smirk form on my face. *I've dealt with worse than you, asshole. Bring. It. On.*

Not much bothers me these days. I don't care what he thinks. I can take him. If he wants a piece of me, who am I not to oblige? The patch on his vest reads "Vice President Phantom Prophets MC", with one-percenter stitched below, and I patiently wait for his pattern move.

"Got no problem with you, man," he finally says.

I acknowledge him with a questioning look, because I know more bullshit is coming. It doesn't take long to prove me right.

"See, here's the thing, Crash. We overheard you talkin' to Gunner about hitchin' a ride. Well, we kinda need him taken to Miami … under the radar. You seem like a good option. Problem solved all around. You make some extra cash. Everybody's happy, right? But, just know, we're Gunner's family, and if anything happens to him, we'll hold you personally responsible."

I continue with a blank stare as the one-sided conversation resumes. He's unaware of the fire kindling inside me. My hands on each side flex open, then close as I try to relax them from forming into a balled fist I can slam into his face. I don't take kindly to threats. My relaxed pose gives nothing away. I need to remain that way to get out of here and stay on point.

"Ain't nowhere you can hide from us. We *will* find you."

Idle threats.

"Not looking for trouble, brother," the VP says.

I nod and I'm saved from replying when the man of the hour rushes forward.

"Heading out, Buzz. Catch ya on the fly," Gunner hastily remarks.

He doesn't feel the tension in the room, oblivious to his surroundings. For a moment I lock eyes with the VP, and an unsaid truce emerges. The anger subsides.

"Consider it done," I promise and walk away.

It's times like these I actually miss having Ollie and Lukas with me. Those guys would have my back. They've proven their loyalty and friendship time after time. The true brotherhood forged in a battle of life and death. I've got to check in with them soon or they'll release the Kraken to find me.

As if thinking about them conjures them up, my company cell phone vibrates in my front jean pocket. I motion at Gunner, pointing at the jacked-up red Dodge Ram sitting under the only lamppost in the lot, click the unlock button for him, then slide the bar across my phone to answer.

"Talk to me."

"We were beginning to worry when you didn't check in," a deep male voice says.

"Fuck-wipes, you know how time passes when you're having fun," I sarcastically reply.

"All the same. What's your twenty?" another voice inquires.

"'Bout to pull out of Perry now."

"Do you have the package?"

"What do you think, Ollie? It's not like I'm going to leave here without it."

"You've been preoccupied with shit lately, man. That's all."

"How's the therapy going, Luc? Roxy?" I sidestep, because I'm not about to touch that subject with a ten foot pole.

"Still therapy, Keagan. A big pain in the ass, but I'm sticking with it 'cause you asked so sweetly. And your baby is barking and slobbering all over me. Can't you hear her?"

"Good girl, Roxy."

A *woof-woof* comes through the line.

"He's got his eyes on a gen-u-ine southern belle," Ollie playfully mentions.

"Not gonna happen, dumbass. She's just my therapist. Nothing more. I told you that once already."

"It could be. She's got the hots for you, Luc. If it was me, I'd wrap my arms around her and get lost in all that southern honey she's so sweetly offering."

"Shut the fuck up, Ols. You don't know nothing."

"I know you need to relax and I'm sure *little Miss Sunshine* would help you with that."

"Ols …"

"We still moving forward as planned?" I interrupt before their joking escalates.

"Affirmative. Nothing's changed," Lukas responds automatically.

"Were you able to get a location on Big Daddy?"

"No. His watch dogs greeted me, but not him. You know he's got eyes watching my every move. I've noticed a tag from the minute I stepped foot in these parts. I expect to meet him soon. Especially with the cargo I'm transporting across state."

"Our clients are eager for a progress report, Keagan. What should I tell them?"

"Tell 'em we are proceeding as planned and should have something more to report in a few days. We told them it would take time. Our plan won't have results overnight, but we will get results. One way or the other. I promise."

My attention zeroes in on Gunner. He's on his phone animatedly gesturing around in the cab of the truck.

"Gotta go for now. I'll check in soon."

I hang up and ease the phone into my pocket as I walk towards the truck. I mentally prepare for the ride and grab the handle on the truck door to open it.

From the crack in the window I hear a woman screaming, "Stay the fuck there, Gunner. Don't be a dumb fucker! We can't afford for you to get caught," blares the voice from his speaker phone.

"I can't risk staying. Too much is riding ..." Gunner's voice fades away as I slam the truck door closed and crank the beast. He glances at me and shifts towards the passenger window. "Can't talk now. Later." Then he disconnects the call.

CHAPTER 4

Jocelyn

Today's not just a routine day in the office for me. The restlessness inside follows the uncertainty of the high profile case I've been asked to handle. Cade and Crystal's case is going to break my resolve to remain impartial when dealing with my clients, even if said clients are too young to protect themselves and need my intervention. From the moment I met the two teenagers, I knew something was off and I still can't shake the feeling. Relying on my experience and knowledge will only go so far, and my gut instinct is screaming for me to reach out and help them.

The fraternal twins are inseparable. When one ventures away, the other instinctively shifts to cover the space between them. They are leery of movement and actions around them. It reminds me of the protective stance Fallyn had years ago for me and Sage.

At times, it's an eerie sight, neither one acting their age but rather beyond it. Their eyes reflect an ocean of sadness. Both teenagers are breathtaking at fifteen. Crystal has long straight black hair and a thin face. Cade's hair is shaggy with black curls engulfing his face, but both share identical blue eyes. They are popular among the "in crowd" and have excelled in academics up until about three months ago.

After their father's death a few years back, their mother remarried the next year. A couple of the teachers have come to me with concerns about their withdrawal from friends and decline in grades. I've scheduled a meeting with her today—in fifteen minutes—and hopefully she will be able to enlighten me as to what is happening with her children.

I glance out the window and peace returns. The sun is shining brightly through the moss-covered trees and the parking lot is full of teenagers rushing around. I smile and hope that my effort is enough of a difference in the lives I come in contact with every day. I've been in Gainesville, Florida since I graduated from the university. My apprenticeship was at a high school here and it didn't hurt that I fell in love with the college town atmosphere. So, when the time came for me to decide where I wanted to live, it was a no-brainer for me; I had nothing waiting for me in Lakeview.

When Fallyn left home, I counted the days until I could get away. After high school, I severed ties with Lakeview, the memories driving me far away to a new beginning. I talk to Grandma, my sisters, and Grayson weekly, or at least I try to. Some continue to call and check on me every now and then. Momma calls on occasion. She tries, and I appreciate her will. Momma is trapped in her own personal hell and no one can help her, so I don't push her away.

Fallyn left me. One day, I had a precious little niece Harper who I adored and a sister who helped me survive living at home, and the next instant she was gone, vanished into thin air. I haven't heard from her since. No one has, except for Grandma. She's the only one Fallyn contacts. I'm not sure if even she knows where Fallyn and Harper are.

She was my best friend, and when I lost her, I lost a part of me too. Eventually, something inside me clicked back into place. I knew then that a fresh start without the hauntings of growing up as a Blackwood was in order.

My gaze lingers on a young teenage couple sitting under a gigantic live oak, the ancestral branches covered in moss reaching out to wrap them in their own cocoon haven as they talk and laugh. My mind wanders back to better days, a time when cheating on a test and remaining anonymous in my dad's thoughts were my biggest concerns … when I was carefree and felt something.

Oh my gosh! I was totally dead meat. I couldn't believe I was standing there in the hallway with Keagan and Mr. Manfurd, our Spanish teacher. He just caught us cheating and he was furious. Keagan was sitting in front of me cheating off Sara Beth in front of him, and he was just simply trying to be nice and help me out. But oh no, I was no good at cheating! I was no good at lying, or stealing, or anything that was bad. I was a churchgoing, God-fearing young lady, after all. Shoot, shoot, shoot! I really stepped in it this time.

I may have been the captain of the junior varsity cheerleading team, but I was no slouch. Appearances can be deceiving. In my case, they certainly were. Clutching my head in my hands in anguish, my mind raced, loudly spewing at my stupid decision to cheat. And with Keagan no doubt. My dad was going to kill me, literally. Mr. Manfurd was going to tell him, I just knew it. This would not turn out well for me. Nope, no way. My dad donated his time in the horticultural department and he'd find him and tell him as soon as he could. I'm so dead! Maybe I could salvage this situation somehow? Okay. Think, Jo. You can fix this.

Using the only weapon I possessed, I divert and tell the truth. I began to plead with Mr. Manfurd. "I'm so sorry, sir. It was totally not cool what we did. I take full responsibility for it. Keagan didn't even realize what I was doing, so please don't punish him for my mistake."

Both Keagan and Mr. Manfurd's jaws dropped as they both looked at me, bewildered, as if I sprouted hooves and a tail. In any other situation I would've laughed, but this was not the time.

I stood my ground because this had to work. It was my only hope.

"I really studied hard for this test. You know I

always get decent grades, but that one question was just so hard, I just wasn't sure."

That's when I let the waterworks fall. It would certainly seal the deal.

Mr. Manfurd's face softened at what he was witnessing. I could sense my plan was working little by little. I should feel guilty. I did cheat. But at that moment, I couldn't. There was no way I could afford for my dad to find out.

He leaned over and put his hand on my shoulder and sighed. Shaking his head, he said, "I'm very disappointed in you, Jocelyn. I would never expect something like this from you or Keagan." Mr. Manfurd's gaze locked onto Keagan. "However, I see how upset you are and I believe what you are saying, so I'll let you both take the test again during your lunch period."

Keagan looked at me, speechless, as I wiped my tears from my face and said, "Thank you sir, so much. I promise it'll never happen again."

Whew! That was a close one. Next, I needed to ask the tough question, to be certain I was off the hook from him.

"Mr. Manfurd, can we please keep this between us?" I appealed to him again with my eyes as tears continued to pool unashamed.

He looked down at me with understanding and replied, "I think we can do that, Jocelyn. But remember, if it ever happens again ..."

The rest hung heavy in the air, and I heard it loud and clear. He didn't have to worry about me. I would never take a chance like that again. It was just not worth the risk. Not worth my dad finding out and grounding me for life, or worse. I couldn't think like that at the moment. Keagan and I received a pass that day. A get-out-of-jail-free card. All was right with the world!

I think about Keagan Fontneau often and wonder if he's fighting the good fight. He joined the Army after graduating. I saw his brother a few times before I left the View, but he never mentioned how Keagan was doing. Sometimes I miss him, his friendship, his witty sense of humor. I received a few letters and a couple of phone calls after he first left. I didn't respond. So eventually, the correspondence stopped. I wanted him to focus on his career and not the baggage that came with being my friend. But such is life. Things change, people change. We grow up and move on. When I take on a case like this one—one that is close to my heart—my memories start to surface.

When Grayson graduates, I will have to go back. I make a point to check on him and Addie. I was there when she was born and send her gifts on the holidays, but I fear she will never know who I am. Not like Grayson. I worry about them being at home in the unhealthy environment of the Blackwoods. At least Grandma's still there to watch over them.

As for me, I've changed since I moved away. I'm still shy and don't want to be in the limelight, but I've branched out and dated a time or two, had the occasional one-night stand when the itch needed scratching. But, nothing serious that gave me the tingling feeling I felt for Keagan. Nope, nada. I fear it will never happen again.

A guy I met in college came close but the sparks weren't there. I almost married him too. I was going to settle, thinking that's the most I deserve, until I caught him in bed with my roommate. Always second best. I decided then and there I wanted to be alone. I would dedicate my life to helping those who couldn't help themselves. That's how I ended up as a psychologist working for the department of health and rehabilitation. My trust fund set up by my grandparents supplements my meager income so I can do what I love the most: helping children.

A knock at my office door stops my reminiscing and Angela pokes her head in. "Miss Blackwood, your four o'clock appointment is here."

"Thank you, Angela."

Rising from my chair, I make my way out to the front office and I'm greeted by a beautiful couple in a heated argument. The man is clearly agitated and the woman is angrily whispering and pointing her finger at him. *Interesting.* He's dressed in a business suit with his tie loosened at the neck and she is wearing an ivory blouse and pencil skirt with four-inch heels. Her

Gucci bag is dangling from her arm like jewelry. They make a striking couple. One of the beautiful people I longed to be growing up. I clear my throat to catch their attention and notice the curiousness on the man's face when he sees me.

"Hello, I'm Jocelyn Blackwood. Thank you so much for coming in today to meet with me." I smile as I approach the couple.

"Hello," they both say, shaking my hand in greeting.

The woman continues, "I'm Calista and this is my husband, Desmond Payne."

The man holds my hand a little longer than what I'm comfortable with, so I start to yank it back only for him to release it. There's a slight glimmer in his eyes that causes me to shiver.

I take a deep breathe to hide my uneasiness.

"It's a pleasure to meet you both. Why don't we go to my office where we can discuss what's going on with Cade and Crystal?" I walk down the hall and gesture at my office doorway, beckoning them to enter and proceed around the large desk to my chair. "Please have a seat and let's talk about the teens." I sit down and fold my hands upon the desk in front of me. "I've asked you here today because of the decline in their grades and social activity. According to a few of their teachers, this pattern has been getting worse. Can you tell me if you noticed this change at home?"

"Darling, those kids are always on the go. They

rarely show up for dinner on time and when they do, they are obnoxious and loud." Calista glances at her finely-manicured nails and smirks. "I tend to believe it's hormonal. They are teenagers, you know."

"I'm aware of their age, but the behavior we are observing at school doesn't coincide with your observations."

I'm interrupted by a concerned acting Desmond. "Do you think drugs are involved?"

"I really don't believe drugs are an issue. Cade and Crystal are shying away from their friends and teachers. Typically peer pressure, a desire to escape reality, or emotional struggles are signs of teen drug abuse. Yes, they are exhibiting bad grades, anti-social skills, and loss of interest, which are stereotypical signs. But neither show signs of fatigue, lack of personal hygiene, bloodshot eyes, or weight loss. I'm extremely concerned. The pattern seems closer to emotional turmoil, which is why I asked if anything had changed at home."

Both look at each other with dumbfounded facial expressions and I fear they are clueless as to what is happening to their children. They seem caught up in their everyday life and are oblivious to what's happening in front of them, but something is nagging at me. Something doesn't add up.

"You mentioned them being late for dinner, right? Do they miss the entire meal or only the beginning? Are they sleeping later in the morning? Hanging out with friends you haven't met?"

"No. They are either at home, school, or the library studying. I drop them off and pick them up. Sometimes, they get a ride home, but normally I'm there to take them wherever they need to go," Calista puffs.

"Hmm, how long are they studying at the library?"

"Almost every day, several hours at a time. If they aren't at school or asleep, they are at the library studying."

"Don't you think it's rather odd they are studying that much, yet their grades are suffering?"

"I … I haven't even thought about it."

"We need to find out what they are doing during their study time. I can talk to them with you if you want, or I can just wait to hear from you. Either way, it's important that we figure out what is going on with them so we can remedy the problem."

"I don't believe that's necessary. We can handle this within our family. Outside interference at this point isn't something needed," Desmond quickly answers.

I beg to differ, but nod my head in acceptance. For now.

"Very well. We can schedule another time to meet in … let's say two weeks? We should have an idea by then if you talking to them has made an impact. Until then, I'll keep posts on their activities from their teachers and if something happens I feel needs your assistance, then I'll call."

"Here's my business card," says Desmond, offering it. "Both office and cell number are listed. You will probably have a better chance getting through to me because I have an assistant answering most of the time. Calista is normally busy with her tennis and clubs."

Strange. Didn't she just mention taking them to and fro when needed?

"Alright then." I take the card from his outstretched fingers and am careful not to touch him. This guy gives me the willies.

We all stand and Desmond turns to leave. I catch a brief glimpse of distress painting Calista's face, as if she has something she needs to get off her chest. When Desmond twists back to us, her mask of indifference is back up. The moment is gone and I'm left with more questions. Does this woman know what's going on with her children? Is she frightened of something? Or maybe someone?

In the rush of leaving my office, Calista is in a tizzy about leaving her purse behind on the table.

"I'll get it, Mrs. Payne. Be right back."

As I walk into my office, I see her Gucci bag laying on the floor by the chair and bend over to retrieve it. I turn around into a wall of hard stone.

"What the …?"

"My apologies, *Miss* Blackwood. I didn't mean to

frighten you." He enunciates the "Miss" and my belly churns hard. Desmond Payne is staring me down with a smirk plastered across his jerk face. No, he didn't. Who does he think he is? Ugh!

Composing my emotions, I tread carefully, "Oh, no. That's okay. Here's your wife's purse."

I hand the bulky purse over to him, at the same time backing up to put distance between us with the chair as my sentry. My skin crawls at the way he caresses me with his beady eyes, lust-filled and dark.

"I just wanted to personally say thank you for watching out for the children. It means a great deal to me."

I'm annoyed by the lack of sincerity in his voice, the careless manner in which he speaks of the teenagers. He seems more interested in my boobs than the topic at hand. *Shut him down, Jocelyn.*

"That's my job. One I'm very good at, Mr. Payne. Thank you for your time. Now, if you'll excuse me, I have another appointment waiting." I gesture to the door.

He strolls out in a huff and I can sense the tension radiating from him. What did he think he would accomplish by coming into my office and making a pass at me? Unacceptable. He may be a good-looking man to many, but I can see the darkness in his eyes, an evil lurking there which emanates from a person who decides to make bad choices in life. I've seen it before many times throughout my childhood, the darkness in my father's eyes. I see a deeper level within him.

I've always been really good at reading people.

My mind begins to build scenarios. Something is off with this man. After meeting him, my instincts are screaming out to me that he has everything to do with the strange behavior of the twins. I could be wrong, but what if I'm not? That's a chance I can't take.

CHAPTER 5
Jocelyn

On the ride home, my thoughts are hampered by a rundown of events surrounding the twins. It appears all the dots are connecting to around six months after Desmond married Calista. Coincidence? Maybe, and the stress of trying to put it all together is wearing me down.

Entering through the stately security gate of Palm Wood Manor, I wave at Chester, the security guard who allows me entrance into the gated community where I live. It's a small neighborhood for the elite where the entrances and exits are monitored thoroughly. A clubhouse, golf course, and several markets and stores are situated within the confounds of the expansive property. A bit over the top? Yes. Few people know I live here. All my mail goes to a post office box at the branch near my office.

My grandma has always taken care of me and everyone she loves dearly, even without my father's approval. She bought this house for me when I decided to stay in Gainesville and insisted on my living here. Honestly, when I first came here, I knew it was outrageous. I've never done outrageous. Then I soon realized it made me feel safe with all of the state of the art benefits. Single woman, living by herself. It's a no brainer. So, I live here for the protection it offers and, of course, to appease my grandma.

I pull up and into the three-car garage of my home right before the sun goes down. My house sits at the end of a cul-de-sac on a two-acre lot. The house is extravagant with its Mediterranean design and Spanish flare. The lightly-tinted terracotta stucco walls, red clay tile roof with a low pitch, sweeping archways, a courtyard, and wrought-iron railings add to my home's elegant character. Its charm adds a romantic appeal that I fell in love with from day one.

Shutting the garage, I put my car in park. Grabbing my food from the back seat, I get out of the car and make my way to the door to punch in the alarm code, gaining access. I glance back over to the last garage bay. Sitting in its spot is my classic candy apple red GTO convertible. My classic car, which was my sixteenth birthday present from dear ole dad, depresses me. It was a payoff or a hush-up present. Take your pick. Whatever it was at the time. Even though it was my birthday present, there was underlying deceit that came with it.

I was thankful to have my own transportation, but anything would've been fine with me. Maybe something less conspicuous, not a showpiece that should be in a museum. But that's the Blackwood way. No, that's my dad's way of showing off his vast wealth, a way to make people think everything is right as rain. What's wrong with just being normal? Even though it reminds me of my dad, I've never been able to part with it. Go figure. I guess I really am a sentimental fool. I'm visibly shaken from the trepidation this case is dredging up in my mind. Sighing, I open the door and enter.

The Pizza Depot is my food of choice tonight. Because of my long hours, I rarely get a home-cooked meal. Kicking my shoes off in the mud room, I make a beeline for the kitchen to grab a bottle of chilled Moscato from the wine fridge and set down the pizza box. One glass of sweetness a night allows me a sense of accord, especially with days like today. Some of the scoundrels I run into in my line of work gives me the creeps.

Meow. Meow. Miss Kitty jumps onto the granite countertop as I'm pouring a glass of wine. She wears a permanent tuxedo, white chest, and paws with a black coat as dark as midnight. Beautiful gold eyes are a stark contrast to the rest of her. Miss Kitty waits patiently for me to finish and feed her. Not before I consume a large gulp of wine.

"Hello, Miss Kitty. How are you tonight?" I express my affection by stroking her fur from head to tail. She rubs up against me, contracting and contorting her lithe body in the feline way. I turn to take her food out of the cherry wood cabinet and serve it up in her favorite pink kitty dish.

She eats at a leisurely pace. I sit on a barstool at

the breakfast bar in my gourmet kitchen, eating my jalapeño, pepperoni, and Canadian bacon pizza, drinking Moscato, and watching Miss Kitty. This is what my life is all about. A great job that I love, a beautiful home, and a temperamental cat who loves me unconditionally.

Later, I change into a pair of my most comfortable pajamas. The cartoon characters, Garfield and Odie are on the front of the tank top with prints of dog bones and fish skeletons scattered all over the shorts. The material is worn a little from the numerous washings over the years. Grandma bought them for me my senior year of high school and I can't seem to part with them. They are my favorite. A stark contrast to the elegance of my bedroom.

After I pull all the decorative pillows off my bed, I pull down the comforter and pound my pillow. I'm tired from a long, emotion-filled day. I tuck myself into the fluffy king-sized bed. My eighteen hundred thread count of Egyptian silk sheets brush against my weary body as I nuzzle in to go to sleep. Sleep doesn't come for me. I toss and turn.

Those twins plague me and consume my mood, reminding me of my childhood, how Fallyn was always in the front protecting me and Sage. I'm closer to this case than I realize. It's bringing back memories. A journey into the past I let go of when I left the View.

Thinking about Fallyn along with the twins causes

a bit of distress for me, feelings I've tried to bury because it releases a helplessness within me I've succeeded for many years to leave in the past. But like a bad penny, it always turns up.

The pizza I ate earlier brings about a whole other round of reflecting, seeing the teenagers under the tree with their easy banter. It brings me back to the first time I got to know Keagan Fontneau. How his friendship became important to me.

We made it to the pizza place across town in about fifteen minutes. Keagan drove slow so as not to scare me, I'm sure. I knew he liked it fast because I'd seen him pull up to school a few times on his motorcycle. The way he talked to me or looked at me reminded of the way a person would approach a scared animal—small steps, measured, and careful. Maybe I was. I was a bag of nerves knowing that if dad caught me, there would be hell to pay.

Keagan ordered us a pizza and drinks, not before asking me what I like and don't like. He ordered everything I wanted: a pepperoni, jalapeño, and Canadian bacon pizza, along with a sweet tea with a slice of lemon. I watched him for a few minutes cautiously sitting across the round table from me. He had a take-charge, no nonsense aura about him. And for some strange reason, I liked it.

I admired the rustic Italian decor of Vino's, baskets hanging from the ceiling and pendant lights dangling over each floral covered table, giving off an ambiance of old world, vintage. The floor was made up of russet colored bricks, an intricate pattern that gives off a timeless sense of beauty and charm. Jutting out from the wall closest to the kitchen was a brick oven composed of stone and stucco. A wood fire burned brightly, crackling underneath the pizzas already in the chamber. Yet with all of its fine dining qualities, Vino's was very soothing and laid-back. This place was perfect.

I felt his eyes on me as I took everything in. Then he asked, "Tell me 'bout yourself, Jocelyn."

I was caught off-guard at first. He's so direct and to the point. My total opposite. I've never been very good at conversations. Ducking my chin to my chest, I inhaled a deep breath, composing my thoughts. As I looked up from my moment of composure, I saw his easy smile and beautiful blue eyes, dancing with mischief. Was he playing with me? Baiting me? I gave him my finest haughty grin I could muster and spun my tale the best I could without giving away too much.

"Well, there's really not much to tell. I come from a large family. I've lived here in Lakeview all my life. My mother teaches elementary school, my dad is a rancher, I love horses, the color pink, and—oh, I'm a Libra," I rambled on and on. "I hate math, I stink at Spanish, and I love cheerleading." Taking another deep breath, I stopped and waited for his scrutiny.

I glanced up and Keagan was staring at me,

taking in my every word. With one eyebrow raised, his face portrayed a person without a care in the world, yet interested all at the same time. His arms were crossed over his ripped chest. The top of Keagan's strawberry blonde hair fell gingerly over his forehead with the sides high and tight. I blushed under his keen gaze. There was something about those piercing blue orbs that gave me the warm and fuzzies.

The waitress came back to our table with drinks and I downed half the glass of the heavenly nectar because my mouth was so dry from my nervous banter. Setting the glass down, I fiddled with the napkin that was laid out across my lap. I was all jittery and shaky from his attention. This kind of thing didn't happen to me. Jocelyn Blackwood was normally the fly on the wall, the one who gets passed up because I blended in so well with my surroundings.

Keagan clucked behind his teeth, garnering my attention.

"What? I was thirsty. I ramble when I'm nervous. My mouth was totally dry. And quite honestly, you make me a little nervous, Keagan."

"Hmmm, you shouldn't be nervous, Jocelyn. Not with me anyway. As long as I've got a biscuit, you've got half." Keagan smiled again.

"Ha! You are not what I imagined, Mr. Fontneau."

"Interesting. I knew there was more to you than meets the eye, Boo," he chuckled and his words eased

my fears slightly.

A few minutes later, the waitress came back with a piping hot pan of pizza and set it onto the middle of the table in between us. Keagan scooped up the first piece and set down in front of me, then served himself. Such manners.

"Thank you. Can you please pass the red pepper flakes? Gotta have them on my pizza."

He passed the jar. "Really? On top of the jalapeños, huh? You must have an iron gut, cher. My kinda lady."

My cheeks filled to bursting from all the grinning I had going on.

"Yep, pepper flakes makes everything taste better. At least that's what I think."

He waited until I finished sprinkling all over my pizza, then did the same to his, along with the parmesan cheese. We dug in. Silence fell between us for a little while as we consumed the delicious meal.

In between the scrumptious oozing, cheesy bites, I made a few noises. "Mmm" and "oh my goodness" fell from my mouth frequently. Peeking up at Keagan to see if he was enjoying the pizza as much as I was, I stopped my chewing. His bottom lip was tucked behind his teeth like he was biting it. I caught a look of lust that's gone as fast as it came. Without missing a beat, he stuck a piece of pizza into his mouth and chewed vigorously as a smirk played wide across his face.

The moment passed and we continued eating while making small talk, getting to know each other one confession at a time. Keagan had a personality that kept me in stitches. He told me stories about his family camping and fishing trips.

"Yep ... she fell right out, trying to pull that fish into the boat. It was a lunker. Next thing I know, my pop pushes me right in after her. No kidding. He said someone had to save her and I was closest. She didn't need any help though. She ended up saving me. I was only ten for crying out loud."

We laughed together. The expressions on his face and hand motions while telling the story made me laugh deep down in my gut, surprising me.

"And what's a lunker?" I asked, bewildered by his unusual words.

"Oh, right. Forgot you might not know what that means, Boo." Keagan's broken laugh is smooth and sexy. "A lunker is any fish that's ten pounds or more. Just like a toad is five to ten pounds and anything less is a chunk." He explained it as if everyone should know that. He was so cute. "So my brother Wade, he's your age, he's really good at playing the guitar. I'm hoping he does something with that one day. He played a few times on the last post where we lived in Texas. He brought in a crowd too. I helped 'em by bangin' on the drums."

"That's awesome, Keagan. My sisters and I love to sing and Fallyn plays the piano flawlessly. We need

to get together sometime and jam."

I was amazed by the dialogue. Nice and easy.

I noticed a piece of pizza caught in what looked like two-day-old scruff, so I leaned over to wipe it off as he leaned in towards me. Our auras seemed to tilt together, intersecting to touch at that one moment in time.

"There's a little pizza caught right here." I wipe it off, startled by my thoughts, and settled back into my seat.

"Oh, yeah. I have to shave every day or it gets like this, cher.*"*

"You really have to shave your face every day?" I asked. "I have to shave my legs daily, but I didn't realize guys had to do the same thing." We both roared into a fit of laughter at the crazy simple things we were discussing. My heart fluttered as my belly took a dip into the unknown. I was struck by the easy chitchat and how uncomplicated it was talking to him. And when he called me "boo" and "cher"*, I melted a little more. Cajun sentiments his pop taught him.*

The table next to us was occupied by an older couple about my grandma's age. The endearing smiles they shot our way gave me a sense of peace. I'd found a new friend, someone who saw me for who I really am. Not one of the Blackwood girls or sisters, but me.

"So why don't you have a boyfriend, Boo?" Keagan didn't pull any punches, as he changed the

direction of our talk. His eyes were crinkling at the corners along with his gleaming megawatt smile.

"I don't do boyfriends." I felt the blood instantly rush up my cheeks, immediately regretting my answer. "Um, I mean I don't have boyfriends. I'm not really allowed to date." Trying to recover from my crazy blunder, I elaborated some more. "My dad is very demanding of certain things and us dating is something that is simply not permitted."

Keagan seemed to assess my answer first with a few bouts of laughter and then he glanced towards me, his face turning serious.

"That's a shame, Jo. Can I call you Jo?" I nod and he continued. "I'd really like to be your boyfriend. I like you. You're fun to hang out with."

My mind was spinning around and around from his admission. This blond, blue eyed sexy boy was interested in being my boyfriend. What would Fallyn do? Oh I knew what she'd say: "Go for it, little sis! You only live once." That's what she does. But I couldn't. I would really love to and Keagan Fontineau was super hot. But my dad would never allow it. And I was the straight and narrow kind of daughter. I could be his friend. That was acceptable. Would he go for it?

As if he could read my mind, Keagan spoke, "You know, Jo. I can be your boyfriend without being your 'boyfriend'." He gestured with air quotes and continued. "I'm a boy, that's obvious, and I wanna be your friend, Boo. So in technical terms, I'd be a boyfriend. Or we could call me a not-boyfriend." He gazed over at me with determination. He was ambitious; I'd give him that. I pondered over what he was offering.

"Boy ... and friend. Well, okay then. Yes. I think that might just work. I guess, I mean it isn't technically unacceptable. Not-boyfriend. Yes. Who knows, maybe we can be BFFs one day."

I smiled brightly up towards his handsome face. I think the BFF may be too much for a guy like Keagan Fontneau to want or need, but he didn't seem to mind. Keagan beamed back at me and I realized this might be one of the best nights of my life.

Why the heck am I thinking about this? About Keagan? I kick at the covers on my feet, annoyed with myself. *Stop this nonsense, Jocelyn.* You can't change the past, only create the future. Thinking about something beyond my control does me no good. I sink back down into the softness of the mattress, rolling over, pillow between my knees. Miss Kitty jumps up onto the bed and snuggles into my arms. I stroke her black, downy fur, soothing us both. The last thing I remember before I succumb to the sandman is Fallyn's smiling face.

In the wee hours of the morning, I wake up startled from a dream, gasping for air. Breath in. Breath out. Breath in. Breath out. I focus on my breathing, letting go of the horrendous nightmare by grounding myself to the here and now. It was one of those dreams that stick with you for a while, not easily forgotten because you experienced it before in a different time.

In this particular dream, I was only five years old. He was hurting her again. Her screams filled my ears even with the pillow covering my head. Like all the other dreams I've had, I was cuddled up on the full-size mattress with my little sister Sage in my old bedroom on the ranch. We had the covers pulled over us hoping he wouldn't see us if he tries to find us. Fallyn stepped in front of me when my dad was questioning me and took the blame for something I had done. She's the big sister and she always ran interference between him and us all the time. It never made sense. She would bait him with her words until he didn't see anyone else in the room but her.

In this dream, this time she was paying the price. It didn't matter. If she wasn't there, it would be Sage, mother, or me. I never meant to get her in trouble. I love her.

He had her counting. "Eighteen." The belt connecting with flesh and Fallyn's voice was hoarse as she released a cry of pain. Again, the realness of the dream is uncanny to the reality that I lived.

My father's voice continued counting. "Nineteen. Twenty."

Her screams became whimpers and I knew he'd

finished giving her twenty licks with his weapon of choice: the leather belt. I hated it. His belt symbolized the brutality and viciousness we were forced to live with daily. He would always tell her that if she didn't move and just took the lashes, then he wouldn't punish me too.

I hated him then, and I still loathe him now. He's evil.

"Go to your room and don't leave until you have my permission. You're not allowed out of this house for any reason," Dad had said, continuing his punishing instructions. "You won't be allowed to go to your slumber party this weekend, either."

I didn't hear Fallyn reply as the bedroom doorknob twisted and the door opened. Fallyn gently walked to the bed and started climbing up onto the mattress. We parted, allowing her to crawl between us to lie down. Like so many times before, we carefully surrounded her and held her hands, not touching anywhere else. It was always the same after the punishments: brutal. The physical damage disappears, but the emotional scars stay forever.

"Are you okay, Fallyn?" Sage had whispered.

She sniffled and faintly replied, "Yes."

That was how Fallyn reacted. She was and still is in my mind the strongest person I know, besides my grandma.

"Do you want a drink? I can sneak out and get you something," I offered, my conscience wrestling with blame and sorrow after what she endured.

"No," she replied, shaking her head. "He would catch you."

"Do you still love me, Fallyn?" I asked her, scared of what her answer would be.

"I'll always love you, both of you. What happened wasn't your fault, Jo. It's his. We have each other and no matter what, that's never gonna change. Remember, we're the three musketeers. One for all and all for one, right?"

We both replied, "Yes."

"I love you, Fallyn."

As the dream continued, she drifted off to sleep and I knew we had to stick together. Growing up, I'd stayed at my Aunt Polly Jean's house and their family wasn't like ours. Her husband didn't whip his daughters like my dad did. I wish he would have been different for us. Every child deserves good parents but not every parent deserves a child; unfortunately for me and my sisters, my dad had three daughters at the time. My mind strays for a second, because now there's Grayson and Addie in the mix. *God help them, I pray.*

The end of my dream was strange this time. And it seemed so real. I was trying to wake myself up from the brutality and legitimacy of the hellish nightmare I lived and survived. A sense of desertion and emptiness enclosed around me. I found myself alone and scared. I couldn't breathe. No Fallyn, no Sage, just me in the hollow blackness. Out from the dark a lone figure walked forward. I could barely make out his face until he got a little closer. It was Keagan. His expression was hard, fierce, but those crystal eyes betrayed him. The beautiful blue aimed at me, regarding only me.

My breathing slows down, sputtering to its normal rhythm. It's been a few months since I dreamed about him. This one was different, but it came just the same. It was like Keagan was there to rescue me. If I was teetering on the edge of whether this case is causing conflict within me, now I know for sure. I need to get myself in check. I'm not the helpless little girl from before.

Despite my normal intake, I still feel as if I can't breathe or catch my breath. It's like I'm suffocating on the inside. It's that need, the urgency to breathe and get out of the house that drives me as I throw the covers aside because going back to sleep is out of the question.

I get up and go to the bathroom and splash water on my face, peering into the mirror. The woman who greets me is the same, but different. The familiar green eyes of a grownup stare back at me. I've filled out with womanly curves from top to bottom. Blonde hair with highlights of multiple shades streak through my tresses. I still keep it long, falling just above my bra line. The bags under my eyes reveal a different story, one that carries the weight of the world.

Pulling my hair tightly back into a ponytail and brushing my teeth, I gather my gear. After I pull the tight spandex running shorts and the *Dri-FIT* halter on, I lace up my pink-and-grey trainers and step out into the crack of dawn. My favorite time of day.

The lightly painted pink sky delivers the sign that rain is coming. A storm is brewing off the east coast, one that is sure to bring with it destruction and mayhem—like my thoughts lately. The sweet smells of geraniums and dew on fresh-cut grass drift around me. This is my heaven, my reprieve from the hectic life I have chosen. Close by, the call of the mockingbird sings as he mocks me with his insistent call. Isn't that amazing? Even birds don't get me.

I set off on a fast pace, pounding the pavement for the four mile jog around my neighborhood. My brain has its own agenda, leading me down memory lane, causing a fissure of pain directly stabbing at my heart and simultaneously filling me with happiness that came with knowing Keagan. Shaking my head from side to side, I smile slightly. Keagan was such a big part of my first high school experience. He wiggled his way into my heart and never left. The time we spent together as friends changed me for the better.

But that was such a long time ago.

I continue through one of the golf course tunnels, amped up, pushing my legs harder with every footfall. The burn in my chest and limbs calm my nerves. Coming out the other side, I catch a glimpse of the horizon over the pristine freshly-cut fairway. I watch as the sun peeks up and out saying hello to the world. I can see it just past the trees, announcing a new day. A fresh start.

Looking at my phone strapped to my arm, I see I've been running for about thirty-eight minutes. Time to finish up and get back home.

CHAPTER 6
KEAGAN

We've been traveling south on State Road 27 for over an hour or so with no conversation. I kinda got the feeling my new best friend Gunner was in some deep shit with whoever was on the other end of the phone call earlier. His mood reflects a kid caught with his hand in a cookie jar, scared he's going to get an ass whoopin' for disobeying. I should know; been there, got that from my maw growing up.

We pass a road sign announcing 40 more miles until Gainesville. We need to stop and gas up and I guess that's a good place to grab some grub. The Pit-Stop is on the outskirts of the city, and a good friend of mine owns the joint.

Ain't it funny how life changes and molds a person into what they became later on? No truer thoughts than the first time I took Jocelyn Blackwood out. That girl still plagues me. Little did I know how much that day would change me and the way I look at life.

Bo, David, and I were waiting on Fallyn and

Jocelyn outside the movie theater. Fallyn had Bo set up this "date" and I was hoping we'd get some time to talk. I wanted to know more about her.

"Hiya, boys!" Fallyn shouted from across the parking lot. She motioned us towards her car as Jocelyn got out from the passenger side.

We walked their way and David wrapped his body around Fallyn, kissing her neck and whispering in her ear. He guided her away from us, walking to his car they got in, and pulled out of the parking lot. Jocelyn was staring at the ground.

"I'm outta here, y'all. Meet ya back here at eleven thirty," Bo commented as he walked away.

We were alone, standing in the middle of the movie theater parking lot staring at each other. She looked delicious. She had her pink boots on and a tank top paired with skinny jeans. I smiled at her. I don't think she realized how beautiful she really was.

"Do you wanna see a movie or go somewhere and talk?" I asked her hoping for the latter.

"Um I ... um ..."

"How 'bout a pizza? My family went to Vino's Pizza Cafe a few weeks back and I'm in love. It's soooo good," I blabbered, trying to loosen her up some.

She smiled and nodded. I motioned to my bronco and she fell in line beside me. I opened the passenger door for her and she slid up and in. I watched her long legs as she folded them and clasped her hands together. I knew she was unaware of the arousing feelings she was stirring in me. Her body language was tense and I liked knowing I was the one that was affecting her.

We arrived at the restaurant and got a table.

"Tell me about yourself, Jocelyn. I know there's more than good looks behind your smile," I used my charming voice and smirked. She looked startled by my words; she wasn't expecting such a direct approach.

That night changed my life. She was all I could think about for the longest time. Last time I heard, Jocelyn had left Lakeview and moved to Gainesville, broken all ties with her family and friends. As many times as I've visited, I've never once run into her. I haven't seen her since high school. And, as much as I would like to see what's she's up to now, I know it's best to let bygones be bygones. She wouldn't know what to think of the fucked-up mess I am today. I guess somehow along life's path, we've changed roles.

She was the lost one when I left the View, not wanting to exist once Fallyn disappeared. I knew they were close. Hell, we all did, but didn't realize she would crawl into such a deep depression. I'm not depressed. I'm pissed. I carry around the guilt of seven men dying on my watch. I need a way to release all my pent-up anger. Killing Mustaff would help, but with the damage he's done to my body, that's something that won't happen for me.

Not only is Gainesville where Jocelyn lives, but it's the city the Army shipped me to from Afghanistan for my recovery at the veteran's hospital in the panhandle, honorably discharged and wounded. My gut churns at the memories that haunt my nightmares. I swore to avenge my brothers who died in the ambush that day, but that choice was taken away from me by the higher-ups calling the shots.

General Fox's last words to me before I left were: "Live to fight another day, soldier. Pick your battles carefully, go to bed with your enemies on your mind, and you'll win the war. Every damn time."

I will never forget those words. I live by them. Every day.

Gunner is cautious of me. Smart reaction from someone who acts like a dummy most of the time. The kid is in way over his head and doesn't realize it yet. He occasionally glances my way and the drumming of his fingers on his upper thigh increases, a sure sign of his anxiety level spiking. The continual roaming of his wide eyes looking for someone to jump out in front of this two-ton moving truck is a telltale sign he's about to freak the fuck out.

He's not sure where I draw the line. He doesn't know me from shit, but the first sign of trouble has him packing his bags and hightailing it out of Perry with an unknown stranger. I know the true reason he left: the brothers allowed it. He's under the radar riding with me.

A police siren blares somewhere behind us, and his body stills. I glance at him quickly and a panic face emerges on Gunner when the red and blue lights flashing in the rearview mirror draw closer. Instantly, he's back and demanding.

"You gotta outrun 'em. I can't be caught, Crash," Gunner exclaims worriedly.

I have no intentions of running from the cops as I ease off the accelerator and slowly apply the brake.

"What the fuck are you doing?" Gunner yells in a panic.

"This baby is fast, but not fast enough to get away from that souped-up Crown Vic engine back there." I thumb at the vehicle over my shoulder. "Trust me, bro. I can handle 'em. Just chillax and let me do the talkin'."

"She was right. Shit, I should've stayed in Perry. I'm a dead man walking. They're going to kill me if I'm caught. Dead," he mumbles furiously.

I release a heavy sigh letting my aggravation show from his less-than-manly behavior. The guy needs a reality check. He's acting like a baby. I edge off the highway, slowly come to a stop, and put the truck in park. The trooper's vehicle stops behind me and the siren sound ends. A car door opens and shuts.

I see two armed troopers walking towards us in the rearview mirror. The silhouette of a large dog in the back seat almost has me smiling. They break apart at the backend, circling each side of the truck.

"Don't panic, Gunner. Stay calm and I'll handle this," I whisper.

He nods and exhales a long breath when someone taps on my driver's side window. I turn and push the buttons, lowering the windows, and the humid Florida air rushes into the cab.

"Howdy, gentlemen. What can I do for y'all?" I ask, glancing from the trooper on my left side to the one on the right side of the vehicle.

"License and registration, sir," the trooper standing at my window requests, eyeing the inside of cab and the man in the passenger seat, too.

"Sure thing, officer. Mind if I ask why you pulled me over?"

"Check point. License and registration?"

I reach for the glove box, intent on retrieving my wallet and the documents requested. Gunner is squirming, so I give him a glare, hoping he heeds my silent warning. He rolls his eyes at me but remains quiet.

I extract my license from inside the plastic holder and hand both items over to the trooper. He nods and returns to the back of my truck to verify on his CB radio while the other one stares at us.

"Nice weather we've been having. Especially with it being hurricane season and all. Usually we've had a hurricane or two swarming the waters by now. Guess we've been lucky so far," the trooper nearest to Gunner says.

"I've had the television channel set on the weather all day long, you know, with Hurricane Georgia out in the Atlantic and all. Forecasters are predicting it to be the worst storm to hit Florida in years. Warning people to batten down the hatches and all. Where y'all headed?"

"South of Miami," I say and catch a slight crinkle in the corner of his mouth.

"Which way you traveling? Interstate or highway?"

"I planned on taking 75 'til we hit the turnpike."

"Well, you might want to rethink that. It'll be packed both ways with people panicking to get out of the state or fighting to get home. You know? Trying to get their homes boarded up and secured before the storm hits. They are saying landfall is expected in the next 24 to 48 hours."

"Thanks for the heads up. I plan to stop in Gainesville, gas up, and eat. Guess we can look at the map for alternatives then. We might have to find a place to stay for the next little bit. I know of a few good stops."

"Yes, sir. That sounds really good. I don't know about you, but I wouldn't wanna be caught when Georgia hits the shore. Never know what she'll be bringing with her."

The other cop returns and hands the papers and

license back to me.

"Everything checks out, sir. You've got a busted taillight. You might want to have that looked at as soon as you can."

"You don't say? I'll have to find somewhere in Gainesville that's open and try to replace it."

They both nod and walk back to their vehicle, get in, and pull back onto the highway. A few seconds later, the Crown Vic's taillights fade away.

CHAPTER 7
Jocelyn

For some ungodly reason, I can't seem to get focused today. My head is on a trip and I feel like a yoyo swinging from one extreme to the next. This case is taking a toll on me.

After my run and a hot shower, I'm feeling a bit better. The tension is relaxing in my shoulders and I can think clearly again. I have to concentrate on my game plan for the twins and try to figure out what is going on. In the end, helping those teenagers find their way is all that really matters to me.

I'm thrust back into the past again to the day I finally realized it was time to move on, the day it was time to pull up my big girl panties and take on the world like I was meant to. Everything changed again for me one more time.

Stretching and yawning in my bed, I pulled the covers away from my body. I glanced to the window and saw that it was still dawn outside. Perfect. It was the time in the morning I could relax and enjoy the fresh air and my horses all alone.

School ended two weeks earlier. Thank goodness. I'd been working on the ranch as much as possible to stay busy and out of my father's way. I figured that if I did, he would certainly leave me be, and so far it had worked out beautifully.

The past year of high school was rough and I was thankful for a reprieve. I couldn't take anymore lingering looks of pity or snickers behind my back. People were cruel. Can't really blame them. It's in our nature, the instinct to lash out before someone does it to you. But it's the choices we make that define who we are in life, like the choice I made to let Keagan go. A twist of discomfort brushed against my heart. At the time, it was necessary. I just felt numb and unsure. He made things brighter, even in my state of darkness. I should've told him so.

I pulled on my jeans and t-shirt and slipped into my old worn riding boots. Heading out the side door so as not to attract attention, I inhaled a deep consoling breath as I absorbed the beauty that surrounded me in the early break of morning. From the roost of the chicken coup near the barn, I heard the crow of Red, the head rooster, signaling the start of a new day. The crickets were chirping their cadence along with the croaking of the bullfrogs down by the pond, sending a signal of peace and life out to the heavens.

During the next few hours, I lost myself in the automatic actions of shoveling fresh hay into the stalls. I enjoyed brushing down Storm and Cyclops, my two best horses. Cyclops was a Palomino, a beautiful breed. He stood a whopping eighteen hands high with a coat that had varying shades of gold. His mane and tail were whitish silver in color. He was high strung and a whole lot of fun to ride. On the other hand, Storm was a Pinto. She's a couple hands shorter than Cyclops. Her white coat was home to large patches of burnt orange and deep chestnut. Where Cyclops was hyper, Storm was laid-back.

After I handed out treats of a few apples and carrots, I fed all the horses, filling their buckets with their favorites: oats, barley, and corn.

When I made it back to the house, I was worn out, exhausted from the chores. All I wanted was a shower and a quick nap before I got at it again. Momma was standing in the kitchen making waffles. The smells of vanilla and almond made my stomach growl. Sage was helping her by cutting up bananas and strawberries. Grayson was in his booster seat at the table, making his own kind of music by banging on the wood surface with a wooden spoon and attempting to sing Old McDonald. He was precious.

"Good morning, sunshine," Momma sang out to me, then continued chanting Old McDonald with Grayson.

"Morning, family."

"Morning sister. How's Cyclops, JoJo? Did he nip at your tushy again?" Sage giggled.

I grinned back at her. "No, not today," I answered, shaking my head. "He's just been mad at me is all. I haven't taken him out for a good run in months. He's cranky. But I plan to remedy that today."

"Sounds like fun. I wanna go, too. I can ride Stormy. Can I go with you?" Sage pleaded.

"Sure, Buttercup. It's a date."

"Oh, Jo. I almost forgot." Momma stopped before pouring more batter into the waffle iron. "Keagan called about an hour ago. He's leaving this morning and wanted to say goodbye."

My attitude took a nosedive from the momentary peace I had found. He was really leaving.

"When? What time? Where?" I yelped out.

"Hold on, Jocelyn, I wrote it all down. I didn't want to forget in case you wanted to go," Momma replied.

She handed me a piece of paper with all the information of Keagan's departure. He was leaving from the bus depot at 10:42 a.m. The clock on the stove indicated I had fifteen minutes.

"I've got to go."

"Of course, sweet girl. Hurry before you're too late. Do be careful." Momma looked at me with understanding as I grabbed my keys off the hook and exited the house.

I didn't even have time to change clothes or brush my hair. The bus station was about ten minutes from the ranch if I didn't have any unexpected stops along the way.

I made it to the bus station just as a bus was pulling away. Exiting my car, I ran as fast as my legs would allow in cowgirl boots, stomping up the pavement like I was being chased by a ghost. But I was too late. I watched the bus as it rounded the corner, falling out of sight.

Sinking to my knees, I grabbed my head and pulled tightly on my hair as the waterworks started. Stupid, stupid, stupid. Why didn't I say goodbye before? Now he was gone and I didn't know if I'd ever get to talk to him again.

I felt a large, yet gentle hand touch my shoulder. My eyes moved to the hand and followed up until I saw him. Keagan's dad. His face wore a mask of indecision and sorrow, a face that bared the remarkable likeness of Keagan.

"C'mere, Boo."

He helped me up off the concrete and guided me to an empty bench out in front of the bus stop. I noticed that no one was around. We were alone. The fact that Keagan was really gone seeped into my skin, causing nausea in the pit of my stomach.

Mr. Fontneau put his arm around me and pulled me in for a comforting hug, but the only thing it accomplished was more tears.

"Is he ... is he really ... gone? I missed him, didn't I?" I voiced through ugly sobs.

I felt his nod as he sniffed then groaned, pulling back slightly.

"Lady bug, you smell terrible. It's like you've been wallerin' around in horse dung. Poo-yee-yi, sugar. My 'pologies, but you stink."

He got a laugh out of me. It was a little bit hysterical, but a laugh just the same.

"Yes sir. I... was doing my chores when I found out. I didn't realize it was today."

"I know. We're never really prepared for change, but it comes just the same," Mr. Fontneau explained. "Why did ya come here, Jo?"

I pondered for a moment, then answered, "I wanted to... I don't know. When my momma told me this was it, I had to be here. To say goodbye. I owed him that much for the friendship he gave me."

Thinking about the question again, I was struck by the fact that Keagan was my best friend. At one time, I thought he would be my best not-boyfriend forever— until Fallyn left and I began to push him away.

"I understand what you're sayin', Boo. There are times we don't realize what we have until we lose it. Now I don't know much about your personal family stuff, only what Keagan shared with me. Do ya mind if I give ya a little piece of advice?"

Mesmerized by his Southern Cajun drawl, I nodded my head for him to continue. This was the closest I could get to Keagan right now, so I'd take it.

"Baby girl, you'll have a chance to see him again. I have no doubt."

His cryptic words cause my head to spin as

another piece of me fell back into place.

"But you gotta pull yourself together. Fix what's broken inside ya. You're no good as a friend or otherwise with this dark cloud hangin' ov'r your head, cher. *I know ya feel abandoned an' ya lost someone ya love the most. That's just life, darlin'. People come and go, in an' out of our lives. It's the impact they leave with us that makes the difference. Yeah? It's what we do with the knowledge that creates the ripples in the pond. Good or bad. Fuh sure," he finished up and looked down at me.*

Words escaped me. I actually heard what he was saying. For the first time in forever, I heard the words of wisdom being given. And within the deep anguish of my heart and brain, I grasped onto every syllable he delivered. Something shifted inside, telling me it was time to release the heartache and move forward.

"Thank you, Mr. Fontneau," was all I could muster, and I think he understood.

Nodding his head in agreement, he squeezed my shoulder once more before he got up to leave.

"Ya know, K is gonna be in the thick of things for a while. Got to keep his head on straight with no distractions, Boo."

I caught his meaning and he was right. I wouldn't be an interference that could get him hurt, or worse, killed.

"Could you give a message to Keagan for me? When you talk to him?"

"Sure thing, cher. *"*

"Would you tell him thank you for being my friend? That I'm going to believe again? And I'll never give up."

"Ca c'est bon, Boo. That's good."

With that, he smiled and walked away from me, leaving me alone at the bus station to think about what I was going to do with my life. My mind was going to war with my heart, and like the phoenix rising from the ashes, so would Jocelyn Blackwood.

Those words Mr. Fontneau spoke to me all those years ago created a defining moment in my life, an expectation I've tried to live up to. Even as simple as they were, the effect they had on my life was monumental. The reason people awaken is because they have finally stopped agreeing with things that insult their soul. This was my logic for moving forward.

I'm curious as to how Mr. Fontneau is doing. Last time I heard he was retired and Mrs. Fontneau had him traveling all over the world. I need to ask Momma next time I talk to her.

I lost Keagan as a friend, lost all contact with him. My choice, of course. Although, the lesson he taught me by being my friend pushed me on the path I lead today. He gifted me friendship and showed me to always believe that anything was possible, that even though I felt alone or felt like part of the shadows, I really wasn't. There was someone who could see me, my best friend who could pick me out of a crowd easily and be happy to do it. That's who Keagan was. He made me feel important. Special, even.

I wanted to help others in that same way. In the background, at a distance, or in the middle, it didn't matter. I transformed myself into the successful psychologist I am today. However, with the job I have, I'm in the thick of it, on the front lines taking up for those less fortunate or in need of help.

I'm curious if he ever thinks about me. What's he doing right now? Crazy, I know. Those kinds of dreams are not in the plans for me. Maybe they were once long ago before everything went to hell in a hand basket. The reason I can't seem to let go is that I still have hope.

Getting comfy on my couch, I open my laptop to start my research. I've got work to do. I need to gather as much information I can about Calista and Desmond Payne. It's the beginnings of what I will need to make my case, if I find out things aren't kosher with the couple. After a few more keystrokes and dead ends, I give up. There is nothing out of the ordinary I can find.

Calista has her hands in many different high society pools. She has won Mother of the Year, Best in Show for her amazing flowers and home gardens as well as being part of several nonprofit cancer organizations. I'm sure those are because of her late husband, father of her twins, who lost the battle three years ago. For all appearances, she seems perfect.

Mr. Desmond Payne is an enigma. He showed up on the social scene about five years ago and has climbed the ranks quickly. He's been featured in GQ, frequents local talk shows at the television stations, and is squeaky clean. Mr. Payne has grown his wealth through tourism. He now owns more than seven luxury resorts in some of the most prestigious places to visit in the state. Destin, Palm Beach, and Miami, to name a few.

I know this is going to take more than average work. I'll need to spend many sessions, one-on-one and together with the twins, to gain their trust and figure out what's really going on in their lives. They lost their dad only a few years ago and their mom's remarrying could be a contributing factor.

Like Mr. Fontneau said, we're never really prepared for change, but it comes anyway. Maybe that's it: too much change is causing the twins pain. It'll take time and I'm committed. I have to help them.

CHAPTER 8
KEAGAN

"So you do know how to talk," Gunner snidely comments as the windows seal and the cool air tunnels from the vents on the dash.

"When necessary," I shrug.

I put the truck in drive and look in my rearview mirror for oncoming traffic. The road is deserted when I accelerate towards Gainesville. We should arrive at the planned stop within the hour, which is enough time to learn more about Gunner and form a new strategy. With all that's at stake here, my patience is thinning and I can't afford it to, not now.

"Well, you handled that situation, and it could've gone south fast. I would've hated killin' them. Make no mistake, Crash. If it came down to me or them, they would've been toast. I ain't going to jail for nobody."

"Big words from someone who almost cried like a baby a little bit ago. You got the balls to back 'em?"

"Yep, sure do. Never leave home without it." He reaches behind him and draws a 9mm pistol. "This here is my insurance."

"Insurance?"

"I'll either kill or be killed. Nobody's takin' me without a fight."

"Sounds like you've got two options, and neither of 'em work for me. I sure as hell ain't ready to die yet. Put that gun away. You can go down in a blaze of glory when I'm not around, mister dead man walking."

"Fuck man. You don't know shit. I've got stuff happenin' and it's real. I'm gonna be rollin' in the dough soon."

"Talk to me."

"Can't."

"Your loss."

I concentrate on driving and ignore the simmering man sitting beside me. A few miles later, a bump in the road jars the truck and Gunner sits up from leaning on the passenger side window.

"I need a vacation. Somewhere on a deserted island with a long leggy blonde with tits the size of watermelons and a never-ending liquor bar. I can imagine it now. Mai Tai and Piña Coladas all day long."

"You're dreaming, douchebag. Those are girly drinks by the way."

"Hardie har har, Crash. You're so funny," Gunner jokes. "Nope. I'm gonna have it. Just as soon as I make this last delivery happen."

"Yeah, must be a humdinger of a delivery to make

that kind of cash."

"Special order from a well-paying client."

I glance at him with a questioning look and return my focus to the highway.

"Some clients have specific tastes. And, this client, well let's just say he's been waiting for this package for quite some time now."

"So, you're just the delivery boy?"

"Fuck you, Crash. I'm more than that. I'm the one who finds a way into the merchandise and delivers the how-tos to get it. This delivery is going to thrust me into retirement, baby."

"You seem confident. What happens when your 'special' client wants more of what you're supplying? Then what are you going to do? Un-retire? Shit, kid. You don't have a clue what you're up against."

Gunner sits quietly gazing out the window at the passing trees. He hasn't answered me back. He seems caught up in his own thoughts and judging from the look on his face, they aren't good ones. Maybe there's hope for him yet. Probably not. His type doesn't learn from words, but actions. So far I'm getting nowhere on this little adventure.

We pull into Grady's Pit-Stop, a one-shop hole-in-the-wall joint, a restaurant, gas station and motel all-in-one. The motel has ten rooms, and the vacancy sign is blinking in the large lobby window. I put the truck in park and turn the engine off.

"Stay here. I'll go get us some rooms and then we

can find some grub."

"Whatever. I got no wheels, so I'll be right here, daddy-o."

I flash him the finger and exit my truck. Stupid fucker. He's got a comeback for everything. I would almost like the guy if he wasn't wrapped up in some scary shit.

I open the glass door and walk into the lobby. There, sitting on the other side of the reception desk, is my buddy Grady "Bulldog" Johnson. Grady and I go way back. His dad served with my pop. We grew up the same, always moving from base to base. We went to high school together in Texas before I moved to Lakeview my senior year. He occasionally helps Trident out when we're in a pinch and need his expertise.

"Well, look what the cat dragged in. Keagan Fontneau. What the hell have you been up to, man? Haven't seen you 'round my neck of the woods in a while."

I clasp his outstretched hand and we bump shoulders in greeting.

"Bulldog, long time no see. Phone call just ain't the same, huh? I've been trying to stay out of trouble. You know the drill."

"How's the family?"

"Pop's driving maw crazy since he retired. They bought a place down south near a little fishing village on the Gulf. They're either fishing or traveling somewhere to fish. She wants to visit Wade and his crew up in Alaska and he keeps saying it's too damn cold to wait for summer."

"Sounds like your pop. Never liked the cold, did he? I remember that year he and Pop did a tour in Germany. He bitched every chance he got about freezing his ass off."

"Yep. He still does every chance he gets. Won't let maw forget it either. He only went because she wanted to say she'd been there. What about your parents?"

"They're good. Staying busy helping Parker with his youngins. Since Missy died, he's been a mess."

"Yeah, maw told me what happened. Fucked up mess."

"You have no idea. Parker about lost it. If they hadn't been there, I don't know what would have happened to my nieces." He glances out the window towards my parked truck and nods. "Gotcha a friend with you?"

"Yeah. We need a place to crash under the radar while Georgia passes through."

"Work?"

"Yeah. He's the job."

"Expecting trouble?"

"I've got it covered. He's not a problem. Wouldn't know his ass from a hole in the ground. Shouldn't be any problem tonight, and we should be long gone before anyone suspects a thing."

"Well, then, it's your lucky day, bro. Only the regulars are here. Got two rooms side-by-side with an adjoining door."

"That'll do."

"Here's the keys. Rooms 8 and 9. Down the hall on the right. Kendall should have dinner ready within the hour. Bar doesn't open for another few, but I don't suspect we'll have many showing up tonight with the weather being as it is and all."

"Thanks, Bulldog. I owe you one."

"No problem, Crash. That's how we roll."

I walk back to the truck and get in. Gunner's got his hackles up again. His fingers thrum along his thigh. He eyes me for a few and then leans back against the window.

"Got two adjoining rooms. We can stay tonight and pull out once the weather is better." I hand him the key to Room 8.

"Fine and dandy, man. I just want a shower and something hot to eat."

"The guy at the desk said dinner would be ready soon. Bar doesn't open for another couple hours. Let's get settled first."

I crank the truck and pull over into the slotted parking space. The wind has picked up in the last few minutes. A gust gently rocks the truck. Gunner grips the "oh shit" handle and I chuckle.

"Didn't grow up around here, huh?"

"Nah. I'm a New Yorker. Born and bred. How did

you know that?"

"'Cause if you did, you would know that's nothing compared to what's in store for tonight. The tail remnants are the worse. Once the eye passes, depending on which side you're located on, can be brutal. C'mon man, let's get you inside."

We get our bags and walk into the tiny lobby. I nod at Grady as we pass by and head down the hall to our rooms. I watch as Gunner unlocks his door and enters the room marked 8. The door closes behind him.

I move further down to the next door. The number 9 is painted in neon orange on a green door. Entering my room, I'm instantly thrown back into the 70s with the cheesy orange bedspread and shaggy green carpet. But what catches my eye are the mirrored tiles placed strategically on the ceiling and, smack dab in the middle, a metallic ball is hanging loosely. *Holy Shit!* Whoever thought the disco era decor was hip should be strung up and shot.

A knocking on the adjacent door echoes in the room followed by Gunner's shout, "Open up, Crash."

I throw my bag on the ugly bedspread and unlock the door. Gunner is standing with his 9mm pointed my way.

"What in the hell are you doing? Did you have a brain fart or something? Put the toy gun away before you hurt yourself."

"Gimme the keys to your truck. I don't trust that

you won't leave me high and dry. Not gonna take the chance."

I give him my best you-are-going-to-regret-this look, then sigh. *You've got to be kidding me.*

"Not gonna happen, fuckwipe." I cross my arms, taking my stance.

A startled expression passes on his face.

"You've got one shot. You better make sure I'm dead, 'cause I'm gonna make you wish you were six feet under if I'm not."

"You are one seriously fucked-up guy, Crash. You do realize I've got a loaded gun pointed at you, right?"

I smirk. "You've been warned, Gunner."

His feet shuffle back and forth as an uneasy expression paints across his face. I patiently wait for him to make up his mind. He takes his eyes off me for a split second and I'm on him like white on rice. He misjudged my speed and agility based on my large frame and build. Too many have before.

I quickly grab the wrist holding the 9mm, shoving him further into the tiny room, and inflict a steady stream of pain until he releases the gun. The gun lands gently on the mattress beside us. He grunts as I twist his arm behind his back and grab his neck with my forearm. I apply pressure to his windpipe, slowing his oxygen intake.

"Listen here, you little assworm from New York, 'cause I'm not gonna repeat myself again.

Understand?"

I ease up from strangling the life right out of him and he draws in air, nodding frantically as he does so.

"I'm not your fucking enemy. I don't plan on leaving your pathetic ass unless you give me a reason to. But if you ever draw your weapon on me again, prepare to meet your maker. Are we clear?"

"Crystal," he squeezes out.

"Good."

I push him away from me and he stumbles to his knees gulping in air to his oxygen-deprived lungs. I reach for his gun and chuckle when I realize the safety is on. I release the magazine and slide the chamber back. Pocketing the bullets, I stride to my room without a backwards glance.

"Get yourself cleaned up so we can eat. I'm hungry."

CHAPTER 9
Jocelyn

My dear friend from college, Katrina Perez is coming up from Tampa to spend the night. Rina, as I like to call her, is a Cuban American beauty. There's a college reunion of sorts happening tonight and she wants us to go, a get-together for business majors who graduated with Rina. We've been planning it for months. It's at a venue out in the middle of BFE on the outskirts of Gainesville, but I'm game. I haven't seen her since last year's girls' weekend and I can't wait.

Although, with all of the weather alerts, I'm still a bit leery and unsure if it's going to happen or not. No one's called it off as of yet, so try we will.

I enter the kitchen and start making lunch when the doorbell rings.

"Just a minute," I holler out.

Opening the door, I'm greeted with a familiar, brilliant smile. Katrina is standing with a hand on her hip, cocky as ever, and a suitcase clutched in the other.

"*Buenas tardes*, Jo!"

Katrina lets go of the bag in her hand, which falls with a thud to the ground, and thrusts forward into my arms. She wraps me up so tight, I can't breathe but manage a giggle of glee.

"Hey, Rina. It's so good to see you."

We go inside and Katrina fills me in on her latest conquest—and it's not the finance kind.

"I've missed you so much, *niña*," she says, laughing, then jokes about me finding a hookup tonight at the party. She reminds me of the first time we met, my first year of college.

Like usual, I was in my own world, studying in the library. I heard a shuffle and looked up to see a tall, lanky girl with long dark curly locks and eyes just as dark, smiling down at me.

"You looked at me like, duh?? Jo, you really had no clue we had world civ together, did you? I still have a hard time believing that."

"Um ... well, I admit that saying I didn't pay much attention to the people in my classes sounded really bad. As in 'I'm a geek bad'."

We both roar with laughter.

"Oh, well, no matter, *mi amiga*," Katrina shrugs, speaking in a heavy Spanish accent. "You called to me, *señorita*. When I saw you in class the day before, I knew we were going to be amigos. My sense told me. And then you were studying in the library all alone. It was a sign."

She smiles and her teeth appear fluorescent white against her tan skin. Katrina is really beautiful.

That day began a friendship forged by many hours

in the library along with lots of espresso from the coffeehouse located right outside the library doors. We became fast friends. I even got to practice my Spanish from time to time. *Mr. Manford would be so proud.*

"You made me go everywhere you went, remember? You said I needed to get out and loosen up. I think you were right."

"*Sí.* You were so *tenso.* I had to do something to help, Jo."

"I was happy to do it. Besides, someone had to make sure nothing bad happened to you, and I was—and still am—the queen of designated drivers." I laugh with fondness oozing from my voice.

We decided to become roommates Katrina's last year of college after the debacle with my ex. I hated to see her go after graduation when she landed a job at an accounting firm in Tampa. We've kept in touch at least once a month and on social media. Rina is a dear friend.

Our career paths vary. Where I counsel children, Katrina uses her talents with numbers to advise in finances. She's an awesome accountant. Her clients include team members of the Tampa Bay Buccaneers, a few golf pros, and even a sprinkle of famous singers, all of whom she can't disclose, of course. Her lineup is very impressive nonetheless.

"It's greatly appreciated, *mi amiga.*"

"I'm so glad you pulled me out of my college

coma, Rina. Now, do tell. Who is going to be at this reunion you so desperately want to go see?" I reply.

"Ah, *chica*," Katrina tsks. "Just someone I lost touch with a long time ago."

"Who?" I whisper.

I'm not sure who she's talking about. I know that Katrina played around a lot in college, at least from the time we met going forward. She never mentioned a boyfriend.

"My old *novio*, Manuel Ortega. We had relations before you and I were friends, *niña*. Manny was my nemesis. We were fire and ice. He's living in Atlanta now. He's been on my mind lately, *sí*? I don't know." Katrina frowns and shakes her head, confused.

Her comment stirs up a feeling of lost friendship for me too. I sigh.

"Well, okay then, lady friend. Let's do this." I put on a determined grin. Who am I to stand in the way of lost love?

For the next few hours, Katrina and I drink a few glasses of wine. I only drink one—designated driver and all—while Rina drinks three. She's real nervous, which is not a trait I usually see in her. We dress in the sexiest garb we have.

"Ooh-la-la, Rina. You look hot!" I comment on what Katrina is wearing. It's a ruby red tube dress that flares right above the knees: elegant and sexy all in one. Her dark hair is ironed straight and falls just below her bra line.

"These babies will pull it all together." She slips into a pair of crisscross ankle-strap platform sandals. Katrina's ready for a night of scandalous behavior for sure and hopefully to catch the eye of one Manuel Ortega.

I watch the weather channel on and off while we get ready. Hurricane Georgia is approaching rapidly. It worries me.

"You see the bad weather coming, Rina? I keep reminding myself that we should be back before the weather turns too bad, or we might need to cut the night short. I hate to think it, but it could happen." I frown at her upturned smile.

"Oh, *sí, niña*. We may have to. But we have some time. Let's not waste *un minuto*. Get dressed, *chica. Vamonos.*"

Grabbing my favorite designer mini dress from the closet, I put it on quickly. The dramatic low neckline plunges to the empire waist. The coral colored fabric hugs delicately to my curves and lands right above my knees. I do love this dress. I place a single teardrop diamond necklace around my neck, along with my favorite bangle bracelets to add to the ensemble. Donning a pair of wedge platform sandals to finish off the carefree look I'm going for, I'm almost done.

We dust our cheeks with a bit of glitter and sparkles, then paint our eyes and lashes to create the smokey look. Smoothing on lipstick, I opt for

Vamptastic Plum and Katrina uses Black Cherry, dramatic yet alluring. Katrina and I look each other over in front of the mirror.

"Damn we look good, *niña*."

"I believe we do, my friend. Let's go."

We leave the house, ready to party. I notice as we leave the house that dark clouds ooze and billow throughout the sky, claiming the evening. It should still be light outside, but the dark blanket in the distance above doesn't allow it. At first glance, it gives me pause. The wind begins whipping around us.

"No worries, Jo. *Vamonos!*" Katrina grabs my hand, the storm forgotten, and we're off on another adventure.

"What road is it again?" I ask for the fifth time in an hour, alarm lacing my voice.

"It's Stratton Drive, *mi amiga. Sí?*" Katrina sounds just as worried.

"I can't see anything around me, Rina, with all the rain and the roads being so dark. There aren't any streetlights anywhere." As I speak, the rain is pelting hard against the windshield and I'm realizing this was a bad idea. "I've got to get us turned around quick or we're in big trouble."

"Turning around is a bad idea, *chica*. The last place we saw was over thirty minutes behind us. We have to pull over, Jo. Let's stop at the next place we see, *bueno*? I still don't have a signal."

I nod in concession. "I agree, Rina. This storm is

getting worse. I'm not sure if it's from the storm or that the cell service sucks out in the middle of nowhere, but we can't call anyone to come help us or direct us to a shelter. I guess the only option we have is to keep going until we find a place to stop and take shelter."

Georgia picked up speed in the last hour. According to the broadcast over the radio, it's projected to make landfall on the coast in the early morning. The frightful weather stems from the bands of circular arms coming off of the storm over the water, which is pounding all over us right now. It's the worst part. Really scary weather.

Up ahead I see bright lights, too big and vast to be headlights.

"Do you see them? Up there? Should we stop?"

"*Sí*. Let's stop and take shelter. It looks like a roadhouse or something like that."

I'm cinched up tight, hands at two and ten on the steering wheel, as I struggle to see through the monsoon wreaking havoc on the windshield. I turn on my blinker out of habit because there's no one behind me on the deserted road. No one is crazy enough to be out in this terrible weather—except, of course, us!

As we pull off the road, I notice the vacancy sign is lit brightly underneath Grady's Pit-Stop. I breathe a sigh of relief. Maybe there's room for us. From the outside, Grady's looks to be a motel and restaurant. From what I can tell through the downpour, it's decent. It's not at all upscale and kinda has a serial killer vibe, but it'll have to do in a pinch. Upon closer inspection, I see a gas station off to the side. There are cars, trucks, and big rigs all scattering the parking lot. It seems packed and I begin to worry there won't be any room for us.

"Let's go see if there's somewhere we can wait out the storm. I don't think we can go anywhere else."

"*Sí*, Jo. *Está bien*. Can you believe this? This totally sucks monkey toes."

We both roll in laughter, feeling delirious, but we don't have much of a choice.

I grab my overnight bag and Katrina clutches hers too.

"Good thing we brought these," I say, holding up my bag, "just in case we decided to stay overnight. So, thankful we thought about it."

"Me too, *amiga*. Now let's run fast."

Katrina opens the door and dashes to the front door.

We run frantically from the car, making it to the overhang outside the lobby door just before another gust of wind almost blows us over. I slip and almost fall when my ankle gives way in my platform shoes from the slippery mud that has collected around the front doorway in a big puddle. Totally not dressed for a rain storm.

Drenched from head to toe, I glance into the glass window and huff in displeasure. Katrina mimics my sentiment. Another round of giggles travel through us both.

"This night is so messed up. We look like drowned rats. No, not rats, *cats*. No, wait. Miss Kitty would look better than us. We're a hot mess."

"*Sí*. We look bad, *niña*. So true."

I open the door to enter and Katrina follows. I'm dripping wet from head to toe, my shoes squeaking as I walk on the concrete tiles. Fantastic. Humiliated from the way my dress clings tightly around me, I approach the front desk.

Ding. Ding. Ding.

"Hello." I wait.

Ding. Ding.

"*Hola*. We need a room," Katrina adds her two cents.

"I'm comin'. Hang on a minute," a voice comes from the doorway behind the desk. A huge titan of a man walks in. Tattoos cover every available space visible, except his face. Serial killer vibe enters my mind again. I feel like a cat on a hot tin roof. I'm confused by the voice I heard and the man standing in front of me. He's a walking enigma.

"Hey there, ladies. Umm." The man stops in his tracks and looks us up and down. I'm sure he's laughing so hard on the inside at both of our untamed corkscrew curls and dripping clothes. A grin erupts across his unshaven jaw. "Wow, you two are a sight for sore eyes. Got drenched out there, huh? How can I help ya?"

He pauses to wait for an answer. I muster up the courage to speak.

"Uh. Ahem. Excuse me. Well, sir, you see, we got lost out there tonight." Gulp. "We can't go back out there, at least not until the storm blows through." I point over to the glass door. I'm panting and shivering from the wetness. My nerves are adding to the shaking in my body. This is the only option. He *seems* nice enough. Katrina's eyes are round and bright. She doesn't seem frightened like me, but intrigued.

"What's takin' so long? Did you run off the guests, hon, or do we have more for the night?" A small slip of a girl walks up behind the man and wraps her arms around his waist, the top of her head touching just even with the giant's pecs. Her smile is stretched across a lovely face and adoration fills her eyes.

"Do you, ah, have somewhere we can stay until then? Let us borrow a towel or two? It might be morning or after before we can leave."

I notice Katrina is shivering in her spot as well.

"Ya ain't kidding, miss. It's gotten pretty nasty out there. Lucky for y'all, I've got one room left. It's yours if ya want it. It's only got one bed, but it's big enough for both of ya."

He hugs the woman back and leans down to give her a gentle kiss on the top of her head.

"You all can get dried up and changed. You'll

miss dinner by the time you get settled, but the bar's open and there's finger foods on the menu, at least until we lose power." He appears to ponder his outburst. "Don't worry too much, though; I've got some backup generators that'll kick on. I think Kendall here can make y'all a plate, though, from the leftovers. You can put it under the warmers. Right, darlin'?"

"I sure can, baby. I'll get on it right now. Welcome to the Pit-Stop."

She's gone as fast as she came. I'm left perplexed that a woman like that could tame a man like him. I direct my attention back to the tattooed man and what he's saying.

"Just find me or Kendall in the common room when you're ready. It's the room we use for the restaurant and bar. All paths lead to it, through that door there." He leans over the desk and points to a door just down from the lobby desk.

"Wow, thank you so much, sir. We really appreciate the hospitality."

My teeth are chattering as I hand over my driver's license and credit card, then fill out the necessary forms.

"*Sí*. Thanks, *senor*."

"It's no big deal. I'm a sucker for helping out the ladies." He smiles warmly and I calm a little more. "Here's the key to Room 10. And your credit card and license. Oh, and if you need extra linens, let me know.

My lady Kendall will take care of you. Should be enough in there for both of you, but if ya need extras." He holds his hand out for me to shake. "Name's Grady. Welcome to the Pit-Stop."

"Nice to meet you, Grady. Jocelyn Blackwood, and this is my friend Katrina Perez. Thanks again."

"Y'all get on now. You might catch a cold if ya stay wet too long. I'll catch ya later."

He winks and turns to walk through the door just where he entered, but at the last minute, he turns and shuts off the switch labeled "vacancy light". *Whew*, we did luck out.

My nervousness lessens as Katrina and I head down the hallway to find our room. We're counting as we go like little girls playing a game. "Six, seven, eight, nine … and here we are! Home sweet home, Room 10. At least for tonight."

I hand over the key so she can open the door.

"Okay, *niña*. Let me see. *Ooph*. The key seems a little stuck. Hang on, there it is." Katrina flashes a smile, proud for her suave actions of opening the door.

"Holy moly, mother of pearl, you've got to be kidding me."

The smells of mothballs assault my nose. As we enter the room, I'm thrust back into the 70s where free love and disco ruled the world. The green shag carpet, mirrored furniture, along with the psychedelic bedspread screams hipster. The dark shades of purple and green splash along all four walls.

"Ah, *niña*. We've gone back in time."

"Oh my goodness. Most definitely." I laugh. "It's like turning back the hands of time. Or Back to the Future."

I shrug, step over to the bed, and lay down my bag. Taking a seat on the worn comforter, I'm surprised by how comfortable it feels. I lie back and relish in the softness, moving from side to side like I'm nesting.

"Alrighty, Jo. I'm taking a shower first. If I'm not back in ten minutes, come after me, *niña*."

"Will do. This bed is super comfy, though. I'll just stay right here and wait."

She smiles as she walks into the bathroom area.

The shock wears off and the nostalgia of the quaint room returns me to another place in time, back to my Aunt Becka's bowling alley.

It's been several weeks since I met Keagan and I can't stop thinking about him. What is wrong with me? We share a few of the same classes, but he hasn't approached me and I kind of want to know more about him. My sisters and I are on our way to the bowling alley for my cousin's birthday party. When we arrive, my Aunt Becka is upset. Sam, her normal employee, called in sick with the flu and she's short an employee. Not wanting her to miss her son's party, I let her know I will hand out shoes at the beginning of the night. She's instantly relieved and kisses my cheek.

I've been passing out bowling shoes for the last thirty minutes when Keagan walks up with someone that looks a lot like him, but younger. Must be his brother. He's staring at me again. It's making me self-conscious, the way he's looking at me. Do I have something on my nose? Then I notice his eyes, and there's something there I haven't ever seen before. A slight shiver rocks me out of my pondering and I ask them for their shoe size. After I get his shoes, he leaves and I'm working again to lessen the line waiting.

When I finish, I exit onto the main floor. I love to bowl. I spot my sisters on the last lane and grab my favorite pink ball to use. I weave in and out of the people jam packed around the fifteen lanes, everyone laughing and knocking down pins. An array of multicolored balls spins down the lanes. The strobe lights are bouncing all around the walls, shimmering off the two large disco balls that hang from the ceiling.

I finally reach my family. It's birthday time.

"Happy Birthday to you ..." we all sing to my little cousin.

He's adorable with his Batman cape, the theme for his special day.

As things end, Fallyn and I get ready to leave. I find a bench and start taking my bowling shoes off. That's when Keagan shows up and sits down beside me.

"You bowl really good. My balls end up more in the gutter." He begins laughing at his ineptness of sending a heavy weighted ball spiraling down an alley.

"I've been bowling since I was able to walk."

"Maybe you can give me some pointers?"

"Um, not sure when I'll be back."

"Maybe we could catch a movie or something?"

"Sorry, my dad doesn't allow us to date."

"How about we get a group of people together and meet at the movies?"

"I'll have to see," I say as I walked out the door.

When we get settled in the car, I notice Fallyn is worrying about something. She's biting her bottom lip.

"What's wrong, Fallyn?"

"Oh, uh ... nothing, Jo. It's all good."

"You know you could tell me anything, Fallyn. I won't tell anyone," I offer.

She sighs. "I've got a lot on my mind and I'm not ready to talk about it yet."

Fallyn worries me. She takes on too much and I know something's not right.

She tries to shift me away from what she's going on and comments, "I noticed you talking to Keagan. He's got a thing for you, sis."

I nonchalantly lift my shoulders. "He asked me to the movies, but I told him Dad wouldn't let us date."

"What? Not cool, JoJo. Maybe we can come up

with something." She's scheming and usually when that happens, trouble follows.

"Whatever. I don't wanna get in trouble."

"We'll see."

"I don't care what you're thinking. It's not going to happen, Care Bear."

She smiles and ends the Keagan conversation. "I need you to have my back tonight. I'm sneaking out because I need to talk to David. Can you do that? Please?" She's begging and I know even though I don't want her to go, I will.

"Yeah, I'll cover for you."

"Knew I could count on you, sis! You're the best."

Later that night, I'm lying in my bed listening to Fallyn leaving. A feeling of dread washes over me. Something is wrong. I close my eyes and pray she knows what she's doing. She hasn't gotten caught yet, but with our dad, you never know.

"Jo, *niña*. Jocelyn! *Estás bien*? Are you okay?"

I'm shaken from the trip down memory lane by Katrina's hands gripping my arms, jerking me from side to side and screeching at me.

"Wait. What? I'm fine, Rina. I'm fine. I'm sorry. I must've dozed off for a moment there. I'm with ya."

"I finished showering and it took longer than ten minutes, *mi amiga*. You were murmuring something I couldn't quite understand. And then I tried to wake you up. You wouldn't wake up. I was scared for you."

I rub my face with my hands, then I sit up and grab hold of Katrina's.

"I guess all the 'excitement' has me a bit overwhelmed. I've had enough today to last me a long while. Plus, there's this new case I've been put in charge of that's constantly on my mind. It's drudging up old memories. I'm fine, Rina, really. I promise."

Katrina eyes me skeptically a little longer and then nods, squeezing my hands.

"Alright, go *ducha, amiga*. Get warm. It'll make you feel much better."

"Yep, you're right, Rina."

One of the hardest lessons in life is letting go. Whether it's guilt, anger, love, loss, or betrayal. Change is never easy. We fight to hold on and we fight to let go. Maybe I can wash away all the lingering memories that have grabbed ahold of me lately.

There's no room for any of it in my life tonight. This one night, I'm off, stuck in a motel in the middle of nowhere thanks to the hurricane that's coming. So, I'm on break with Katrina and I'm going to loosen up and have some fun.

CHAPTER 10
KEAGAN

Sometime later, Gunner opens the adjoining door and strolls into my room ready to go eat. He's again dressed like a college kid, but he's added a bowtie. What the fuck? Seriously? I'm still amused from his shenanigans earlier. I'm hoping he knows what to expect from me now. I'm not a pushover and I will take you out if you fuck with me.

Nothing or nobody is going to stand in my way.

I agreed with Ollie and Lukas when we took this mission. The risks are high. Too many variables. We would be acting alone at times and in our business that's a dangerous thing. The situation may arise where you have to step outside your comfort zone. Lines become blurred, and knowing where the line in the sand is marked isn't always easy.

I've got the television on and the local newscaster is blabbering about Hurricane Georgia and all the preparations the state is doing for the storm's arrival. By the way the winds are howling outside the room's window, I would think that if you haven't already battened down, you're screwed.

The shutters on the windows outside are locked, readying the Pit-Stop for the storm. The flapping noise from the shutters increases as the wind picks up.

"Of all the times for a storm to come through …" Gunner mumbles, watching the window.

"My pop always told me growing up when a storm rattled and howled outside not to worry, that it was just God bowling with the angels upstairs."

"Yeah, well, that don't sound like bowling to me at all. More like the sky is falling and we're gonna be pummeled into the ground like a pair of fuckin' squished bugs."

"You crack me up with the stuff coming out of your mouth. Let's go."

Televisions are blaring with news on Hurricane Georgia's latest coordinates when we walk into the large room used as a restaurant during the day and a bar at night. We make it just in time to eat. The tables are full with anxious people worried about where the eye of the storm will hit. Grady flags me down and I make a beeline towards him when I see him point at two vacant chairs. Kendall is sitting on his lap whispering in his ear. She stops and looks up, smiling.

Kendall leaps from Bulldog's lap and hugs me. The tiny slip of a woman has a firm grip on my waist when she says, "Holy Shit! Keagan! Where the hell have you been? You've been hiding from us too long. We sure have missed seeing you." She keeps hugging me.

Bulldog reaches over and gently extracts her arms from around my body and lifts her back into his lap. He laughs at her welcome and places a kiss on her forehead.

"Let the man breathe, darlin'. I told you earlier, he's been busy."

"I know. It's just so good to see him again. Like old times."

Kendall and Grady share a relationship many would be envious of. At one time in my life, I wanted something like what they have, someone to share my life with. Now I can only dream because I'm too fucked up to take care of myself much less care that deeply for another person. Revenge and hatred are all I want. They keep me going. That's my bitch. Mustaff shattered those hopes when he killed my men, men that depended on me, men who I let down.

The two of them look as much in love today as they did when I went to school with them in Texas. Damn, that was years ago. We use to call them the odd couple. He's a hulk of a man and she's petite. He's tatted all over and her pale iridescent skin is blemish free. He's rough around the edges and she's as sweet as they come, a free spirit. Complete opposites.

They were dubbed "Couple Most Likely to Marry First" growing up. Funny thing is, neither one of them want to tie the knot. They are happy just the way they are, being together, something about them not needing a marriage license to be the real thing.

I notice Gunner is standing off to the side watching the scene unfold. He looks confused and I'm sure questions will follow soon.

"Bulldog and Kendall, this is Gunner. I'm giving him a lift to Miami. Gunner, these fine folks here are the owners of this fine establishment, Grady's Pit-Stop. You won't find a better southern home-cooked meal anywhere else in the entire state of Florida."

I wave my hand between them. Gunner stumbles through the introductions, preoccupied with his thoughts, and slides into one of the vacant chairs. I take the seat beside him and three winks later a piping hot plate of food lands in front of me. The smell assaults my senses as my stomach growls causing everyone to laugh. Cubed steak, new potatoes with summer vegetables, and a large glass of sweet tea.

Fast as lightning, she's back delivering the same plate and drink to Gunner. She saddles close to Grady and ends up back on his lap. Smiling at the two of them, I cut a piece of the battered-fried steak and spear a potato onto my fork. When the food hits my mouth, I moan in satisfaction.

"Mmm. Damn, Kendall, you know the way to my heart."

"I remember the path runs through your stomach," she says, giggling. "I seem to recall you always were a human garbage disposal. You better save room for dessert. I've got homemade peach cobbler and ice cream."

"She's trying to fatten me up," I jokingly reply.

"Some things never change," Grady chuckles.

We finish eating listening to the weather updates on the television and conversations around us. Old man Kelsey is yapping about Hurricane Frederick and the storm surge he had to endure a long time ago when he was stuck in The Keys. Gunner's eyes continue to roam around the room expecting the boogieman to jump out and get him.

"You ready for Georgia?"

"As much as we can be ready for a cat-four hurricane. Maybe she'll lose steam once she makes landfall. I know it's going to be ugly here for a while. We'll probably lose power."

"They're predicting she'll get in the Gulf and grow to a five. God help the people when it hits, if that happens. Where are they thinking she'll go?"

"Anywhere from Galveston to Tallahassee," Kendall answers.

"Most models are predicting Pensacola. Damn shame mother nature got herself in a tizzy," Grady says.

"How many generators do you have?"

"Enough to keep the fridge cold and minimal lights when needed."

"How many people are here?"

"About twenty-six."

"You got enough supplies to handle that many? I

wouldn't think you'd get power returned fast being so far out from the city."

"Yeah, man. We've got a well-stocked pantry. Just gonna be a bitch when the humidity hits and the AC's off."

"What do you mean no AC?" Gunner pipes in.

"No power equals no air. Pretty simple, dwindle dwarf."

"You've got to be jokin' with me, right?"

I shake my head no and the heavy sigh he releases could blow out the candles on the table.

"I'm really beginning to hate the south."

We all laugh at the forlorn expression on his face. Grady's phone releases a series of annoying beeps and he turns the sound off with a swipe of his finger.

"Well, y'all enjoyed dinner, but duty calls. Some poor soul must be lost."

"What do you mean?" Gunner asks, shaken.

"That's our front door alert. Grady has the door rigged to his phone in case we have customers showing up during our busy times. We don't have to stop taking patrons in. You wouldn't believe the times I've went to the lobby and there were people waiting to get a room. So, Grady fixed it," Kendall replies.

"You want me to follow?" I offer.

"No. Probably just somebody needing directions or wanting shelter from the storm. I've only got one room left and then we'll be filling this room. Don't wanna turn anybody away with Georgia out there. Just not safe."

He makes his way around the tables to the hallway.

"I gotta clean the kitchen in case the power goes out. Last time a storm blew through here, I didn't, and the entire motel stunk to high heaven. I really don't want a repeat."

Kendall stacks the dishes from our table in a neat pile.

"We're just gonna sit here and chill, hon. Go ahead and take care of business. We'll be here when you get done."

"Sure you don't want to help with the cleanup, Keagan? I seem to recall your obsession with cleanliness after your momma got a hold of you."

"No way. I outgrew that thinking thanks to maw, among other things."

We both laugh at the joke. My maw tanned my hide when she got home from work one day and I hadn't cleaned the morning dishes. I tried to explain to her that dishes were a woman's job, but the minute those words left my mouth, I knew I was a goner. I washed every dirty dish by hand for months. Didn't matter if I had friends over or had been at school, the dishes would be waiting for me and the automatic dishwasher had apparently met its maker because I wasn't allowed to stack it.

The straw that broke the camel's back was when I came home and she had made her famous enchiladas.

There wasn't a counter not covered with dirty, caked-on dishes. I know she used every casserole dish she owned. I gave up and kindly told her I had rethought my stand on washing dishes: it was an equal opportunity job.

"What's so funny, Crash?" Gunner inquires.

"Long story from when I was kid. Let's just say women are smart, sneaky, and can hold a grudge, so beware."

"My momma wasn't around much when I was growing up. My grandparents told me she had the voice of an angel. I kinda remember her singing to me when I was young," he reveals with a shrug.

"Had?"

"Yeah, my dad came home one day and found her with the next door neighbor. He shot 'em both, dead."

"Shit, Gunner. Didn't mean to bring up bad memories."

"Happened years ago. That's how I ended up meeting Buzz. He's the VP of the Phantom Prophets. We were in the same group home until he turned eighteen. I lived with my grandparents until I was eight. They died in a car accident on the way home from Christmas shopping. I really hate that time of the year. That's the year my life turned to shit."

"You didn't have any other family?"

"None who wanted the responsibility of an eight-year-old. My momma was an only child. When her parents were killed, there wasn't anyone else, and let's just say dear ol' dad's family wasn't in the picture."

"The state couldn't find you a new home?"

"Nope. Ended up bunking with ten other kids. The only thing that saved me was Buzz. He kept the older bullies away."

"You and Buzz are close, huh?"

"Yeah, man. He's the reason I'm with you. He's the only one that took an interest in me. He got me the gig working for his MC. Computers and networking always came easy. I could escape from this world into a new one. One of the workers at the home I was stuck in was gonna throw away this old desktop they used. Buzz snuck it out of the garbage and found me a secret place to be alone. I took it apart, got it running. Eventually I started writing code. Don't ask me how I know what buttons to push; it just comes naturally."

"I've got a friend like that. He's a genius and can make any system purr like a fattened up kitten on cream. Is that how you got in the mess you're in now?"

"Well ..."

"Unbelievable. You're a fuckin' *hacker*?"

"I done told you, I wasn't talkin' about that with you. Look, I can't. They would kill me if they knew I said anything now as it is."

"You need someone watching your back. I can promise nothing will happen to you. I've got connections."

"Oh shit. You don't know what you're sayin'.

These guys don't play. They'll kill ya and won't lose sleep over pullin' the trigger. Just let it go before you're sucked into their web. 'Cause once you're in, only death releases you. And, from what I've heard, you'll wish you were dead before it's all over." He takes a deep breath and exhales. "That's why I play nice. Do their biddin' and get the fuck out. Buzz will protect me."

"You're in way over your head, kid."

"Can't deny it. But that doesn't change a thing for me."

"Then trust me. Let me help."

"Why are you so worried about me? What's in it for you?"

I brace my palms on the top of the table and lean in his direction, speaking in a low voice because I don't want anyone to overhear. "It's not about me, you dumbass fucktard. It's about what your so-called clients are doing. The devastation and destruction they are causing along the way isn't a pretty picture. Do you even know what you are supplying?"

He shakes his head slowly left to right.

"That's what I thought. You really should take a closer look and then come find me. Hopefully, I will still be in a position to help you out. But don't wait too long."

"Why won't you tell me if you know so much?"

"Because you wouldn't believe me if I did. Follow your own trail, Gunner. You need answers."

He's startled at my statement and opens his mouth with a retort. Out of the blue, lightning cracks and thunder booms somewhere very close. The lights in the huge room flicker on and off, and the televisions that were announcing Hurricane Georgia's arrival grow silent. A hush falls over the people gathered in anticipation of what will happen next. Grady strides through the entrance of the large room and maneuvers his way to the bar in the corner where Kendall is standing. He reaches for the remote she is offering and the room fills with weather updates.

An edge lifts when he announces to the room, "Georgia's about to knock on our door, folks. We've weathered rougher storms. We're ready."

CHAPTER 11

Jocelyn

Thirty minutes later, I've managed to wash away all the coldness that had seeped deep into my bones. I'm feeling normal again.

Normal. I'm not even sure what that means. I've never had the typical normal life. Yes, I come from a wealthy family, pillars of the community, but with hidden secrets of shame and abuse. Appearances on the outside can be very deceiving.

Most people look at a distance and think the Blackwood family is amazing. Perfect, even. They envy us from afar, aside from the scandal that went down with Fallyn, which was easy enough for the infamous Harold Blackwood V to sweep under the rug. And now it's as if it hadn't happened or she didn't ever exist, which cuts me deeply. Only those closest to the family know the truth, and those people are very few.

Katrina is one of the privileged. Well, I shouldn't call it a privilege, not really. I wouldn't say knowing about the Blackwood family drama and wrongdoings is any kind of benefit. She's always been easy to talk to and Lord knows I've needed a friend all these years.

She and I have so much in common. We both come from a large family, we're second in line in the sibling department and her grandmother, the matriarch of her family, is one of the most important people in her life, just like me.

However, where Katrina comes from a similar background, the abuse is not an issue in her family. According to what I've witnessed, her family is the genuine article, a family that loves without abandon and judgment. You can actually see it in their faces by the way they express their emotions through touch and kind, gentle words. Although her dad rules the family with stern constitution, always expecting greatness, there is a loving temperament in which anyone can feel radiating, surrounding the family like a tangible being.

That's very different from my own. I grew up in a world where as long as you follow the rules, walk the straight and narrow line, or in other words do whatever my father deemed appropriate, you are accepted by him. Well, most of the time, anyway.

Sometimes even that wasn't enough. There was and always is a motive behind his actions. "You do this and I'll give you this or let you do this" was the common theme. A continuous vicious cycle which he will never break. In detaching myself from *him* and leaving Lakeview, I'm breaking the cycle.

I have vowed never to kowtow to anyone ever again.

When I was a little girl, I wanted a family of my own one day. It was a little girl's dream of happiness. Fallyn, Sage, and I would play house with our baby dolls for hours and hours. Well it seemed like hours for a small child. At the time, we were all innocent to what the world truly held for us. Not to mention the power and poison our father embodied. However, some things will never change, and I'm not sure now if my dream can ever come true.

I won't be a doormat like my momma was.

Maybe one day I will find someone to love me completely, to see the real me and love *her*, not just some idea of who I need to be or what they expect me to be. A partner in all things, an equal. I'm not giving up hope yet, because anything is possible if you just believe it, just like Keagan always told me.

After my shower, I dry my hair and pull my bangs back away from my face with a rose petal hair clip. Clean face, clean clothes, and nothing wet. I'm revived and ready for anything.

I've changed into a pair of medium washed skinny jeans and a light pink ocean inspired patterned tank top, along with my pink cowgirl boots. The boots are a lot like the ones I had when I was younger. They ground me.

Katrina has changed into similar attire, lying sprawled out on the bed and watching the news. Plastered across the nineteen-inch screen is Hurricane Georgia. The newscaster and weatherman are discussing the path and landfall points.

The lights flicker and then go off. We sit in the dark. Nothing but our breathing is heard.

"You okay, Rina?"

"*Sí*. Didn't the guy say they had generators?"

"Yep. Let's hope they get them going soon."

Within a few seconds, the lights stream back to life.

"Whew, that was a bit unsettling."

"No doubt. Georgia's slowed down, *chica,* and gaining strength. They say it's basically standing still and going to move slowly for now."

"Seriously? That doesn't suck at all. Ugh!"

"True. I think we are here for a while. Might as well make the best of it. *Sí*?"

"Agreed." Sighing, I sit down at the foot of the bed. I clasp my hands tightly, then release, clasp, release.

"What, *amiga*? Are you okay? I mean from earlier, during your siesta. It seemed to bother you. You were mumbling incoherently and the only word I understood you to say was '*Fallyn*'. Her name, you murmured over and over. Are you still having bad dreams, Jo? You know we can talk about it," she urges. "I'm always here for you, *mi amiga*. Have you heard anything? Still nada?" Concern laced her voice.

I shook my head back and forth.

"Nope, nothing. And I continue getting those unknown number calls like before. I still always answer, too, without question. When I say 'Hello, this is Jocelyn' I get zip, zilch, or nothing but static on the other line. I try to say hello a few more times. Hold my breath. Hoping and wishing, ya know?"

"Ah, Jo. I know that can be very frustrating for you. *Mi pobre amiga.*"

"Yep, very depressing. I always hang up the phone feeling frustrated every single time. Like I've told you before, I've been receiving these weird phone calls for a while now. They started not too long after my graduation from college. It's always the same, too. Unknown number. Sometimes I can faintly hear someone breathing on the other end of the line. Other times it's just static. I keep wondering if it's the signal I've been waiting on? The 'everything's gonna be alright' code? You know, what she used to say when we were little. Is she trying to reach out to me? In my heart of hearts I want to believe it's her. I want to believe it's Fallyn. I wish I could tell her how much I care about her and miss her most in my life."

I wipe away a stray tear. I hadn't even realize I was crying. The mind is a tricky organ. It's the supreme ruler of the body, even when the heart longs to go in a different direction. The strange thing is if your mind believes it, your heart will follow. It has to. I guess that's the reason I have the feeling it's her. It has to be her.

"I can't even imagine what you're going through, *niña.* I would be devastated if something happened to one of *mi familia*. Or if I couldn't talk to one of them whenever I wanted to. But one day, *mi amiga*. One day everything will be alright."

Katrina moved to sit beside me on the bed. Grabbing my hand and squeezing, she smiles at me after using Fallyn's words. No, it's not my sister sitting beside me making everything better. Although if I had to have one person by my side right now other than Fallyn, I would pick Katrina. She always seems to know just what to say.

"Thanks, Rina. Ya know, I've often thought about how chance brought us together and I'm so glad that we became friends. Because when it hurts to look back and I'm too scared to look ahead, it's nice to know I have someone in my corner. You're the best, *mi amiga*." I use her favorite phrase, letting her know how much her kind words and love mean to me. She hugs me hard, like she always does, grounding me again to the present.

Katrina releases me and leans back on her hands, watching the television again. We don't dwell; we just move on.

"Oh, by the way, that shower really rocked my world, Rina. It's exactly what I needed."

"I told you it would be *increíble*. Much better being wet naked than wet with clothes on. *Sí*? Hey, you're looking good, Jo. I love the way you're rocking those boots. Like a boss," she snickers. "You ready to go?"

"Thanks. Not too shabby yourself, lady," I compliment her. "Yes, let's get a move on. I'm so starving, I could eat a horse right now. The sooner the better. What about you?"

"*Sí.* I'm hungry. The common room is calling my name. I hope they have something good."

"Beggars can't be choosers, Rina," I say, trying to sound like a mother scolding her child as I smirk. "But I'm crossing my fingers for some fried chicken and mashed potatoes."

"Or some *ropa vieja with congri*. Yumm."

We exit room 10 laughing. Things are good once again. Loud voices coming from down the hall lure us in the direction. As we draw closer, the laughter and shuffling of chairs carry out into the corridor.

"Sounds like a party, *mi amiga*. Maybe we'll have some fun tonight after all."

"I can't imagine a party going on in the middle of a hurricane, but I'm definitely up for it. Let's do this."

Katrina enters the room first and I follow behind.

I stroll into the room with food on the brain as my tummy growls and rumbles for the third time in the past few minutes. My eyes zero in on the hanging lights scattered around illuminating the large dim area and the multiple televisions suspended from the walls in various spots, each of them blasting out the weather and what's to come with Hurricane Georgia. Tables are jam-packed into the space and full of people. There's a countertop in the corner where drinks are being mixed up and served by Grady's lady, Kendall.

"There's Kendall over there, Rina. We can ask her about the food. Follow me."

"Okay, *niña*. I want to get some food, now."

As I weave in and around the tables packed with people, I get the strange feeling that someone is watching me. Scanning the room, I don't see anyone who stands out or who I might know. *Hmph.* We continue to the corner of the room, hopefully to find the promised hot meal.

"Hey, Kendall. I'm Jocelyn and this is Katrina from earlier, in the lobby."

"Hi, girls. Y'all look much better than before. Storms rough out there. I guess y'all are ready to eat, right? Give me just a sec and I'll go get your grub. I hope you like country food."

"Sure thing. No problem. Thanks," I say.

I focus on Kendall as she finishes mixing up a drink and passes it to an elderly-looking man. He's wearing a button-up sports shirt untucked from his khaki pants and a fedora with a feather on the side.

"Now take it slowly tonight, Mr. Jenkins. We don't need any repeats of last night. Right, hon?"

"Ah, shucks, Miss Kendall. I'll be good. Gotta keep my wits about me with the storm comin' and all. I might be needed to help."

His smile is cheerful and light as he turns around carefully making his way back to his table, careful not to spill a drop of the most certainly tasty drink

Kendall made for him.

"That's Mr. Jenkins. He's a permanent resident here at the Pit-Stop. God love him. Good. Now where was I? Oh, food. Hang on, girls. I'll be right back. Have a seat right at the high-top table. The one over there." She points at the tall lone table in the corner as she exits through the door behind the makeshift bar.

I like this woman already. She radiates a good heart. No wonder Grady snatched her up. I'd sure like to hear that story. With the weather getting rough, I foresee a good old-fashioned girl's gossip hour.

Within a few minutes, Katrina and I are sitting at a table in the corner, scarfing down cubed steak, new potatoes, and steamed veggies. Kendall is an excellent cook. Same caliber as my momma. It's all simply delicious.

I finish up the last piece of cubed steak on my plate and take one more drink of sweet tea when I feel someone staring at me again. Pushing a stray piece of hair behind my ear, I glance up and lock eyes with fierce unyielding blue ones. Beautiful eyes that belong to a baldheaded, tattooed hulk of a man. His look gives nothing away. He seems indifferent to the fact that we have locked gazes. Then, in contradiction to his appearance, his mouth quirks up with a lopsided grin, barely revealed from the goatee hair on his face, and I look away. *Son of a biscuit eater*. My heart is pounding rapidly, caused by this bad-boy biker-looking man a few tables over.

"Are you all finished, *chica*? I'm going to take these to Kendall and see about getting us some drinks. What's your poison tonight, *mi amiga*?"

"Yeah, thanks." I'm fidgeting with my napkin and diverting my eyes left and right. Old habits die hard. "Well, hmm. I'm sure they don't have any Moscato here, so I'll take a rum and coke. With an extra shot of rum, please. I need something to calm my nerves."

"You got it, *chica*." She glances in the direction of the table with the smokin' hot bad boy I've been making eyes with. "Oh. Don't look now, but I think you have an admirer. And his friend's not too bad either. I'll be right back. We'll have to go chat them up when I get back."

Katrina walks off, leaving me with that last piece of information. Always the cheerleader in my corner. Daring myself to see if he's still watching, my eyes look up. *Yep, he's still staring at me.* This time, he looks away to speak to the other guy at his table and I'm gifted the chance to study him for a brief time. His features are hard, tired and worn, battle weary. This man has been to the dark side. The scowl on his handsome face portrays a man of action with a badass disposition. Hottie McHottie is an understatement to his masculine beauty. I'm sure he has many stories to tell, or maybe he wouldn't want to. I'm suddenly wanting to know. No—I'm *needing* to know more about this mysterious man.

His eyes. It's his eyes that give me pause. I'm

puzzled by the familiarity. It's like I know him, yet I know that's impossible. I've never seen this man before tonight and he's not really someone I would hang out with, even though I've never been one to judge a book by its cover. Those eyes, though, they're a haunting blue. They remind me of Keagan, although his eyes were never haunted. Keagan's blue eyes were full of happiness. They would sparkle with mischief and life. I have never come across another person who had the same color eyes like his. This man is the first. Aside from his rough exterior, his eyes seem to tell another story, calling out to me and drawing me in."Ha, I knew you had your eyes on him too, *chica*."

After she sets down a red solo cup full of rum and coke, no doubt, I scoop it right up without comment and take a long swallow, feeling the burn as it goes down gently. Boy, does it feel good. Then I take another just because. I look up and see Katrina studying me suspiciously.

"What? I know it's not my usual thing, but it's been a crazy day, right? I need a little liquid courage right now."

"But remember, you've got to take it slow this time. You don't want to get sick."

I'm not bothered in the least by her comment. I'm in control. My eyes wander to the tattooed hulk again; I can't help myself. His bright blue gaze ripping holes deep into my soul.

"Why don't we go and join them? We're in this

for the long haul tonight, so let's have a little fun, *niña!*"

"Wait! Rina!"

I grab hold of her and she falls back into her seat.

"What? Jo, come on, *mi amiga*. It's okay to live a little. No harm, no foul. Right?" Katrina's wisdom is whiny and impatient. I really can't blame her.

I sit there for a few minutes, analyzing her frankness. She's correct. I know this to be true. I'm the cautious one. I find it very hard to just let go and loosen up. For so long I've kept up my guard. After everything that happened with Fallyn and then when I finally trusted someone again, my ex-fiancé, well we all know how that turned out. And before that, the only boy relationship I ever had was with my best not-boyfriend Keagan. I just never wanted to trust anyone completely again.

But this isn't really about trust, is it? This is about living a little and having some fun. I'm still young, even though I act like a senior citizen sometimes—careful, safe, and above all, never getting too close to anyone, ever. I have a selective circle of friends and that's the way I like it.

Katrina is the only person who ever broke down those walls I have erected around my heart quickly and without much effort. We're soul sisters, someone I can trust completely.

"Okay, Rina. But we need like a code word. In case one of us wants to leave or something goes wrong. Ya know? Just in case."

Beautiful laughter erupts from Katrina. She thinks this is funny. Maybe she's right. I'm not twenty anymore.

"Alright, *mi amiga*. Just like when we were in college, huh? Okay, how about pink? That's your favorite color. We can say 'pink' if we get in too deep."

I hold up my hand and make a slashing movement while shaking my head.

"Nope, no can do, Rina. I like pink too much and it could come up in conversation. You know my boots are pink, right?" I laugh heartily. "Let me see. Maybe … headache. Yes, headache. It would be easy to leave if one of us had a headache. What do ya think?"

I spy Katrina's full on smile as she says, "*Sí, amiga*. That's perfect. Headache it is. Now *vamonos*! Up and at 'em, Jo. Let's go live a little."

I take a deep breath and finish off my rum and coke. Then I slide off the stool as Katrina grabs my hand and pulls me towards the table where the Hottie McHottie bad boy is sitting, his eyes on alert as we approach.

CHAPTER 12
KEAGAN

"What the ...?" *This isn't happening.* "Of all the fucking places," I whisper to myself, knowing Gunner is hearing the verbal rant and not giving a flying fuck either way. I can't believe my luck. *The luck of the Irish, my ass.* Luck hasn't been my friend for the past several years of my life. I've got the scars to prove just how shitty my luck is. If something can go wrong, it does. *Murphy's Law.*

Unbelievable! Now's not a good time. Why couldn't I be in the View when this happened, possibly sitting at the bar drinking a beer at The Rock Salt with Lukas and Ollie? Or better yet, eating breakfast at Tropical Palm? No, I'm just one unlucky bastard with a black storm following me around, waiting to rain on my parade. Yet just like back in the day, in she strolls wearing those sexy pink cowboy boots and painted-on jeans without a care in the world about the problems she's causing me.

Jocelyn Blackwood. M'aingeal.

Memories from the first day of high school flood me: her trademark boots, the day I met her ... Little did I realize she would change me.

When I was younger, I thought she was the one for me. I use to dream about her wrapping those sexy boots around my waist as I thrust deep inside her. She would scream my name from the pleasure I caused her body and vow to never let me go. A foolish dream of my youth. I know better now. Women like her aren't for me.

She never wanted more from me than friendship. She never understood how much she meant to me. I was just another guy trying to date one of the Blackwood Sisters.

But, she wasn't that to me. She was more. I saw more. The real *Jocelyn*.

She was all I cared about throughout my senior year of high school, but she wouldn't allow me in. I made a commitment to serve my country and when the time came for me to leave the View, that was the hardest choice I ever made because I was leaving her too. Subconsciously, I guess that's one of the many reasons I live there now and run my business from there—to be closer to her.

She was angelic. Pure. Sensitive. Beautiful.

I knew she was easily spooked, but I couldn't stay away from her from the moment I laid eyes on her.

She possessed an aura of innocence that drew me in. I was a fish out of water when she was around. Awkward little Keagan Fontneau. I couldn't express my true feelings, so I came up with the not-boyfriend phrase to ease her fears. The phrase worked for a while and I was her best friend.

Her dad was an asshole. He frightened her the most. When Fallyn left out of the blue my senior year, all his anger focused in on Jo.

I'll always care about her. When I was stationed in Afghanistan, I often wondered what she was doing, how her life was going, if she had found happiness or did she still suffer from the loss of Fallyn abandoning her. My eyes roam the room and stop to linger on her. She's sitting on a barstool talking with Kendall and another woman laughing at something one of them said.

I can't help but stare at her. The priceless masterpiece in front of me is even more beautiful today than when she was sixteen. Age has fine-tuned her luscious body. Her curly waves fall loosely around her face and softly over her breasts. Long fingers gesture at the television, then her red lips move and I inwardly groan imagining them touching me.

Her eyes look the same, but hold a different story. Something is missing in the green depths. *Eyes are the doorway into the soul,* my pop always says. She's smiling and laughing, but it doesn't reach the full-on Jocelyn smile I know.

She stops talking to her friend, lost in her own thoughts. Her pert little nose scrunches in deep concentration. She leans back on the stool and carefully brushes her hair from her cheek, hooking it behind her ear. She searches the room as if she can feel my eyes boring into her soul, needing her to know who I am. Our gazes collide and, like a vortex in the center of a tornado, my tunnel vision zooms in on her. There's no one else but us. A familiar ache surfaces, one I thought I had outgrown long ago.

For a split second, I see something in her stare, maybe the slight flicker of awareness or her deep intake of air, but I think she recognizes me. The moment ends when her friend snaps her fingers, drawing her away from me and back into the conversation.

"*M'aingea l...*"

"What the hell are you saying now?" Gunner interrupts my drifting thoughts.

I've forgotten where I'm at. She's done that to me before.

"Nothing, man."

"What does 'magel' mean? C'mon, dude. I need to know."

"You're butchering my language. It's *M'aingeal*. You pronounce it 'Mayn-gel'." I snicker. "Maw's Irish Catholic and Pop is Cajun. Let's just say, growing up in my house was never boring."

"You're full of surprises."

"Hoo-ha you have no idea, kid. My little bro is a natural born hellion. Tell him the sky is blue and he'll argue that's it's not just blue but white, grey, and black. Any other color he can think of. Pop says he's got too much of Maw's Irish side in him. I wouldn't disagree out loud or she would box my ears good."

"Damn, I'd forgotten all about those times my Gramps boxed mine. Jeez. Feels like another lifetime ago. She was strict. Never let me sit down at the table without my hands washed and shirt tucked in. She even made me say 'Grace' before eating. I miss that woman."

"Funny, the little things that bring you 'round."

"Ain't that the truth. Is that why your ears look so funny? Your momma's wrath? They stick out like Dumbo," he jokes and takes a swig of his beer.

We are both laughing, releasing some of the tension that's circled us since we left Perry. Maybe he's salvageable. Maybe he can help us find the missing pieces after all.

We abruptly stop laughing when Gunner slaps my shoulder and nudges his chin upwards. That's when I see her. I look into her eyes and wonder why she doesn't know me. Have I changed so much that she can't recognize me? *C'est la vie*.

"Can we join you?" the beauty standing before Gunner asks him.

I can't take my eyes off of Jocelyn. She's making me want something I was sure I had lost overseas.

"Well, I …" Gunner stutters and shoves me again.

He's such a douchebag.

I glance at him and sigh. "Pull up a chair, ladies. We're just enjoying the wonderful Florida weather that's brought us all here. Can we get you something? I'm sure the selection isn't what you're normally used to, but I'm sure there's something we can find that you might want on the menu." I wink.

They share a smile and a faint tinge of pink appears across Jocelyn's cheeks as she makes her way to one of the vacant chairs. She sits down in the one closest to me. Placing her elbows on the tabletop and her chin between her hands, she leans inward. *Fuck!* The upclose view I have of her sends shockwaves through my system. My memory didn't do her justice, and this near, the sprinkle of angel's dust along the top of her nose and cheeks has me fighting the urge to touch her.

I'm snapped out of my lust-filled moment when Kendall approaches our table.

"Hey, girls. I see you found—"

"Crash, name's Crash. And this is Gunner," I say, nodding in his direction.

Kendall frowns at me and I plead with my eyes for her not to say anything else. A disapproving look follows, but she doesn't correct me.

"*Buenas noches*, amigos. I'm Katrina, and this is my friend, Jocelyn."

"Hi," Jocelyn quietly says.

"So, does anybody need a refill?" Kendall inquires.

"Mojito, please."

"I think I'll have another rum and coke."

"I'll have another beer," I say, and Gunner seconds my order.

"I'll go grab them and be back in a jiffy."

Kendall wanders off, stopping a few times to talk at tables on her way to where Grady is manning the bar. He leans over when she motions him downward and covers his ear. He looks at me and then back down at her, intently listening to what she's saying. He shrugs his shoulders and says something back. Apparently she's not happy with him because she turns and walks into the kitchen area without a backwards glance. I wait for him to head over, but instead he looks at me smiling. What the hell did she say to him?

She's probably pissed, thinking I'm going to hurt her *new friend*. If she only knew the history behind my decision to remain anonymous, she would be chasing her away from me. The baggage I carry is for only me and I don't want to share it with anyone, especially Jocelyn. She's too good and innocent to be able to understand what drives me now. I'm not the same guy she knew in high school, carefree and happy.

I haven't been that way since reality set in.

Back before I left on my last tour of duty, I wouldn't have given my actions a second thought. I can only imagine scooping her up in my arms, feeling her body against mine, and holding her close, not letting her place a foot on the ground. I would hold her until I had my fill and only then would I let her out of my sight. I'm so messed up.

Gunner's goofy grin has me focusing on the convo. He's got his chin propped on his hand, staring at the ladies. I follow his stare, making sure he's not ogling Jocelyn. I will knock his ass to the Georgia-Florida line if he tries flirting with her in front of me. The thought of her with someone else sends waves of anger flooding my brain.

I relax my posture when it registers that he's watching her friend like a lovesick puppy. Wimp.

"*Si*. I'm serious. We were drenched from the pouring rain. Jo's hair kinked even curlier than normal when the cool air conditioning hit it, as if that's even possible, with the corkscrews she's got."

"Jeez, Rina. Thanks for the visual."

"Well, you looked like you had stuck your finger in a light socket," she stutters and busts out laughing over her own joke.

"I wasn't the only one! You were sporting kinky ringlets from the eighteenth century, too."

"My hair isn't as thick. Yours is so thick. So juicy, *niña*." She giggles, eyeing the man beside her.

"Here you go, folks. Drinks for everyone," Kendall says and hands a tallboy to me.

"Any news on the roads clearing?"

"Sheriff radioed and they are working on securing Route 441 near Twin Lakes. He's talking to Grady about using sandbags in some places. We're close to the dam and possible flooding is always a worry."

"Sandbags? Shit. Why me?"

"Honey child, you think sandbags are a bad thing? You ain't got a clue," Kendall answers and spins away.

"I guess the weather's going to get worse, huh?"

"Maybe. Maybe not. You never know with hurricanes. Some are as fickle as women. One minute she's moving directly for you, you blink, and she's gone. You never know what direction she'll go."

"Hmph. You use 'she' like *she's* a real living, breathing person," Jocelyn says while sipping her drink.

"Well, it *is* Mother Nature we're talking about here," I point out.

"Pleeeeeeease. Men can be fickle, too."

"We can, can we?"

She leans in close to me, licks her lips, and whispers in a low sultry tone, "They always seem to want more than what they can handle. I'm sure you know my meaning, Crash. How boys will be boys, and boys like their toys and stuff. Well that goes for older boys, too, sugarplum. Seems like a never ending battle for y'all to always want to play with fire."

I position myself even closer to her and reply, for her ears only, "Oh, but darlin', I'll let you in on a little secret: For the right woman, I want to burn."

She inhales a deep, shaky breath when I nip her earlobe and softly nuzzle her cheek with my nose. I'm hard as fuck now thanks to the beauty sitting beside me. I want her in the worst way. She's the one that got away. The one I wanted desperately when I was younger. I need to get her out of my system once and for all.

She pulls away from me, but not before briefly sharing an unspoken yearning of primal need and want.

Leaning back, I reach for my beer and study her closely. She's rattled. Her eyes dart around the room, looking everywhere else but on me. She gulps her drink and places the empty glass on the table. Her friend and Gunner are in a deep conversation of the best places to eat in Miami when Kendall shows up again with a fresh drink for Jocelyn. I'm still nursing the warm beer from earlier and have no intentions of losing control.

I need to get out of here and away from her soon before I do something fucking drastic, like losing the tiny thread of sanity I have left.

A guy I don't recognize is eyeing her up and down like a delicious tasty morsel of chocolate. He winks at her and she blushes. When she smiles at him, I almost go caveman on her ass. I want to beat my hands on my chest, throw her over my shoulders, and find the nearest bed to fuck the living daylights outta her. *She's mine.*

She's stirring feelings that have no place in my life, especially now. I need an easy exit, stat.

Three drink deliveries later, Jocelyn stands, bumping the stool which causes it to teeter, then sways to one side almost touching the floor.

"I wanna dance."

I jump up to help steady her and she awkwardly bows her back so that her head is resting on my chest.

"Think you've reached your limit, darlin'."

"I'mmmmm okaaaaay," she says, patting my forearm. "Just needa find a baf room."

Before Katrina can offer, I slowly begin walking Jocelyn towards the doorway.

"Where ... do ya think I'm going?"

"We're gonna find you a toilet before your dinner comes back up and all that liquor you've consumed in the past hour or so."

"Mys head's spinnin' round and round ... Stop twirling me!"

"You're gonna have one hell of a hangover in the morning."

"I'ms not drunk. I's never do that. I's a gooood girlz."

"Mmm-hmm, sure you're not."

We barely turn down the hallway towards my room when she stumbles and tries to sit down in the middle of the floor. Shit, Kendall did this on purpose, feeding her drinks left and right. She made sure Jo was slammed enough not to be with me tonight, which was her way of ensuring nothing happens to her newest charge. Son of a bitch. I try to help her stand, grabbing her behind at the waist, but she's boneless, making it hard to keep her upright. Her boots are pointing to the ceiling as her legs give way, forming a V. She slides down the front of my aroused body, wiggling to the floor.

"Jocelyn, baby, you can't sleep here. C'mon, let's find your room."

"No. Can't move. Spinning. Whoaaaa."

I bend and place one hand behind her back and the other under her knees, then lift. I cradle her in my arms, cussing Kendall a new one. I should have known she would do something like this to protect Jocelyn from me. I manage to get the key into the door and the 70s decor slams my situation home.

I've got Jocelyn in my room, drunk as a skunk, and all I want to do is sink balls-deep into her. I'm so fucked! If it was anybody else, I'd be laughing my ass off.

A moan from the woman wreaking havoc on my system jars me into action. I place her on my bed. Turning, I search my bag, finding two little white pills, and return to her side with a bottle of water.

"Jocelyn, you need to take these. Here. Open up and swallow them down."

She doesn't open her eyes when I slightly lift her head, but her lips part when the pills touch them and she swallows them down. I place the bottle of water on the nightstand for later.

I cover her and lie down facing her, then watch

her breathe in and out. I can't believe she's here with me.

"Good night, *m'aingeal*."

I place a kiss on her forehead and close my eyes, letting the wind and rain lull me to sleep and praying my nightmares don't visit.

CHAPTER 13
Jocelyn

Deep, rolling, pounding thunder and gusts of high winds whistle outside reminding me of the looming hurricane surrounding Florida. The rain is peppering the window in my room with a nonstop, consistent melody, lulling my overactive brain with peace. I stretch my arms above my head and push my toes as far down the bed as possible, just like Miss Kitty does when she's waking up. My body feels refreshed on account that I slept all night without any dreaming. Wow. The storm was my lullaby.

My eyelashes flutter open, although they feel thick and heavy. A dull ache is creeping up the back of my neck into my frontal lobe, bringing on a headache, certainly from the over drinking which took place last night. *Jeez, I know better.* I carefully open my eyes as flashes of the night before inundate my brain. The drinking, the company … the sexy, Hottie McHottie bad boy with the beautiful eyes.

As I finally gain access to the use of my eyelids and pry them fully open, I turn my head to the other side of the bed and gulp. The alluring, tattooed bad-ass that I met in the common room is staring hard at me. *Oh my goodness. What did I do?* My eyes wander around the motel room and I realize that this isn't my room. Nope, I'm not in room 10. Although, I'm still fully clothed.

"Good morning, *m'aingeal.*"

A smile has crept up his beautiful face and I'm captured and stunned by the rawness I see there. Familiar, yet foreign. Wait, what did he just call me? My angel? No one has called me that since … Keagan. He gives me a knowing look and it sucker punches me right in the gut, causing a rush of butterfly emotions.

A flicker of remembrance flashes me back to the bar last night right before things got really hazy and I passed out. Crash—or that's the name he gave me— leaned in and nibbled on my ear telling me he would want to burn for me.

I bolt upright out of the bed and scramble to get away from this stranger … or whoever this person is who's staring back at me. Limbs flailing, covers bunched around my feet, I trip and fall out of the bed. I'm really not sure what's real and what I've dreamed at this point.

I compose myself the best I can, because I feel like someone just walked all over my grave. I squawk, "What the heck! What did you just call me? Who are you? Why am I in your room? You've got a lot of explaining to do, mister."

Pushing my hair back out of my face, I shake my finger boldly at the man lying on the bed, acting like he hasn't a care in the world.

Chuckling, he says, "So many questions. Just like you, *cher*, to go all twenty questions with a side of crazy."

Then he laughs. He's laughing at me? *The nerve of this man!*

"Don't act like you know me, *Crash*. Is that right? Didn't you tell me your name is Crash?"

I wait impatiently for a response, tapping my foot frantically on the carpet as I clutch one of my hands into a fist by my side while the other is placed firmly on my hip—my stubborn stance. I'm crazy mad right now. But all I get out of this maddening, sexy man is a laugh. I want to pull out my hair from his arrogance. He continues with a deep, lingering chuckle, which does something wild to my insides, bringing back a feeling I left behind years ago … an ache I've never really let go of.

And there's only one person who ever yielded this type of response from me: Keagan.

After his bout of laughter subsides, his gaze once again finds mine. Those eyes. This can't be happening. I must be dreaming. I rub my fists over my eyes and then I even go as far as to pinch myself.

The pinch garners a yelp. "Ouch! Shoot. That's gonna leave a mark."

He chuckles again. "Silly girl. Jo, come sit down. I won't bite. I'll explain everything to ya."

His voice holds a tender note, which is

unexpected from the looks of this man. But what if this is Keagan? *My* Keagan. Can it be? I inspect the man lying on the bed a bit further—his slick head, tattoos covering his arms, and probably other places I've yet to discover. Totally not the same boy I remember from so long ago. His face has softened considerably since last night, but he's still scary as heck. I'd be totally unsure if it weren't for those crystal bluish gold-flecked eyes. I study them again and recognition dawns on me.

"How? Why? … I don't understand what's going on here. Am I dreaming?"

"No, Jo. Just come sit and calm down. Please. C'mere, Boo."

He pats the side of the bed that I vacated, beckoning in a commanding way for me to comply.

My mind is reeling from the possibilities. If this is my Keagan, it's a miracle. I never thought I'd ever see him again. Although, if it is him, why would he lie to me? Play like he didn't know me or ever met me before? I think about the way he bored holes in me from across the room last night, watching me cautiously and anticipating my recognition.

I have to know. I need to know. I walk back to the bed cautiously and sit down with one butt cheek hanging off the edge and the other planted firmly on the mattress, just in case.

"It's me, Jo. Keagan. You know it is. All you have to do is believe it."

Understanding wallops me right in the face with his admission, and before I realize what I'm doing, I smack him straight across his gorgeous, goateed face. Then I punch him in the arm. I snatch my hand back, pulling it to my mouth as if I touched a hot pot and heave deep breaths in and out, shocked at what I just did.

"What the fuck, Jocelyn?"

He rubs his jaw with his huge paw because I'm sure the punch to his arm didn't hurt him at all by the throbbing of my hand. Hand had met steel.

"Well, um…" I'm at a loss for words. I never speculated the first thing I would do if I ever saw Keagan again was hit him, but doggonit, he lied to me, playing like he was someone else.

"It was you the whole time and you didn't tell me? Why would you trick me like that? I knew you were familiar to me. I was drawn to you. You reminded me of the boy I knew years ago, but I didn't think that was possible. And you've changed so much … Keagan. What did you expect?"

"Damn it, woman, you're right. But what the hell? You didn't have to hit me."

"Well, that's what you get for deceiving me like that, Keagan. 'What the heck' back at you!"

He shakes his shaved head back and forth with a slight smile quirking his lips, running his big hands over his smooth skull. I succumb to the fantasy of my hands there instead, touching him. I'd give anything to know what he's thinking right now.

His next words startle me.

"Of all the places in all the world, you had to step into the same motel I did. What are the chances of that, *cher*?"

"Jeez, I don't know. Crazy, right?" I blush under his scrutiny. His gaze making me squirm and I close my legs tighter to stove off the burning itch that's tickling between my thighs. *Get yourself together, Jo. You're mad, remember?* Hormones are a bitch.

Keagan was always very good at reading me and he recognizes the discomfort I'm sporting because of him. So he diverts the conversation, a tactic Keagan always excelled in. And I'm grateful at the moment. The next words that come out of his mouth squash my resolve a bit more.

"I couldn't believe it was you last night and I was so damn glad to see you again, Jo. It's been a long time. And when you smiled at me, I was a goner. Even when I latched onto the fact that you didn't recognize me, I couldn't stop it. I wanted to be close to you again. I'm on a job and I can't say more than that. It's dangerous, despite the short time we have. I missed you."

Son of a gun. What do I say to that? I hear the words I've longed for and yet...

"*M'aingeal.*" His endearment is a whisper on his lips as he gently lifts his hand to my cheek and strokes softly back and forth, moving his thumb across my lips and then down my neck. He settles his huge palm over my heart which is beating ninety to nothing—a rhythm no doubt created by this moment of reconnection with Keagan. It's such a tender gesture from the harsh man sitting in front of me.

"What are you doing?" I'm breathless, anticipating what he'll do next.

This Keagan has grown bolder since we last saw each other years ago. I loved how forthright he was and his dominating presence back then, which kept me on the edge of my seat. But now...now I'm sucked into his vortex of the older version. Gaining a bit of sense, I gently remove his hand and hold it in mine. I have questions that need answering and I'm confused.

"What's going on, Keagan? Why did you play off like you were someone else? I have to know."

"Don't." Just that one word speaks volumes to the insistence he commands, but I can't help myself as I push for more.

"Please, Keagan."

"No, *cher*. Not this time. Enough. No questions and answers. Just you and me. I've waited long enough to have a taste of you and I'm not wasting this chance. Now you can roll the dice with me or walk away now. But if you stay put, I promise, I'm gonna make you scream like you've never screamed before, Jo. You can count on that. The rest can wait for another time. Are ya with me or not? I want you. Now."

He grabs my hand and places it on his massive erection which is clearly busting at the seams behind his zipped up jeans. *Oh my gosh.* His face is a mix of passion and need.

I begin to pant and my breathing becomes hard. I want him too, I always have. Should I take this chance? Spend some surely unforgettable time with the man I've fantasized about for years, or do I walk away? He played me, but he obviously has his reasons. Right? I'll get it out of him later. Are we going too fast? Can I even do this? Yes, I want him. I always have. At one time long ago, he was my best friend. I can trust in that. To heck with what happens later. I need to know how good I think it can be. This is my fantasy and today it's going to come true.

Thunder booms and claps loudly outside. Seconds later, a bright flash of light rivets straight through the window and appears to disappear on the shag green carpet beside the bed. I jump. I'm startled by the hazardous sounds and eerie bolt. Keagan takes the opportunity to pull me closer to him where he's lying on his side of the bed, rooting me to his side and folding me up into his imposing, hefty arms. At first I reluctantly move into his space. Then I snuggle in deep because I'm scared. *Right?* My nose is seized by the masculine scent, only belonging to Keagan.

"Whatta ya say, *m'aingeal?* You ready to see what it's like between us or do you want to run away again?"

"Whatta ya say, *m'aingeal?* You ready to see what it's like between us or do you want to run away again?"

A distressed gasp fills the stale hotel room as her eyes narrow on me. She moves away from the bed, walking over to the secured window as if she's able to watch the turbulence of the storm outside despite the fact that the raging one inside of me is even more dangerous to her.

The furrowed brow on her lovely face worries me. I've pushed too far. I rise up from the prone position and attempt to wrap her in my arms again. She brushes my arms away and turns to face me.

"Run away? It's called depression, Keagan. I closed down. Too painful dealing with life at the time. I thought you understood me. That if anyone understood what I was going through, it was you."

I start to interrupt her and she holds her palm up facing my direction. Moments pass as she collects her thoughts.

Her posture eases from the tautness in seconds,

and she says, "You really have a way with women, huh? You do realize what a jerk comment that was?"

I nod and patiently wait for her to decide which way she will go. Inwardly, I cringe at my attempt to stab her back with hurtful words. She didn't know the pain she caused me all those years ago. She was young, naïve, and drowning in her own problems.

Tentatively, she moves in my direction and places her hand over my chest.

"Oh, Keagan, honey, I've dreamed of this moment so many times. This isn't how I pictured us. Not our first time together." She lowers her stare to my chest and pauses.

I barely breathe, waiting for her response.

"So, I guess to answer your question, yes, I'm ready, and no, I won't run away from you." She absently strokes my chest. "From this thing between us."

I still her hand laying on my chest stroking her fingers intimately.

"I want you. Skin to skin. Nothing between us. I want to map your body. Find your pleasure points and drive you insane for hours upon hours. I need to feel you, Jocelyn."

The indecision in her eyes fades away. She lifts her lips to me and I don't hesitate when she offers them to me, answering my plea. I slowly rub her bottom lip with my thumb and cradle her head in my other hand. Time stops, suspended. With eyes locked on each other, so much is relayed in the brief seconds that elapse. Longing. Need. Desire. A slow burn kindles within. The moment stirs intense emotions.

The precious gift she's offering almost sends me to my knees. I'm not worthy. I'm damaged goods. She deserves better. Her eyes seek a promise of tomorrow, of more than today, something I'm not able to provide her with. I'm a bastard wanting her this way, knowing a future with her isn't possible, but I can't make myself walk away. I'm weak.

Her mouth caresses my thumb with tender nips. The softness of her lips touching my rough skin ignites a burning flame within my gut. I groan when she opens and teeth rub the length. Her eyes bore into mine with a promise of things to come as her warm mouth envelopes my thumb again, applying pressure and creating a suction. Blood rushes to my aching cock, needing relief.

This Jocelyn standing before me is bold, confident, and driving me crazy. The woman is daring me to claim her body.

I remove my thumb, tugging, impatient for my first taste of her. Framing her angelic face, I lower my mouth and reach for the promise of heaven I will find there. A groan escapes as she welcomes me home. Sweetness fills my mouth when her tongue circles mine and her lips move passionately, building a yearning that requires more.

I hold her steady, demanding more. She meets my

unspoken demand with one of her own. A frenzy of teeth gnashing ensues and a battle for dominance unfolds. Her nails latch securely onto my ass, pulling me even closer to her body. Her pebbled breasts massage my chest seeking release from the restriction of clothing we have between us.

She tugs at the shirt I'm wearing, lifting it up.

"Take it off," she demands. "Now. Take it off."

I release her, allowing her to push the shirt up and over my chest. The desperation in her voice escalating my need. I take over, discarding it to the side. Her hands come back, roaming over my torso. I'm lost, craving her. She levels her eyes with mine and touches a puckered scar.

I had forgotten. For a small blip in time, the past was just that: the past. It didn't linger. She was the reason. Now she was seeing my imperfections, touching them.

"Keagan."

Her eyes shimmer with moisture and affection as she weaves a trail of kisses from scar to scar, following the path around my disfigured body.

Marking me, branding me everywhere she touches, turning the memory of pain and failure into something beautiful.

She lowers to her knees in front of me and unbuckles my belt. I'm mesmerized by her movements. I've fallen into her trance. The button on my jeans snaps open and the zipper lowers. She's intent at her task, removing my clothing. Her hands slip between the jeans and my skin. She strains, trying to pull them down my thighs. I easily push them down, waiting for her next move.

She lowers my boxers, scraping the sides of my hips with her nails, a combination of pleasure and pain. My thick cock springs forward, thumping against my abs. Dainty hands wrap tightly around me and stroke from root to tip, over and over, pumping and priming the muscle. The action is pure heaven.

When her tongue licks the small drops of pre-cum off the crown of my dick, my knees threaten to collapse under me. Fire. I'm burning alive inside, her every touch sizzling through me like the fiery storm raging outside. I throw my head back as an overwhelming feeling of pleasure courses through my body. Warmth closes around me as I sink into her willing, open mouth. She's captured me, owns me.

I watch the intimate act trying to remain in control. She's a siren beckoning me. I'm caught in her sexual web of pleasure. When her teeth rake over the tip of my member and her hand squeezes and massages my sack, I react. I grip a fistful of her curly hair pulling her mouth away from me.

"Jocelyn, you've got to stop, baby. You're driving me crazy."

The sight before me steals my breath away. She's kneeling, eyes glassed over with desire and lust, lips puffy, red, and panting. Exquisite, the things dreams are made of.

Extending my hand, she accepts, and I wrap her closely in my arms, inhaling her unique scent. The moment washes over me. Here we are, stuck at the Pit-Stop waiting for Hurricane Georgia to pass, the rain pounding outside the window being a constant reminder. My jeans are hanging off my ass, but I have my angel in my arms. Her scent surrounds me. I don't want to let her go, but I need more.

I maneuver us near the bed and sit down with her standing directly in front of me. Her breathing is returning to normal.

"*Cher*, you will be the death of me if I don't remove these boots."

She flashes a smile as I finish removing the last of my clothes. Standing before her, aching with desire, needing her to end the primal yearning deep down inside, I remind myself we only have tonight and I need to satisfy the craving for her.

"C'mere, angel," I tenderly command, waiting for her submission. She willingly steps into my out stretched arms.

"You're naked," she whispers.

"And you have way too many clothes on," I snicker. "I'm fucking buck-ass naked. Shouldn't it be the other way 'round?"

"You always did like to strut your stuff."

"I'll show you."

Peals of laughter wrap around me. Her happiness

assaults my senses, pushing me into action.

"Angel, do we need protection?"

"No. I'm on the pill. I don't want anything between us."

I grab a handful of her top and yank it from the inside of her wrinkled jeans. Her laughter stops as the howling of the wind outside plays a thunderous melody. The material bunches, revealing inch by glorious inch of her creamy skin. Her voluptuous breasts encased in the silky satin material lure my focus to the dusty nipples straining from the restriction. I thumb the front clasp and watch as the silky bra falls to the floor. I'm overcome by a longing to worship the beauty of Jocelyn Blackwood.

Pulling her close, feeling her skin against mine, it feels so right. My hand curves around the soft mounds of her rear to tuck her hips into mine. Her warmth seeps under my skin. The gentle sound of her voice coaxes me closer to her in every way possible. Body. Mind. Soul.

I nip the lobe of her ear lightly, causing a shiver. I cascade kisses down her long throat as my fingers probe and stroke her nipple. Round and round, building the sensation. I lightly pinch her erect rosy nipple, sending a jolt of pleasure through her body. Her moans increase in volume, matching the thunder and rain outside.

She rubs her pussy on my throbbing cock and my hips roll and thrust, seeking refuge in her heavenly body. Her head lolls back, stretching her neck as I continue to nip downwards, adding a sting only to lick the same spot with my tongue. She offers the other side, chasing the pleasure.

Finding our way to the bed, I lower her, keeping our bodies pressed together. My mouth latches onto her nipple, biting down and adding to her already aroused body. I need to hear my name on her lips.

My fingers search the slick folds through the curls finding her swollen clit. Lightly tapping, I simultaneously tug on her mouth-watering breast. She starts to come unglued in my arms, twisting and turning, bumping and grinding against me.

"Keagan. Oh my god! Please. Don't stop. More. I need …"

I suck harder and thrust my finger into her welcoming heat. Tightness engulfs my finger as her muscles ripple and squeeze, seeking relief from the intense pleasure swarming her body. I insert another finger and her hips violently bump against the palm of my hand. She's become a hellcat, wild and untamed, chasing her pleasure and determined to let nothing stand in her way of satisfying her body's need.

An unknown feeling overcomes me. Need. Possession. Her swollen breasts heave, seeking oxygen for the deprived lungs within and the restlessness of finding satisfaction. I need more. Crawling into a lower position on her body, my mouth latches on to her core and my tongue spears into her.

"Keagan!" she screams.

Her fingernails dig into my smooth head, pushing her pussy upwards for more. My tongue strokes her intimately and I zone in on her sensitive clit. Sucking the swollen nub into my mouth, I insert my fingers into her and hook upwards, hitting the spot that sends her tumbling into sexual oblivion. Moisture washes over them instantaneously. Her body trembles.

Possession. Intent. Longing. I clench my teeth as the need for her surges through me. My body responds balls tightening, cock aching for her to satisfy. She's boneless in my arms, a slight film of sweat, glistens over her flushed skin. Her eyes open and she focuses on me. Before words can form, I'm pressing into her, and a husky moan escapes from the moist lips I'm devouring.

Piece by piece, inch by agonizing inch, I bury myself into the depths of her welcoming body, stretching her tender muscles. The crown of my thick, engorged cock leading the way through the fiery heat. Finally. My angel. The pounding of her heart against my chest draws my gaze back to her. Her darkening eyes blaze with desire and yearning.

She looks between our bodies, where we are joined, staring between her thighs as I take her body. In. Out. Slow. Precise. My erection is covered from the dampness her body produces each time I withdraw from inside her. She flings her wavy hair, arching backwards, while pinching and cupping her breasts.

Short quick breaths escape from her lips when she grits her teeth at the excruciatingly slow pace I've set.

Ecstasy. The feeling of completeness washes over me. I know I'll never be the same. She's changing me minute by minute, second by second, my shelter from the raging storm inside my mind.

An edge of uncontrollable need takes over and I'm relentlessly pounding into her haven. I fuck her as if my life depends on the next stroke. I want her to remember tonight, forever branded into her mind. Thrust after thrust, stroke after stroke, my hips move in accordance to hers, both of us fighting for the ultimate pleasure.

Her legs circle my waist anchoring her ankles above my ass. I've lost all sense of finesse. My only thought is Jocelyn and the sexual fulfillment we're racing towards. My pace increases. I'm driving into her harder, faster with every plunge. Her cries fill my senses as her pussy tightens around me, sucking me into her climax. I thrust one more time, hard, deep, and explode as a powerful orgasm rips through my body. Unimaginable pleasure courses through me.

I collapse out of breath and energy. Gently, I pull her into my side. After what we just shared, I need to feel connected to her. Stroking her backside, I wait for our breathing to return to normal. It doesn't take long. Jocelyn recovers first. A smirk forms across my face. She's fallen quietly into a peaceful rest.

What the fuck just happened? I'm wrestling with

unfamiliar emotions. I knew it wasn't smart to mess with Jocelyn. From the first day I met her, she's held an uncanny ability to bring out strong feelings. I know I can't offer her a future—not now, not with the baggage I carry and the crazy life I live. For now I'll have to be satisfied with tonight and all we shared.

My phone vibrates on the bedside table and I know my time with Jocelyn is coming to an end. I've known for years she was the only one for me, and being with her confirms this. I wish I could make her the promises she so desperately needs, but I can't. I'm not sure if I will ever be able to. There's too much water under the bridge. Reaching for the phone, I open the text from Gunner, which reads: *We need to talk. My room ASAP.*

Sighing, I easily extract myself from her and roll out of bed as quietly as possible. She doesn't stir from her slumber.

I locate my jeans and slide them on. I unlock the adjoining door and open. What I find blows my mind. The television, radio, and some other electronic devices have been torn apart and reassembled into a makeshift computer of sorts. The phone jack is wired into them. A keyboard is attached and Gunner is feverishly typing. He glances from what he's doing when he hears the door behind me close.

"We've got to leave. They're on their way. I know these people here are your friends. You don't wanna bring this trouble to their doorsteps."

"Slow down, kid. Explain it me. What trouble and who's coming?"

"The Phantom Prophets and some of the people who are working with them. They must suspect something, or maybe they just wanna ensure I deliver the goods before I find out what they are up to. Not sure." He continues rambling, "I located the target for the client and you're right. I wouldn't have believed you. This is one fucked up mess I'm in."

"Have you contacted them?"

"No. I entered a back door, checking the files I had stolen for them. I needed to know what they were doing with the data. I thought it was all about guns and laundering money. Money, for shit's sake! But, they're connected to some major players in the middle east. Terrorists. Ties to the mafia. You were right, Crash. I'm a dead man walking."

"If you didn't contact them, then how do they know where you are? I need answers, Gunner."

"I tapped into the convos. I've been listening half the night. Couldn't sleep with the weather beating shit out there."

"What the fuck did you do?"

"You know, found their station and listened. Didn't take long after that to follow the trail. And they know you were sent to get me."

"You're shitting me, right?"

"No."

"Stay here. Clean this shit up, little MacGyver.

I'm going to get us some different wheels. Be ready to split in thirty."

I walk back into the room and Jocelyn's lying there asleep in the same position as I left her a little while ago. She looks like an angel. Her golden locks of hair fan the pillow creating a halo effect. The slight sprinkle of freckles on her nose has me wishing for more time, but she's in danger now, danger that I've put her in the middle of. She's suffered enough and I can't drag her with me.

Once I've finished the travel arrangements with Grady, I quietly shower and dress. This is going to be so hard on her. I remember the months of thinking about her when I left the View and we were just best friends, or like she thought of me as her not-boyfriend material. Maybe when this is all over, I can find a way to be a part of her life.

After picking her clothes up off the floor and packing my bag, I memorize the image of her sleeping for later when my tormented nights return.

Leaning over, I kiss her lips. "Until later, *m'aingeal,*" I whisper softly.

I need more of Jocelyn. I can't make her any promises, but there will be a *later*, because I'm not satisfied with just one night of ecstasy in her arms. Then I leave, locking the door on my way out.

CHAPTER 15
KEAGAN

Knocking on the psychedelic orange eight, Gunner opens it with his bag swung up on his shoulder.

"Let's go. Grady's found us some transportation. Two bikes."

"You want to ride a motorcycle in this weather? What's wrong with using your truck? We would at least stay somewhat dry."

"They've all seen the truck, and with the taillight busted, we're an easy target. This way they won't be expecting us and it'll at least give us a head start outta here 'til we can meet up with reinforcements. Besides the weather's let up and we've got a dry spell to ride."

"What do mean 'reinforcements'? You didn't tell me you were gonna involve outsiders. I mean, uh, besides us."

"Sooner or later, you're going to have to trust me. I know what I'm doing. I plan on keeping you and me safe and alive."

"So, you've got a plan to keep us alive?"

"Duh, fuckwit. I always have a plan."

"We'll have to go slow."

"Follow me and you'll be fine."

I head in the opposite direction of the lobby. We need to get the hell outta here. I can feel the net closing in on us. Even with the bad weather, evil will find a way, and the people hunting Gunner are playing for keeps. They won't let a hurricane stand in their way.

This place hasn't changed since the last time I'd visited before shipping out to Afghanistan. I had bought a bike and needed Grady to work his magic. He's known around these parts as Midas for his golden touch on customizing motorcycles to match the personality of its owner. I purchased her a while back and only Grady could make her mine.

I open the door marked "Garage" and walk through. A few guys are sitting around talking. They glance our way. I notice one of them is the son of a bitch who smiled at Jocelyn last night. He better stay the fuck away from her if he doesn't want a fucking knuckle sandwich. He's not good enough for her. She belongs to me. My only problem is she doesn't know it yet, even if we don't have a future.

Grady enters from the back, wiping his hands with a rag, and motions us towards a black Suzuki GSX.

"I made a few adjustments, but she's ready. Got this one for him, too," he mentions, nodding in Gunner's direction. "Took the governor off, so speed won't be an issue if you get in a bind."

"What the hell? You can't be serious. You want me to ride that to Miami? In the rain? It's almost three hundred miles away. They're made for racing, not long distance travel. They'll be calling me Bowlegged Bob by the end of this trip," Gunner whines.

"It's the only bike I've got available fast enough to keep up with Keagan's. You'll have to make do, little Bob," Grady smirks.

"Shit. This keeps getting better and better."

I'm restless, needing to get on the road and removing Jocelyn from the danger coming for us.

"Stay alert, Bulldog. Not sure what trouble's coming your way."

"You know me. I'm always ready for trouble. Won't catch me with my pants down."

"Phantom Prophets ain't something to laugh about. I've seen with my own eyes what they are capable of when they want info from unwilling people. It's brutal. They mean business," Gunner intercedes.

"Boy, you don't know much about me or you wouldn't be worrying. I can handle my own. I use to eat boys like that for breakfast." Grady chuckles and slaps Gunner on the back.

"All's the same. Keep your eyes open and your finger on the trigger."

"I hear you loud and clear, Keagan." Grady glances around the garage area and finds several of his men listening. "Anybody fucking stupid enough to come here looking for a fight won't be disappointed."

"Good enough."

"What about your lady friend from last night? You want us to look out for her, too? Whew. She's a looker. Kendall wasn't very happy about you talking with her. Thought she may shoot you herself."

"No shit. She made sure Jocelyn was taken care of. She passed out before I got her to the room. Can you make damn sure she isn't seen? Hopefully, she'll be long gone before they show up. If they even do. I don't want them seeing her." Pointing to the guy that smiled at Jocelyn last night, I say roughly, "She belongs to me, so stay the fuck away from her."

He's shocked I called him out, and Grady busts out laughing. I may not be able to have her with me now, but I damn sure won't let anybody else stake a claim on her.

"Finally going back for seconds? Didn't think we would ever see the day when Keagan Fontneau might double dip."

"Shut the fuck up, Bulldog. Don't need this shit right now. Where's my ride?"

A genuine smile forms on Grady's face and he turns, walking a few feet away, lifting a tarp off my bike and revealing the beauty before me. "I've made sure she was cranked weekly. She purrs like a lion. Shouldn't have any problems."

That's when I see my Black Beauty shining in all her glory, like coming home.

She was an old 80s model sportster, first bike I ever bought as a soldier. I fell in love. Black Beauty. She was matte black and sleek. When I'd returned home before my last tour, I hooked up with Grady about changing her up, customizing her to my way of thinking.

Now, she's beautiful. A mobile piece of art. Metallic black paint with lightning streaks of red and gold encircle the gas tank. It's not too much, but subtle enough to show off the storm that's brewing when I'm on her: endless heat and badass fuckery.

Grady replaced the knucklehead motor with a twin cam engine, 96 cubic inches of pure power. The bathtub-shaped motor allows for more efficient combustion and higher compression. The potential to run speeds of up to one sixty plus miles per hour. My kind of ride. The faster the better.

I've longed to feel the rumble from the engine between my thighs. The wind on my face with a long stretch of road in front of me. Freedom. Freedom from the worries surrounding me.

"Thanks, man. I owe you one."

"Nope. That's just how we do things 'round here, brother. Watch your back 'til you meet up with the others, Keagan."

"Gotcha. You ready, kid?"

"As ready as I'm gonna be. I've ridden one of these babies before, just not in this kind of weather. Should be an experience I won't forget."

"Make sure you stay behind me and follow my lead."

"10-4, daddy-o." He mockingly salutes me.

Smothering a smirk, I ignore the fuckwit and straddle the magnificent bike. Inserting the key, the rumble from the engine soothes the storm raging inside.

We pull away from the Pit-Stop heading east out of Gainesville on highway 20. The wind is rough, and even though the rain has slacked off, the puddles on the road concerns me. Looking in the side mirror, Gunner is hunched over catty corner from my location at four o'clock. He seems knowledgeable enough of the machine he's riding. He's steady and strong enough to keep the bike upright. The kid is growing on me.

My plan is to ride the opposite direction of Gainesville, setting an easy trail for the ones following us. I want to draw them as far away as possible from Jocelyn and the others.

She's going to be spitting fire mad at me for leaving without saying goodbye—or at least I hope so. I recall her depression when Fallyn left and curse the stupidity of my actions. Fuck. I don't want to hurt her, and think maybe I should call her. No. Can't drag her on, making her believe we have a future together when there isn't one.

She has her life in Gainesville and I have mine in Lakeview.

A bolt of lightning flashes in the distance followed by an awareness of rain starting to fall. We round a sharp curve and a black utility vehicle comes into view, parked on the side of the road. The doors open and three bodies appear. Downshifting, I motion Gunner and maneuver towards them, stopping. Leaving the engine running, I dismount and shoulder bump the soldier in front of me.

"Rocky, man. You're a sight for sore eyes. Been way too long."

"You're telling me. Can't help it, Keagan. I was born with this beauty."

"Fuck. You asked that fine woman of yours that question lately?"

"Yeah and she tells me she's not worthy of this fine ass," he says, chuckling.

"You're not right. I'll be sure not to mention that to Sara Beth next time I see her. I told Ollie you were the man for the job."

"Wouldn't be anywhere else. I owe you."

"No. I vaguely remember telling you over and over, we're even."

"Not after what you did for me. Life debt. Ain't going away."

His kid brother had returned home from Iraq missing both legs. They needed the money and the combat veterans motorcycle club I ride with helped raise the funds for his prosthetic legs and therapy. He would have been stuck in a wheelchair. The only thing

I did was request the fundraiser ride. My brothers did the rest.

It doesn't hurt that our body builds are identical. We could pass as doubles..

Shannon and Ollie stroll our way. The rain is picking up. I hear Gunner curse and a smile threatens me again, a questioning look from Ollie instantly sobering me.

"We've got our orders from Ollie. With the weather the way it is, we need to get on the road," Shannon reports. He's the one who keeps everyone in sync and on time.

"See you boys back at ground zero in twenty-four hours," Rocky supplies.

He revs the engine on my Harley and speeds away with Shannon following closely behind on Gunner's borrowed motorcycle.

"Let's jet," Ollie says, walking over to the driver's side.

I reach for the passenger door handle and somewhere behind me Gunner yells, "Shotgun."

Ollie releases a hoot of laughter.

I just shake my head, open the door, and get in. Stupid fucker's getting under my skin.

Ollie makes a U-turn and we are on our way back to ground zero, the safe location Ollie acquired for this operation. The rain is steadily falling and my thoughts drift back to Jocelyn. She should be in her home in her comfy little bed enjoying her comfy life without me.

Fuck me. She's getting under my skin now too.

CHAPTER 16
Jocelyn

For some crazy reason, a chill has settled deep into my bones. I grasp at the covers again and pull them up over my head, trying to alleviate the coldness. The smells of sex and Keagan wash through me as I snuggle down into the softness of the extra pillow I'm clutching.

Pillow? A pillow rests in my arms in place of the whopper of a hard, solid body that was lying next to me earlier.

I sit up in the bed quickly, untangling the covers off my head and peer around the room. Hair falls forward into my face and I brush it behind my ears. My gaze never finds its target. The black duffle bag that was sitting on the corner chair previously has been vacated. Not a stitch of clothing or anything at all remains, just my own clothes laid neatly across the foot of the bed. Not a trace left of the man I spent the morning making love to. The bad boy, Hottie McHottie Crash, who turned out to be Keagan. My Keagan. Vanished. The same man that kept his bold promise and made me scream over and over again.

He's gone. It's as if he was never here and it was all just a beautiful dream. Sorrow seeps in and my eyes well up from the pain of it. What was I supposed to think? That we'd reconnect and it was fate? I would finally get my happily-ever-after? Dreams are for children. I dash away the tears that fall down my cheek. *Buck up, Jocelyn.* I knew the risk when I said yes.

I scramble out of the bed and knock over the bedside table lamp with my clumsiness.

"Ugh! Shoot me right now. I'm such a klutz."

I rub my hip that hit the corner of the side table, along with my elbow.

"Coward!" I holler out to the empty room.

I'm furious at myself for what I allowed to happen, even though I wanted to know what it was like to be held in his arms. I needed him after all this time, consequences be damned. That's just it. I was so caught up in the moment and the pleasure he evoked, I didn't stop to really think about how it would affect me. Totally my fault.

But walking out without saying a word or goodbye? That's a new low in my book for this new rough and tough bad boy version of Keagan.

I stand naked as the day I was born hovering over my neatly folded clothes. He took the time to fold my clothes, but couldn't have the decency to wake me up before he left? Ugh! What a jerk. He's nothing like the boy I knew long ago. That person would've hunted me down and tried even harder to make me smile, even when I couldn't give him what he wanted at the time.

Why did he call me *m'aingeal?* What was the point if he was going to walk out without a backward glance? The first time he called me that to my face was the same night my life plunged into darkness. But his beautiful words, I will never forget.

My grandma's most-loved time of the year was Christmas. The entire Blackwood family gathered at her new home in town and she put on a shindig unlike anything you can imagine. Strings of colorful lights adorned every inch of the house and the smells of cinnamon filled my senses. I was surrounded by laughter and conversations as one by one we filled plates from the buffets of food on the festively decorated tables. My anticipation spiked at the presents piled around the ten foot live tree in the center of the room. Grandma buys gifts year round and takes extra care in finding unique gifts to fit a personality. I couldn't wait to see what she had in store for me.

I paused when Fallyn appeared in the archway. She'd been missing for most of the party and I noticed her eyes were red and puffy. She'd been crying. That was not good. I got up, made my way to her. I was hoping she would help me sneak away for a little while tonight to see Keagan and give him his Christmas gift. We'd become really good friends since our "pizza night" and, just like Grandma does, I had

*found a special gift for him. I wanted to give him my
gift and by the looks of things it wouldn't happen.*

"Fallyn, what's wrong?"

*"Sorry, Jo. I can't talk about it right now. Please
let it go." She hugged me tightly and said, "I love you,
little sister," before turning around to find a place to
sit.*

*I heard her whisper, "Everything's so messed
up," and a feeling of dread from when we were
younger seeped its way into my body. I couldn't help
but wonder if she just told me goodbye.*

*Knowing she wouldn't relent and tell me what was
going on until she's ready, I gave up and walked back
to my seat. I'm enveloped once again in holiday cheer,
yet my anxiety was overwhelming my thoughts. Fallyn
never cried unless he hurt her. I plastered a fake smile
on my face and join in singing carols as my grandma
passed gifts around the room.*

*A short time later, the doorbell rang. I was sitting
on the couch talking to my cousin Saul. He's a few
years older than me, a fierce saxophone player and a
ladies' man to boot. We were in the middle of
discussing his acceptance letter to Georgia when I
caught his voice. Keagan was standing in the front
entryway of my grandma's home, eyes focused in on
me. My inner voice began an excited chant of "yes,
yes, yes!". I was smiling as I walked to the door to
greet my best not-boyfriend Keagan.*

We walked outside and sat down on Grandma's

porch swing. The crickets were singing a lullaby. Even in the winter in the south, life was still ever present.

"Merry Christmas, Jo." Keagan handed me a beautifully packaged box with pink paper and gold ribbon trim. "I hope you like it."

I was shocked by the gift. I was shocked he was here; he came and found me to give me a gift. My eyes began to water at the intensity of this moment.

"I have something for you too."

I stepped back inside to retrieve the gift I got for him and needing time to compose myself from the deep emotions I'm harboring. When I came back, I handed Keagan the small Santa Claus bag, entwined at the top with red and green ribbon holding the handles firmly together.

"What's this?" Keagan sounded a little stunned that I purchased him a gift as well.

"It's something to always remember me by. No arguments. Now let's open them at the same time. Ready? One, two, three."

I tore into the sparkly pink paper like a kid in a candy store while keeping track of what Keagan was doing.

The box was small and my hands began to shake in anticipation of the possibilities the contents in the package contained. I was about to open it when I hear Keagan.

"Jo, this is ... wow. It's extraordinary, Boo."

He holds the gold coin up to the light, revealing a masculine scripted K on the front with a star above the letter encased in emeralds. On the other side of the coin are angel wings with the words "Always Believe and Never Give Up".

Keagan was leaving at the end of school this year and his plans were to enlist in the military. It was his dream to serve like his dad and mom. I wanted to give him something that would be easy to carry with him, but at the same time, special and unique, just like he was. So when I talked to Grandma about getting Keagan a gift, she led me in the right direction, like always. She told me about a coin that Grandpa kept with him in his pocket—one his father had given to him. He carried it everywhere he went. And so sprung the idea of crafting a coin just for Keagan.

"This is too much. And perfect at the same time, Jo. Just like you."

He leaned in and gently kissed my cheek as he encircled me with his arms for the hug I've longed to receive from him. I felt like I was floating on a cloud. I was so happy that he liked my gift.

"Your turn, cher. *Now I can't wait for you to open up your gift," Keagan said as he leaned back, gripping his new coin in hand, and watched patiently for me to open the box.*

Slowly so the magic didn't disappear all at once, I opened the small box to reveal a set of diamond angel wing earrings. My throat clogged up and tears threatened to spill as I carefully took the delicate jewelry out of the box. The wings were made up of diamonds with tiny pink stones outlining the wings, each one crafted in beauty and grace.

"Oh my gosh! Keagan, these are beautiful. And they're angel wings. Almost like the ones I had carved on your coin. So the angels would watch over you always."

My emotions were on overflow. A tear escaped the corner of my eye and I dashed it away quickly with my fingertip.

Chuckling and shaking his head back and forth, Keagan replied as he looked into my eyes, "Funny isn't it? But mine aren't to watch over you, Jo. I picked them because you are m'aingeal, *my angel. Since the moment I saw you, I knew you were going to be special to me. You're my best friend. My best not-girlfriend. Thanks for that, Boo."*

Unable to contain my joy any longer, I launched into his arms and kissed his cheeks. Not gently like he did to me, but with an urgency for him to know how much he means to me. Keagan didn't move except to hug me back. Such a gentleman.

"Thank you for being my best not-boyfriend, too. Merry Christmas, Keagan."

Shoot! Dang memories. I'm confused and pissed off. Though the more I stew over it, the madder I get. "Gentleman" my ass. Son of a biscuit eater. Who does this Keagan-upgrade think he is? Not my best friend, that's for darn sure, misleading me and then taking advantage of my vulnerability. It was too fast. I feel used … and it's all my fault. Nothing new. The ones we care about the most always leave.

I get dressed in a hurry, scuttling out the door while pushing my feet firmly into my boots. I've gotta get out of here, find Katrina, and vamoose. I stumble into the hallway. A few doors down I spot room 10. Knocking vigorously on the door, I shout through it.

"Rina! Are you in there? Rina."

I hear scuffling and the door swings open wide.

"*Sí*, Jo. No need to shout, *chica*. I'm up."

Katrina is holding her head with one hand. Her eyes are sleepy and she looks disheveled. I walk through the door and look around.

"Are you in here alone? No, never mind, it really doesn't matter. We have to go. Let's get our stuff together and leave. Hurricane or not, I'm not gonna stay here another minute."

"Wait, *niña*. Hold on. Slow down *un minuto*. Are you okay? Did something happen, *mí amiga*? Who do I need to hurt?"

I burst out laughing. I mean, really? Katrina is obviously sporting a headache and she's looking a little on the rough side, a sign that her night was more than likely as interesting as mine. But she's worried about me. I continue laughing and hug her up tight. I love this lady.

"I'm soooorry," I giggle again. "You are ... such a cutie when you get all hot tempered, Rina. Hahaha. Thank you."

"Hmph. Well, you came in here all crazy weird, *chica.* I'm ready to take someone out if needed on your behalf. *Hermanas*, remember?"

"Okay. Understood. You know you're the best, Rina? And no. No one to take out."

I laugh hard again at the irony of the situation. Long ago, Keagan was in my corner just like Katrina. He would've done anything to help me. I wasn't invisible when he was around. Gee willikers.

"Not necessary. I've just had a ... well, it was a very interesting evening, to say the least. I'm gonna tell you everything when we're on the way back to my house. Okay?"

Katrina's dark gaze is a set of laser beams, boring holes through my head: her new favorite look when it comes to my shenanigans on this trip. She relents when she sees the something she's looking for in my expression.

"*Sí*. Let's pack it up and head out. The storm has moved over us. I've been watching the news, *niña*. There's still some bad weather out there, but it's better. The flooding is what they're saying to watch out for. Let's do this. But you've got a lot of explaining to do."

We pack up and go to check out at the front desk. As we approach, the lobby is chalked full of ginormous tatted men in leathers with scowls on every one of their faces. What the heck? I slink back into the hall but Katrina grabs my hand and makes her way through the crowd of testosterone.

"Don't give me fucking bullshit, man. We know they were here." The scariest one of the bunch is leaning over the counter, trying to intimidate Grady.

"Not sure what you're talkin' about, man. No one by that name or script has been here. Ya know there was a hurricane out there, right?"

"That red Dodge out on the road tells me I'm right. Now you've got a few options here, Bulldog. Either you tell me what I want to know, or we make this real hard on you real quick."

At that, Katrina pivots us around and back to the hallway, hiding out of the way. We listen carefully as the banter continues.

"Maybe they called someone for a pick up. I don't know. I was tryin' to be patient with ya. But let me tell *you* somethin', *Buzz*. You've got about ten seconds to get you and your mangy dogs off my property or it's gonna get real hard, real quick for you."

With that, Grady pulls out a sawed off shotgun from under the counter and points directly at the chest of the one called Buzz. Oh my goodness. My eyes roam to the movement from both sides of the lobby as five other burly men come out from around the corner, guns in hands, surrounding the scarier-looking biker dudes.

I hold my breath and look to Katrina for assurance. Her eyes are peeled on what's going down. She turns her head to me and puts a finger up over her lips. *Not a word, I get it.*

"Whoa, hold on, bro. Wait jus' a minute. No harm, no foul, Bulldog." He holds his hand up in surrender as he scans the room.

"No harm, no foul? Not today, Buzz. You came into my house. Not cool, man. I'm not your *bro*. Turn your ass 'round now and don't ever let your boots cross my path. Yeah?"

Buzz wears a perverse smile which gives me the hebejebes.

"Okay, Bulldog. We'll play it your way. You win … today."

He backs out slowly then turns and pushes the front glass door open, exiting into the parking lot, along with the rest of his posse. A couple seconds later, the rumble of motorcycles cranking up and roaring onto the main road echoes in the room, alongside the rain falling hard, as the sounds vibrate the panes on the front of the motel.

"You ladies, alright?"

Startled, I screech, "Oh!"

I didn't even hear him approach. Grady chuckles.

"You okay? Sorry 'bout that. We usually don't get the likes of those in here. It's not allowed. They were on the hunt."

"On the hunt?"

"Yeah, looking for someone, or a few someones. Don't worry 'bout it. They won't be coming back any time soon. Anyhow, what can I do for you?"

I glance around and notice it's business as usual. The giant men with guns are gone. Kendall has appeared out of nowhere and is standing behind the front desk. Her smile is contagious and I smile back at her, the intimidating and creepy guys suddenly on the back burner of my mind.

"We're ready to check out, *hombre*. Time for us to leave."

"Yes, we're gonna try to make it back home now," I confirm.

"Well, come right over here then and we'll get you gals on your way. It's been a pleasure having you here with us, even if it was under bad weather circumstances."

The hostile stand-off earlier is a distance memory, apparently.

"You were lifesavers. Thank you so much for taking us in."

"Anytime. Y'all come back, if not to stay the night, then to come for dinner or drinks. For sure."

Kendall smiles again and I can tangibly feel her warmth and sincerity.

"You make a mean mojito, *niña*. They were *perfecto*."

"That's my baby. She's good at all kinds of

things." Grady wraps his meaty arms around Kendall's tiny waist.

"Thanks, Rina." Kendall blushes from the attention.

"Oye. What happened to the two guys we were drinking with last night? Gunner and Crash, *sí*?"

I visibly gasp and all heads turn in my direction.

"Oh, sorry. A'hem. I've got a frog in my throat. I need some water."

"Here ya go, darlin'." Grady hands me a bottle of water from the mini fridge as he answers, "Yeah, well they had to leave earlier. Said they were on a trip and had a timeline."

Grady and Kendall glance back and forth between each other. I'm struck by the waves of emotions I see pouring off the couple. I find it a bit odd. Kendall's face is marred with frustration and worry. Do she and Grady know Keagan?

"*Sí*, makes sense. Gunner was droning on and on about some job or something. *Bueno, gracias*."

"Yeah, well. They'll be alright. But you two, y'all be careful out there. The weather's still rockin' and it's floodin' too. Which way ya headed?" Grady asks.

"We're going back north to Gainesville. I live on the upper northwest side of town."

"Good. The floodin' seems to be more down here and more south. Y'all should be good."

"Here's your receipt, girls. Like I said, please come see me. It was a pleasure to have some normal people around," Kendall says with a laugh, then comes around the counter and gives us both a hug like we're old friends. Nothing like a storm to bring people together.

"Thank you for everything. We'll see you around," I say right before we push through the front door.

We leave Grady's Pit-Stop in the rain the same way we entered, except this time I can see where I'm going. Once again, I've been changed from the experience at the roadside motel. Now I carry with me the knowledge after all these years of what it's like to be with Keagan Fontneau. I'm so screwed.

CHAPTER 17
Jocelyn

The drive home was much shorter than the way over, only about thirty minutes with traffic. Katrina and I talked about what happened. Well, I chatted and she listened patiently and didn't say a word until I was completely finished. I laid it all on the line for her without sugarcoating any of it. I replayed the whole Crash being Keagan, all the way up to the amazing sex we shared. Katrina just nodded and smiled, which was totally uncharacteristic of her. She never gave me her opinion about it until right before she was ready to leave: "Well, *mí amiga*, sounds to me like something happened back there. *Sí?*"

I glance over as she's shutting the trunk of her car, all packed up and ready to go back to Tampa. The rain has decided to give us a break, but the sun is still hidden behind the dark stormy clouds.

"It feels *loca* right now. Someday, everything will all make perfect sense. But for now, laugh at the confusion, *chica*. Smile through those distractions, and keep telling yourself there is a reason for everything that happens. *Sí?*"

I hug her tightly. She's important to me. Katrina's words comfort my weary heart.

"Absolutely," I nod. "Thanks, Rina. Now you be safe out there. Call me when you get home. Oh, and if the weather turns south, pull over!"

"Not a *problema*, Jo. Take care, *mí amiga*."

Katrina pulls out of my circular drive and onto the main street, waving erratically at me as I blow kisses and gesture with my hands a goodbye like a Looney Tune.

She passes out of view and I whisper, "Until next time, *hermana*. I'm gonna miss you."

Alone again, I walk back to the front door and enter my home. I shut the heavy wooden door, lock the deadbolt, and turn on the alarm. Going into the den, I lie down on the couch as my thoughts swirl around all of the interesting people I met or came in contact with the past couple of days. The striking blue eyes of the grown up Keagan play over and over in my head.

I pull the fluffy plush blanket over my body, curling up my legs and arms. Katrina's thought-provoking words get me to think and reflect big time, wondering what can hurt the most in life: saying something to someone you care about and wishing you hadn't, or saying nothing at all and wishing you had? I have no regrets.

Everything happens for a reason. I believe it. If you believe hard enough, anything is possible. But did Keagan and I go too fast? We just saw each other again after all those years and after the way things ended when Fallyn left. We never had that kind of relationship. Maybe it was the storm raging outside. Maybe it was the storm raging within us both. I really don't have a clue. The simple truth is, we were two people with a need to fulfill and that's exactly what happened.

Do I believe fate played a role in bringing us back to together? One extraordinary night full of intense passion? I felt the connection, the one I had longed for. Yet without a thought, he up and left. The big jerk! The big, strong, beautiful, sexy, Hottie McHottie, tattooed-up jerk! I'm nuts.

I stroll into the bedroom, into my walk-in closet, and reach my jewelry box. Pulling out the drawer I'm seeking, I grip two dainty angel wing earrings in my hand. The pair are beautiful. I remember the sentiment behind the gift. Although, as a teenager, it was the most perfect present I ever received. As an adult, I can't make any sense of it.

My thoughts aren't taking a break and it seems I'm doomed either way. Time to pack up the craziness and go to my relaxing place. A jog around the neighborhood will help. It's not early morning like my usual, but I need to release some pent up frustration.

Donning my favorite grey and pink trainers, I head out the door to run away the pain that's blasting my heart to pieces. It's bad enough that the case with the twins had me reminiscing into unwanted territory. And now, seeing Keagan in the flesh has my emotions spiraling out of control on a whole new level. I'm mega pissed off at him, and if he were to show up right now, I'd give him a "what for?"

The sun has made an appearance out from behind the clouds and a light sprinkle has started up again—a fox's wedding, a sun shower. It's beautiful. As each drop falls down onto my weary body, cooling my overheated skin, my sanity slowly returns.

Lost in my thoughts, I come around the next bend in the road and catch sight of a lone figure jogging my way. I cautiously glance over to make sure I'm not in his path, a bit leery of being out on the streets alone.

"This is a safe community, Jo," I mumble to myself. "People are watching everywhere."

At first sight, I can only see the outline of a hood. No face. No features. I'm spooked, but my worries ease as I see another jogger trailing behind him. Ducking my head and picking up speed, I attempt to pass by.

An arm reaches out and grabs hold of me. I react instinctively, punching the anonymous culprit who grabbed me as hard as I can. I catch him in the shoulder and then assume the "don't mess with me" pose.

"Whoa, wait a minute! That's some punch you have there, *Miss* Blackwood."

Like fingernails on a chalkboard, the voice of Desmond Payne pierces my ears. He holds his hands up, palms out in the universal surrendering pose.

"What? What are you doing here?" I call out between breaths, because let's face it, I've been running two miles.

"What does it look like? I'm taking a run. I'm allowed. This is a free country." His timbre reeks of deceit, but I let it go. This has to be a coincidence.

"True, free country and all. But this is a private community, Mr. Payne. Do you live here?"

"Are you alright, Miss?" The other jogger I saw trailing comes to a stop right beside me. He's taken a defensive stance and I'm struck by how sexy he looks with his dark hair clinging to his sweaty forehead. Ear buds hang around his ears and my eyes head south to his shirtless muscular chest and lickable six pack abs. He's decorated with sleeves of tattoos wrapping up around his shoulders and torso. Holy mother of pearl. Jerking my eyes back to his, a smile plays across his handsome face. I blush because I've been caught, darn it.

"Yes, thank you. I'm fine." I catch my breath from the run and the hot guy standing beside me.

I level my stare on Mr. Payne. He's dressed in a hooded rain jacket zipped up tight with sweat pants, and leather mid-top sneakers. If I was a bettin' gal, I'd say he's dressed for a gym workout, maybe. But a jog? My mind races as to why this man would be on a street that I run every day, in *my* gated community. It's the same street I've never encountered him on before.

"Okay, if you're sure," the sexy jogger guy says, nodding his head and moving just slightly to the side behind Mr. Payne, not too far off. For a brief second, I wonder why.

Then I hear the sickening voice of Desmond Payne and I'm grateful.

"I apologize if I startled you. It seems I do that to you quite a bit." The hint of sarcasm in his voice grates over my skin, but I don't let him see how he affects me.

"It's fine, really. I, uh, apologize for punching you. You know, a woman running on the street alone, can't be too careful." I allow a half smile and it doesn't reach my eyes. I glance over to the jogger who has taken up stock on the sidewalk not far away, settled behind Desmond a few yards back. He's doing stretches as he keeps his eye on us. For reasons beyond my comprehension, I'm grateful.

"Well, that's all fine and good. Don't worry your pretty self over it. When I realized it was you, I just wanted to say hello." He sounds off in a snarky tone.

"Do you live here? In Palm Wood Manor, I mean. I've never seen you around, but that doesn't mean anything, really." I avert my eyes over his shoulder to the sexy jogger because I already know the answer— seen the file, got the scoop.

"No, Miss Blackwood. I live at Charles Town Estates, the next community over from this one. But you already know that, don't you?" His eyes are challenging. "I have a gate pass for all four properties owned by the franchise. I like to play golf, among other things, and this one has an excellent course. But the view here for running is like no other. So I come here often to run when I'm looking for a change. It is a wonder we've never run into each other before."

I don't like his answer and I sure don't appreciate the way his eyes have taken up residence of staring at my ta-tas.

"Ah, sadly I must be going. Have a good run." He turns to leave and then stops, calling over his shoulder, "You might want to think about carrying some mace or even a baseball bat when you jog, Miss Blackwood. This may be a safe gated community, but one can never be too sure of these kinds of things. Your punch and pose would do nothing to a man who wants to have you."

And then he's gone.

What the fudge? My mouth gapes open, eyes wide with shock. I can't believe what I've just heard. I stand there for a few more minutes, absorbing his finishing line. The warning starts a feeling of dread in the pit of my stomach. What does this man want? He has to have a few loose screws.

"Are you okay, ma'am?"

I'm startled and completely jump out of my skin. Heart pounding and goosebumps pimpling across my skin, my cheeks heat to red with embarrassment.

"Holy macaroni! You scared me to death, mister."

"Sorry, the name's Oliver Bishop, ma'am. But most people call me Ollie." He reaches out to shake my hand.

"Nice to meet you Oliver, Ollie. I'm Jocelyn. New to the neighborhood?"

"Yes, ma'am. It's beautiful here. Aside from the hurricanes, football team, and mother nature included." His friendly demeanor matches the beaming white teeth he's sporting with his grin. He pauses and surveys the area. "I wanted to make sure that you were alright and the creeper had exited the area before I vacated."

"Well, thank you, sir. I mean Ollie. He was a creeper. I'm glad I wasn't alone. Are you in the military? I mean, it's none of my business, really, but you seem all 'yes ma'am' and using words like 'vacated'. You sound like you might be."

Ollie laughs and I instantly smile back. I feel at ease talking to this stranger; he has that affect. He gives off the impression he's one of those people everyone gravitates toward—easy and familiar.

"Yes, ma'am. Well, not anymore. I served two tours in the middle east. Glad to be back home."

"Thank you for your service." I raise my right hand over my heart in reverence. "Two tours? That must've been rough for you. I have a not-boyfriend who served over there." This time I laugh at his expression. "I know, I know. Sounds strange. I haven't seen him in years, since high school. Until a few days ago, in fact. He's so different now. War really can change a person, huh?" I can't believe I'm talking about this with a total stranger, like we're best pals.

"Ya know, it can." Ollie's eyes suddenly appear mournful. "The things that have to happen in the midst of chaos can rattle even the strongest soul. That's all a bit depressing, isn't it? I'm thankful I made it out and intact. Your *'not-boyfriend'*, too," he adds, making air quotes with sadness etched across his face.

I can't help but ogle his abs as they ripple and bulge as he speaks. When I spot a puckered pink scar on his shoulder solidifying his statement, a wave of guilt washes over me. His posture reminds me of Keagan. Time to go.

"Well, me too, Ollie. And I'm grateful you were here just now. Thank you again."

"You got it, Jocelyn. Now I have to get back to my run. It was nice meeting you. Maybe I'll see you around."

"Bye!" I shout out as I eyeball his fine backside while he jogs away. Thank goodness he was at the right place at the right time. What a nice guy, the same way Keagan was way back when he cared.

My psyche keeps sinking further into a heap at the back of my brain. So much for taking a run to clear my head. I'm a mess from the inside out. It was better when I dreamed about him on occasion. Now, I'm beginning to struggle. The deeper I go, the harder it will be to crawl out from the cavern with a K that's consuming my heart. Although, I may never see him again. That one thought drives me to sadness. For some reason, deep down, I believe I'll see him down the road. My head keeps reminding me I'm super pissed off, but my heart is playing a whole other tune. *Darn it all, Keagan Fontneau.*

The frightening run-in with Desmond Payne didn't help either. As I jog back to my house, my head is on a swivel as I survey my surroundings. I can't be caught unawares again and I certainly can't take any chances with Mr. Payne in my neighborhood. What the heck? The more I think about the encounter, the more disgusted I feel. He was threatening me or giving me a warning of sorts, as if he was attempting to intimidate me. If I'm honest with myself, I'd say he succeeded. I'm just thankful someone was there to intercede on my behalf. I hate to say it, but I wouldn't want to be caught in a dark alley or otherwise with the likes of Desmond Payne.

At the same time, I need to tread carefully. Obviously I've either uncovered something Mr. Payne is desperately wanting to keep hidden or I'm his newest obsession. Neither scenario appeals to me.

When I make it back home and I'm all locked in again, I'm relieved. I've learned to be stronger over the years and not be scared of my shadow like I was when I was younger. Yet, I can't help but think about how wonderful it would be to have someone here to share the burden. A certain someone to make me feel safe and cared for. A blue eyed devil with tattoos.

Ring, ring, ring.

Thoughts interrupted, I answer the phone.

"Hello?"

"Hi, Miss … Blackwood? Hi, umm, shoot," a whisper of a female voice sputters through the line. An undercurrent of panic and courage reaches out to me.

"Yes, this is Miss Blackwood. Who is this? Crystal? Is that you?"

I've only spoken with the twins at their school on one occasion, but my gut is screaming it's her.

"Yes, ma'am. I…umm. I wanted to call and see if you could meet with Cade and me. Our mom said that we should call you if we wanted to talk, she said it would be okay. We could both really use some advice."

I hear a muffled gruff voice in the background and can only assume it's Cade from the tone and the words spewing forth. It sounds as if Crystal has placed her hand over the speaker to smother the conversation, but I'm able to hear the ranting anyway.

"I don't want to, Crys. You can't make me. No one can help."

"Hush up, Cade. This is different, she is different."

"Hello, Crystal. Are you okay? Is Cade alright?"

"Yes, ma'am. It's all good. We just, well, it's time for us to make things right. Can you meet us at school on Tuesday next week?"

"Sure, Crystal. That'll be great. Are you sure there's nothing I can help you with right now?"

"No, thank you, Miss Blackwood. Tuesday will be great. We both look forward to talking to you then. Thank you."

"Speak for yourself, Crys," floats through the line in a garbled murmur.

"Alright, then. I'll see you both at your school on Tuesday. Goodbye Crystal."

I hang up and feel even more confused. I've always considered myself an expert in my field, good at reading people, and therefore able to excel at helping those who need it, making the appropriate recommendations and fixing what's broken—as long as the ones who need the help desire it. I was reborn or remade into the woman I am today because I longed to help others. I couldn't do that for Fallyn or Harper, so I had to try a different approach to keep my own sanity intact. The more and more information I gather on this case, the less and less I know. And I feel as if I know everything about nothing. Crazy, right?

Where strange conversations go, this one was one of the strangest I've had. And from a teenager, no doubt. What did all of that mean? Is Cade harboring a secret that Crystal wants to help reveal, or is it something more simple? Losing their dad, hormones, a stepfather such as Desmond Payne, the look of indifference on Calista's face at our first meeting … all of it whispers through my mind. The list goes on and on. But one thing's for certain: the kids wish to talk on Tuesday. I'll be ready to listen.

Something has to go right. Is it too much to ask for one thing in my life to go smooth as silk? For one circumstance to be easy-peasy? Like the old saying goes: learn from yesterday, live for today, and hope for tomorrow.

I guess I'll have to wait and see what tomorrow brings.

CHAPTER 18
KEAGAN

Twenty-eight hours, thirty-one minutes, ten seconds and counting. That's how long I've been away from Jocelyn, and time seems to drag on and on. I know in my mind I did the right thing for her and me, but the look on her face when she gave herself to me has me doubting my actions.

Roxy vying for attention drags my thoughts back to the present. Her head is nudging my hand, begging for me to pet her. We're sitting around the makeshift conference room table waiting on Ollie to return from his surveillance of one of the players in this game. He's been trailing a major benefactor, someone we believe will lead us to Big Daddy sooner or later. It's a lead. We are running out of options and time.

Rocky and Shannon returned late last night. They were sure no one was the wiser and the Phantom Prophets are on their way to Miami. Shannon reported they gave them the slip around Fort Lauderdale.

Gunner and Lukas have their heads together whispering shit. When Gunner arrived, Lukas wasn't too happy when he took apart one of his computers.

The kid has a lot to learn.

Lukas swats Gunner's hand from his computer. "Don't touch another damn thing, boy. This is expensive stuff. Didn't you learn any manners growing up?"

Gunner rubs his hand. "I'm trying to optimize the operating system and free up some memory. If you let me add this booster program too, you'll be a flying ghost on the web. Not like you don't have enough problems running what you have from that thing."

"Listen here, you little runt, I know exactly what I have. I've been doing this longer than you've been alive and this is state-of-the-art equipment. Some of this shit isn't even available on the open market."

"How 'bout you let him help some, Lukas?" Rocky interjects. "Couldn't hurt. We're on a time crunch and two heads are better than one."

"Whatcha got, *boy*?" Lukas unhappily sulks.

"I can tweak the existing toolchain bypassing the usual API with a fast-path interface. This will optimize the programs I'm going to add and enhance the performance so the search should take less time and we can beat them at finding what they are trying to find. I know my stuff, Lukas. C'mon, we've got to locate them before he does. I couldn't live with myself knowing I had sent them in their direction."

"I have no idea what the hell he just said, but sounds like a viable option, Luc. Let him try it. What can go wrong?" Shannon adds before getting up for another cup of coffee.

"Plenty, but I'm game. We need answers. I'm watching you," Lukas reluctantly agrees, gesturing his two fingers from his eyes to Gunner's.

The elevator door opens. Ollie walks forward dressed in gym shorts and a t-shirt.

"You're not going to believe the gall of this egotistical dumbass I'm following. He's a piece of work," Ollie begins as he grabs a bottle of water from the refrigerator and finds a place to sit down.

"Bad, huh?" I ask.

"He likes bullying women. It's sick, man. It took a lot of restraint not to haul him off and deck the motherfucker." He takes a swig of the cold water and continues, "And the woman was a natural beauty, too. Hourglass figure to die for and, damn, *her eyes* … I haven't seen a pair that green before, like emeralds. She almost decked him flat on his ass, so she's got spunk."

"Did you get pictures?" Lukas glances up from where he and Gunner are working.

"Yeah, here you go." He hands over what looks like a man's sports watch. It must be another one of Lukas's homemade camera toys.

"Gimme a sec to upload the data and we'll have a visual for your report."

"Sure." Ollie continues his rant over his newest interest. "I'm seriously considering when this is over, finding this woman and asking her on a date. Bet she's a hellion in bed, especially with that swing. She's the whole package, boys: brains, beauty, and boobs."

We all chuckle at Ollie's comments and hand motions. He constantly tries to keep everyone relaxed and off kilter with his crazy ass comments. He's the unofficial jokester of the group. When we returned from overseas, he was there, wounded, keeping me and Lukas in a good frame of mind, never a negative word, only encouraging us to get our shit together. I'm not sure I've ever seen him blow up. Don't get me wrong, he can kill someone as efficient as any of us, but he prefers diplomacy first. His danger comes from his brain.

Lukas glances up and I focus on the screen in front of me. What I see releases years of pent-up fury. Seconds later, I'm exploding from my chair, grabbing Ollie by the front of his shirt, and yanking him to his feet.

"When and where the fuck did you take this?"

"What the fuck, Keagan?" he says, pushing me away from him. "Palm Wood Manor. About an hour or so ago."

The room is silent. You can hear a pin drop. I've never reacted that way before, especially with my brothers, but something snapped inside of me seeing Desmond Payne with his hands on Jocelyn. Her being so close to someone that dangerous sent tremors of fear to my heart.

I take a deep breath and right the chair I had been

sitting in only a few seconds before.

"That's Jocelyn Blackwood," I state more calmly.

No other words are necessary. Lukas and Ollie know who she is to me. You share a lot of shit when you're in the trenches on the front line waiting for the next explosion or ambush to occur. We all had. They both share glances back and forth. I sit back down and rub my hand over my head trying to shake the anger away.

"Hey, that's the girl from the Pit-Stop," Gunner says. "What's she doing with Dez?"

"You know the man in the photo, kid?"

"Yeah, Crash. He and Buzz are business associates. I've been with Buzz a few times when he had to meet up with him for new orders from the big boss. Some bar outside of Daytona." He shrugs.

"Fan-fucking-tastic. Luc."

"I'm on it."

"Ollie, report."

"He seemed to know her well. Addressed her by name. She was uncomfortable. I stayed close by until he left. I only overheard bits and pieces of the conversation, but he was definitely threatening her. Why? I'm not sure. I checked on her after he was gone and she was jumpy. I caught up with our boy here about thirty minutes later and followed him to his office."

"I'm going to find out why the fuck Desmond Payne is talking to her."

"Keagan, you need to calm down before you go charging over there," Ollie, the voice of reason, quietly says. "You don't want to scare her."

I send a look his way and don't reply. Wasn't he just talking shit about how fine my angel is only minutes ago? He shakes his head in defeat. He knows me, and my mind is made up: I'm going to see Jo now.

"Here's an access badge into the property." Lukas hands me a white card that looks almost like a credit card I have in my wallet. "You'll need it to gain entrance or you would have to get permission from her. The guard at the entrance is a nuisance."

"I'll be back later. Keep looking, Luc. Use the kid. He knows his shit. He's a little MacGyver like you. Find the missing link."

Thirty minutes later, I park my bike in her driveway, impressed at the massive home before me, and jog up the steps, ringing the doorbell. Several minutes pass by. Finally, she opens the front door and promptly slams it in my face before I can stop her.

"What the fuck, Jocelyn? Open the fucking door. Now."

"No. Go away, Keagan. I have nothing to say to you."

"Angel, I need to talk to you. I'm … uh, fuck. This ain't easy, Jocelyn! I'm fucking sorry I wasn't there when you woke up, but I had good reason. It was work. I had to take care of some things, and when I came back in to tell you goodbye, you were sleeping so peacefully that I couldn't wake you up." Leaning against the door, I sigh, "Come on, Jo. Open up."

Seconds pass and I bang my head on the door. Nothing. I'm about to leave when I hear the knob turn and the door opens.

"You have thirty seconds and then I'm slamming the door again."

"You look so good, angel, standing there in your sexy little pajamas. Let me in, baby. I need to talk to you without the chance of someone else hearing what I have to say."

She briefly stares at me and the indecisiveness is written all over her expression.

"You know you want to let me in." I wink.

"You are a menace to society, Keagan Fontneau! I can't believe in good conscience that I'm allowing you into my house, but holy guacamole, I am!"

"Oh, *cher*, you know your body craves what only I can deliver."

"Oh, you! You, you, you …"

"Now, now, pretty thing. Come on over here."

I lunge forward, wrapping my hand around her waist and yank her into my arms. Her arms fly to my biceps and push away, trying to dislodge the firm hold.

"Sweetness, when are you going to realize you can't get away from me?"

"Keagan, you are crazy! Let me go right this

minute!"

My lips lock onto hers, stopping her tirade. I move inside the doorway, slamming it shut with my foot. Leaning back, my hips push between her thighs and find home when her legs circle my waist and lock behind my back. I press her back closer to me, and her unrestrained nipples flatten on my chest. My tongue manipulates hers as she matches me stroke for stroke, nip for nip. She's made for me. When passion ignites, her body seeks relief and her traitorous body responds to mine as my hips thrust back and forth, rubbing against her aroused body.

"Angel."

She relaxes and fists my shirt, pulling it up. We stop kissing to discard the unwanted shirt. I slowly lower to the floor and she straddles me, my rigid cock straining against the zipper of my jeans. She rocks her hips, rubbing her clit and grinding into my erection.

My hands flex and massage her ass, easily lifting her to move her against my pounding cock. Her nails rake across my shoulders and I'm dying to feel her sweet cunt again. I nip her bottom lip and devour her mouth. She's my heaven. Grabbing my jeans, I move my hips until my restrained cock is freed. Moving her flimsy pajama bottoms to the side, I lift her hips and sink balls-deep into her tight hot body. She's so turned on, my thick long dick needs no lubrication.

I rip my lips from hers before I bite her. "Fuck, Jo! Ah, fuck!"

She doesn't respond as she comes up on her knees and slowly rocks, swaying her hips side to side and grinding down. She's out for revenge. I'm so close to losing my shit. I flip her to the hard tile, grab her rounded ass, and thrust deep.

"Keagan!"

She twists and turns, searching, begging for release.

My palm flattens by her face and I watch as my cock drives home into her warm, tight pussy. I keep a steady rhythm, pounding harder and harder into her. Her fingers dig into my ass for something to hold on to. I'm sure I'll have marks tomorrow. Adjusting my hips slightly, I find her spot and hammer home.

She throws her head back, screaming my name. It echoes off the walls in the large foyer. I thrust deeply into her again one last time and groan when her pussy grips my dick so hard, I'm yelling her name.

"You're mine, Jocelyn. You may not want me as fucked up as I am, I may not be ready … but damn it, woman, you belong with me."

CHAPTER 19
Jocelyn

The last time I felt this safe was … never. Keagan has always had a take-charge quality about him. I always trusted him completely when we were younger even during my extreme state of loss and darkness, hence this afternoon surprise. Just when I thought I may never see him again, Keagan shows up out of nowhere and rocks my world. Deep trouble.

My body betrayed me. *It was delicious!*

Keagan is sprawled out on the floor in front of the couch with one hand propped up behind his head, all his beautiful, intricately-painted tattoos on display for my greedy eyes. I'm curled up and around his big frame, smelling the delicious fragrance that's only his and following the patterns with my fingers. I garner a shudder or laugh once or twice. Keagan is ticklish. Caught in the moment of bliss, my heart melts into a puddle. Looking back over our time as youngsters, the warmth and emotions filled us both to the point of bursting, simultaneously adding fuel to the flame that has burned brightly over the years and brought us both to this point in time.

"You okay, Boo?" His deep voice is like liquid velvet, enclosing me up in a bubble of pleasure and yearning.

"I am. I feel pretty good right now. Even though I'm still mad at you, ya big lug."

Play-swatting at his chest, he mocks me by pretending it hurts. A deep chuckle fills the room. I can't stop the smile that falls across my own face.

"A psychologist, huh? That's huge, Jo. So damn proud of you, baby."

"It just seemed right, ya know? You played a big part in that decision, too. I wanted to help people, the same way you helped me a long time ago. Anyhow, it's what I do."

"Really somethin', Boo. I'm sure Fallyn would be proud of you."

"I kinda like to think so." My body language turns into sorrow and I'm grateful when Keagan changes the subject.

"I came over here to make sure you were okay, Jo. There's somethin' else. How do you know Desmond Payne?"

The look on my face must give off the confusion from the out-of-left-field comment he's thrown at me. I squint my eyes in his direction with a rebuttal because this line of questioning is getting me all kinds of pissed off again.

"Better question is, how do *you* know Desmond Payne, Mr. Fontneau?"

He shakes his head, rubbing his large palm over his face. "Can't talk about it, Jocelyn. But he's a motherfucker. Someone you need to steer clear of."

"Ha! That's nothing I don't already know, Keagan. And I can't talk about it either, it being my job and all."

"You're not involved with him are you? Or have been?"

He appears a little worried. Interesting.

"In his dreams maybe." I roll my eyes. "Seriously? Do you honestly believe I'd stoop to the likes of that slimy, no-good snake? He's nappy. With a capital N. Think that little of me, huh?" I question, the fire beginning to boil my blood. "Nope. Strictly professional. Again, I can't talk about it with you." I turn my head because I don't want him to see the hurt he's caused.

"Jocelyn, Boo. I just worry about ya. He's a snake in the grass, lying in wait. I just don't want to see you hurt."

I swivel my head back in his direction, studying his worry lines and determination, trying to figure out how he knows Desmond Payne.

"Stalemate, huh?"

"Yes, sir. I'm afraid so." I mimic a salute.

"The storm's lettin' up, Boo. How 'bout we go for a ride?"

Keagan changes directions again. My brain commences in a pirouette from his back and forth.

"A ride? A ride on what? I thought we already did that." Blushing under his continuous stare, I'm not sure what he's talking about or what he wants to ride. My mind still reels from the warning he just gave me.

"My bike, baby. Just got her back and I want you on the back. Grease the wheels, Boo."

"Oh, I don't think so, Keagan. I've never been on a motorcycle and I'm pretty sure I'd be scared to death. I've had enough of that here lately, thank you very much."

"C'mon, Jocelyn. It's not real scary. I'll go slow." He smirks, his blue eyes dancing with mischief. "Besides, you've got to meet Black Beauty. She's almost as perfect as you are."

And there you have it. His way with words always traps me deeply and yanks at me hard, convincing me to forget everything else.

"Well, I don't know. It's really wet out there. The roads are still bad. I don't know."

"Come, let me show you. Take a chance, Jo. You never know how perfect somethin' might turn out to be. If you try. And … I'm not takin' no for an answer. You're gonna love her."

He's like a kid on his birthday, so excited to show off his new toy. I score a glimpse of the old Keagan, the boy I knew long ago.

"Alrighty, I'll take a look. But no promises, ya hear?"

Not sure why I made the last remark because honestly, I'd follow him anywhere.

Keagan pulls up off the floor and takes me with

him. I go into my bedroom closet to put on some clothes. I opt for my skinny jeans and favorite pink boots. I'm pulling my hair back into a hair tie and stop short as I come out of the closet, my eyes landing on the behemoth taking up space in my bedroom. Keagan had followed me into my room. I do a double take. He's yummy and delicious, and I eat him up with my eyes. He's dressed again in his ass-hugging jeans and biker boots, followed by a black t-shirt with "FUBAR" in red letters ironed on the front. How did I not see that shirt before? He's leaning against my bedpost … right where he belongs.

"I love those boots, Jocelyn." My name on his tongue generates flip-flops in my belly.

"Thanks. I love your boots, too." Shoot! I just said that. I'm losing my mind. Get it together, girl.

"Ya do, huh?" Keagan glances down at his black leather boots. He grins, shaking his head. "C'mon, *cher*. Let's go stretch out our legs."

He circles me in his brawny arms and laps me up like he's trying to get to the center of the Tootsie Pop. I'm lost. Once more, he licks and nips on my bottom lip, then grabs my hand and tugs me out the door.

"Whaddya think, Boo? Beautiful, yeah?"

Sitting on my red brick driveway is the biggest, menacing-looking two-wheeled machine I've ever seen in person.

"Holy mackerel, Keagan. That thing is a beast!"

"Yeah. Grady fixed her up right. She rides smooth

as silk and takes the corners with ease. Zero to sixty in less than ten seconds."

"Grady, as in Pit-Stop Grady?"

Keagan chuckles again. It's an all-familiar sound from our childhood dipped in manly spice. I love it and can't get enough of it—or him. I want more.

"The one and the same. We go way back. My pop and his were buddies in the service. Served together. Brought her to him right before my last deployment. Wanted the bike to match the man."

I smile at the sparkle I see. Boys and their toys. I was right.

"You're full of surprises, Mr. Fontneau. Hmph. Makes sense, the funny eyes they were giving me. I got the feeling Kendall and Grady knew what was going on when I left there."

"Yeah. Gonna explain more. But right now, I want you on my bike. Get to it, Jo. Let me see what you look like on her."

Timidly, I walk forward and run my fingertips across the tank, down the black stitched leather seat, and to the back fender. The motorcycle is painted a sparkling black with red and gold glimmers of lightning scattered all over. Nothing over the top; it's a perfect storm. It's chromed out from top to bottom. On the tip of the tail right above the fat boy tire, written in a cryptic script are the words: "De Oppresso Liber. Defectum Est Non Bene."

"It's magnificent, Keagan. What does this mean?"

I softly touch the Latin phrase.

"'To free the oppressed. Failure is not an option.' It's a military thing." He half-smiles and I see his dimple peeking out to say hello.

A beautiful tribute. Enough said. My mind skips to the bullet holes I witnessed, scattered on his stomach. I'm curious to know more. What happened to this strong man standing in front of me? Keagan walks over during my musings, placing a large black half shell helmet on my head, obviously belonging to him, judging from its bulkiness. He buckles and snaps it into place. The weight is heavy on my head as I lift my chin up to his.

"Just in case, *cher*." He places a kiss on the top of my nose.

He walks to the side and slings his powerful leg across the top of the seat, settling onto the leather, both feet planted firmly on the ground. He pulls the machine upright.

"Hop on, Jo."

I grip the bulky helmet in my hands, heart beating erratically as I bite the inside of my lip. The anticipation of his handsome mug is my undoing as I walk over to the side of the bike.

"Where am I supposed to sit?" Looking down at the seat, I notice there's not much room left since he got on.

"The fender. Half on, half off. You'll fit. Stop stalling, Jocelyn."

"Oh, well alrighty then. That's going to be peachy," I say in a smarty-pants voice.

"Put your foot right here." He guides me to get on. "It's a lot like mounting a horse and you've done that plenty. Just use me as the harness."

Firmly placing my foot on the ribbed rubber floor pad, I swing up and come to rest right up against Keagan's hard back. My girly parts whisper a delightfully sultry tune being this close to him. He grabs my arms and anchors them around his waist.

"Hold on tight, Jo. Don't let go. I'll take care of you."

The deep rumble of the motor cranking up rips me wide open with excitement. I've never done anything like this before. Cheek situated on his back, I begin to grin as I clutch Keagan hard. Before I realize it, the majestic machine lurches forward and we're off.

My senses are on overload as we travel down the neighborhood street. Good to his word, Keagan takes it nice and slow, getting me used to the way the bike sways from side to side in its movements and maneuvers. As we pass by the guard shack, Chester steps out and I wave with one hand, the other gripping hold of Keagan's bunched-up shirt. The loud roar of the monstrous motor causes the passersby in cars to rubber-neck. The security guard eyes me questioningly at first, but when I shoot him a big smile, he shrugs and goes back into the security booth.

Keagan pulls out onto the main road and lights

Black Beauty up. I squeal as I feel the throb and quake between my thighs. It's like the feeling of running, but on steroids. I'm scared to death and thrilled all at once. My knuckles are white from holding on tightly to his taut stomach. The vibrations from his laugh course through him and into me, as if we are one.

The sensations of no limits, no worries, and total freedom astound me. The shifting of the gears are exhilarating. We pass by a field and I'm enveloped by the sweet distinctive smell of honeysuckle. I'm surprised by another encounter of the savory aroma of a grill cooking somewhere close by. This is what freedom feels like. With Keagan's help, I'm being brave, taking risks and allowing the unexpected to happen. It's amazing and I love the feeling. I never want this to end.

Little by little, I'm learning to never take life too seriously. Nobody gets out alive anyway.

The more time I spend with her, the more I realize I've been kidding myself. This isn't just a fly-by interest, here-today-gone-tomorrow thing with Jocelyn.

I hit a pothole and wait. Her arms wrap tightly around my waist, pressing her heavenly body closer to mine. I gun the bike and she squeezes harder as we speed down the highway back to Gainesville.

I'm aching for her. I can't seem to get enough of her.

I'm concerned Desmond has set his sights on her. I know she doesn't understand what people like him are capable of. She's lived a somewhat sheltered life from the harsh reality of crime and mayhem in the world. I'm sure she's dealt with some cases that would curl my toes, but the actual culprits I'm dealing with here scare the shit out of me to think what they would do to her if they had the chance.

An unfamiliar ache grips me; the thought of never hearing her laughter or listening to her give me hell isn't something I can deal with right now. Making my mind up, I decide to keep her with me, at least until I've talked with the guys and get an update of what they've found.

We pull up in front of the two-story building. Jocelyn lifts her head from the center of my back and a contented sigh escapes her lips. I turn the engine off and hold my hand out for her to dismount. When she's standing beside me, desire explodes inside. I grab her hand and pull her close for a kiss.

Initially, it was to satisfy my body's craving after having her up against me for so long on the ride. But passion ignites zero to sixty in a flash when our tongues collide and my hand fists in her curls, bringing her as close as possible, exchanging breath for breath. Her tongue circles mine, tantalizing me, begging for more. I grab the firm globes of her rear and yank her into the cradle of my thighs. She returns the favor, holding me as tightly.

A throat clears somewhere nearby and I reluctantly open my clasped fingers one at a time and stroke her hair. Leaning my forehead on hers, I let out a loud sigh.

"This better be fucking good, Ollie. You're interrupting me and I'm in the middle of something very, very important."

"Yeah, Keagan. They found something you're gonna want to see."

Jocelyn looks at Ollie and gasps. "You?"

He chuckles and offers his hand. I swat it away.

"Jo, this is Ollie Bishop, my business partner and used-to-be friend," I say, giving him a stern stay-the-fuck-away look.

He laughs harder at me, grabbing his clenching stomach. "Oh man, you've got it bad. We've already met. Good to see you again, Jo."

"It's Jocelyn to you," I remark, not being able to stop myself.

"I think I can speak for myself, thank you very much," she says, giving me a stern look. Turning, the sassy little minx smiles at Ollie. "Hi, Ollie. Glad to know he's actually got a friend these days. I was worried."

I push past the hysterically laughing Ollie and grab Jo's hand.

"C'mon. Let's get inside."

He's still chuckling softly when we enter the building. Lukas and Gunner stop what they are doing and stare. I wrap my arm around Jocelyn's waist.

"Hi, Jocelyn," Gunner greets her with a wave of his fingers.

"Lukas Rogers, this is Jo."

"I kind of figured that and all, Keagan." Lukas stands, making his way towards her and wrapping her in a burly hug. "Hiya, Jocelyn. It's nice to finally put a pretty face with the name."

"Um, well okay. Hello. You know, you're really tall, right?" she mumbles with her chin extended up.

He smirks and steps back as Roxy comes

barreling towards us. "I've been told a time or two. Here comes his other baby."

I snap my fingers and Roxy sits.

"Jo, meet Roxy."

Dropping to her knees, she opens her arms. "You didn't tell me you had a Rottweiler, Keagan. She's adorable."

I motion for Roxy to come forward. As she starts licking Jo's face, the room erupts in laughter.

"You thirsty, Jo?"

"Now that you mention it, I could use something cold to drink."

"Hey, kid. Can you show Jo? I need a minute real quick with these guys."

"Sure thing, pops." He rises from the chair and motions her towards the kitchen area. Sooner or later, I'm gonna get him and his smart aleck comments. I watch as she strolls away. Damn, those boots have me wanting her in a bad way. The image of her wearing nothing but her pink boots while I'm taking her from behind has me shifting my stance. When they are a little ways away, I turn my attention.

"Ollie mentioned you found something?"

"We broadened the search. You know we've been using the Cabricci family and known associates. After Desmond confronted Jocelyn, we decided to include the Blackwood name."

"What the fuck?"

"Hear me out, Keagan."

"I'm listening. Haven't lost my shit." I lower my voice.

"We knew there was a possibility we would find something. Desmond Payne doesn't make a move without their approval. And, with him chasing Jocelyn the way he did, got us to thinking. What if the connection between them is one of her clients?"

"Tell me something I don't already know, Luc. Talked to her about him and she's not saying a word."

"Gunner also found that Matilda Blackwood purchased several properties across the United States the year Fallyn Blackwood went missing under the alias of Matilda Rice."

"She purchased my home the same way. No biggie. That's how she keeps her properties separate from my grandfather's. Her attorneys have had her doing it that way for years," Jocelyn interrupts and shrugs her shoulders.

"Jocelyn," I rumble.

"Keagan," she sarcastically mimics.

"You shouldn't be listening in on our private conversation."

She shrugs again and places her balled fists on her hips. Fucking wonderful. I know that look. We're about to go round and round.

"Why are you running a background check on my grandmother? She's not involved in anything illegal."

"Jo, you can't be involved in this."

"Why not? You're discussing *my* family."

"It's business. We don't want to mix business with pleasure."

"Whatever, Keagan. I'm not going anywhere. I want to know why you were talking about my grandma. So, deal with it."

"Jo, this isn't a good idea. I don't want to dredge up bad memories."

"Good gosh, Keagan. I'm an adult. I think I can handle anything you *dredge* up."

"Keagan, she could help us," Ollie inserts. "Why don't we all sit down and talk about this?"

He gestures at the table. Jocelyn doesn't hesitate to sit down. Well, shit. This isn't how I wanted to spend my day. I wanted time alone with her, just the two of us. I reluctantly walk over and take a seat.

She drums her fingers on the table. I clasp her hand and pull it into my lap.

"The case we are working on involves a large crime family from the west coast," Ollie begins. "For years, they've been known on the black market as the ones to go to see if you needed illegal firepower. We're not talking average guns for personal use, but heavy weapons used for war, terrorism. Sizeable shipments."

"They lead the drug-trafficking here in the states," Lukas interjects. "Their connections are endless."

"Yeah, they hire illegal gangs and clubs. Keep 'em on the payroll as distributors for their stock," Gunner pipes in. "That's how I got messed up in this shit, Jo. They needed a hacker."

She nods. "So, what does this have to do with me? My family?"

"Well, here's the tricky part. Our client didn't hire us for those reasons," Lukas states wearily.

"Then why?"

"They've added a new product to their repertoire," Ollie hesitantly says with an uncomfortable expression.

"Okay."

"Human trafficking," I announce, getting tired of all the tiptoeing around the subject bullshit, "or more specifically, children."

"Whoa. Hold on a minute here. Did you just say selling children?" she squeaks, rubbing her arms.

"Yeah. I didn't realize what I was doing for them. Never would have done it, had I known it was selling babies," Gunner answers, visibly upset. "But, I'm gonna fix it. I was able to find out the date to the upcoming auction. It's next week."

"And you think my grandma is involved in something as horrific as this? You all are out of your ever-lovin' minds!" she yells and slams her hand on the tabletop. "This is absolutely crazy. We can settle this right here, right now. Where's my phone? I'll call my grandma and she can tell you just how nuts all of you are."

"Hold on there, Jocelyn. No one said your grandmother was involved in the kidnappings," Ollie calmly responds. "We are just covering all the bases, and with Desmond sniffing around you, we needed to check."

"Okay, I know something is going on. First, Keagan questions me about Desmond, and now you say that. What does he have to do with that family?" she demands.

"He gets his orders from the top."

"Fantastic. Just what I need. A moron with organized crime connections on my trail. What's next?"

"Nothing. C'mon. Time to get you home, Jo."

"Wait a minute, buddy. I'm not finished here."

Not replying, I secure my arm around her waist and lift her out of the chair.

"Put me down, right now."

I nod at the guys and stride out the door to my bike. Putting her feet back on the ground, I straddle the bike and give her my "get on the fucking bike now" look. She huffs and puffs and accepts my hand, climbing on behind me. I start to crank the bike and hear her mumble, "Two can play that game, baby."

CHAPTER 21
Jocelyn

As we walk into my home, Keagan is holding my hand in a death grip like he's scared I'll turn tail and run. Does he even know his own strength? Jeez, Louise. I squeeze his hand as hard as I can with both of mine to send the message because I'm just not talking to him yet. He briefly looks my way, worry written on his beautiful face, and eases up a bit. My hand is thankful.

Tonight was full of shock and awe. I uncovered some pretty disturbing things I'm not sure how to handle thus far. I'm exhausted mentally and fuming mad due to the lack of responses given by a certain someone who is pulling me through the house at this very moment. I want answers.

On the ride home, I had a chance to cool down a little with the wind whipping my hair, the sweet smells of Florida inundating me. It was heavenly.

I learned some things out of pure luck by overhearing the guys talking. My grandmother bought homes all over the United States, and she did it all under the name Rice—her maiden name, barely traceable if you didn't know what you were looking for. That's the way she's done things for years, so it was not real surprising.

The guys pretty much shut down after my question tirade and Keagan dragged me out of the door, so I quit talking to him. Yep, didn't say a word as we walked to the bike, got on, and sped through the streets. Just sat there like a stump on a log—while gripping him tightly, of course.

But a couple of things are really bothering me, aside from the fact that my family name is being looked into by Keagan and his cronies. Unbelievable.

Number one: Fallyn left right after Harper's birth, so is that a coincidence? Two: Human trafficking. Children, at that. And three: The creeper, Desmond Payne, is connected to all of it. I have to talk to Grandma.

Keagan leads me through the long hallway to the back of the house into my bedroom. His eyes are laser beams focused solely on me. Decisive, resolute. Stopping a few feet from of my bed, he sighs. I pull my arms up and cross my chest as I huff and jut my hip out to the side.

"Angel. How long ya gonna stay mad at me?" Keagan props his large paws on my shoulders and playfully shakes me back and forth. "C'mon, Boo."

He lets go, backs up a little, and strikes a pose. Oh my goodness. A mouthwatering muscle-mania pose like he used to do when we were kids. *It was just to see me smile,* he'd always say. Gosh dang it. He's bringing the big guns out. Literally.

I can't help the smile that begins to curve on my mouth, so I turn my back on him.

"Ugh!"

"Ya can't hide from me, Jo," he adds in his sexy voice as he moves his beautifully constructed body around until he's in my view again. The only thing better would be him naked. Keagan commences to modeling his muscles and I've had about all I can take.

"Spill it, Keagan. I need to know what's going on. It's just you and me now."

"There she is. *M'aingeal.*"

"I want to be mad here, Keagan. Stop that!"

I gesture to his posing. He gives me one last pose, then sighs with sadness playing across his features, and he quits.

"It's complicated, Jocelyn. There's so many players at work here. It's not all black and white. Let's sit."

He guides me over to the chaise lounge in front of the window and sits down. I reluctantly follow suit.

"Well, I'm waiting." I stretch my knee up across the lounger and face Keagan.

"The client who hired our firm has a six-month-old. He was taken two weeks ago, and we know who has him. We have a handful of days to find him before he's lost to them forever. I know you want answers. I honestly don't have them for you. But I promise that when I do, I'll share them with you."

I understand what he's saying. No answers today.

"Those poor people. I'm sure they're going out of their minds with worry. What kind of monsters would take an innocent child?"

"There's evil in the world, Jo. I've seen it, been 'round it, got the scars as proof. C'mere."

He reaches over and uproots me from my current position. Cradling me in his lap, Keagan strokes my back and runs his fingers through my hair.

"*M'aingeal.*"

My head against his chest, I listen to the solid beating of his heart. *Thump-thump, thump-thump.*

"I think I'm in love with your bike Black Beauty."

"Yeah?"

I feel the reverberations of his voice in his chest.

"I loved going fast, the wind caressing my face and the power of freedom that comes with it. Riding with you was exhilarating! Even if I didn't have much of a seat." *Just adding another piece of my heart to what's already yours.* I keep that tidbit to myself.

Laughing, he says, "It's made for one, angel. But you did good."

"I hope I get to do it again. I'd like that."

"Let's get you naked, baby," he whispers in my ear as he redirects the conversation.

Keagan stands up and puts me on my feet. He kneels down in front of me and begins to take off one pink boot at a time. Slowly and methodically, he pulls them off and discards them on the floor.

"One day soon, I'm gonna fuck you with these on. That's a promise, Boo."

A shiver rocks down my spine all the way to my lady parts. The possibilities are thrilling.

"I'll hold you to it, Mr. Fontneau."

Keagan winks and smiles up at me. When he's done with my boots, he stands back up and reaches out to grab my shirt. Ever so gently like a man with purpose, Keagan tugs it up. He stops when my shirt has uncovered my breasts and still covering my face, arms caught above my head. He nips and licks his way around my bra, teasing and taunting me. I squirm. He chuckles as he removes my shirt the rest of the way.

Unsnapping my jeans, he hooks his fingers around the sides and slides them down my legs, taking my underwear along with them. The last piece left is my bra and he circles me up while he unclasps it. My skin is sensitive, overheated from his foreplay when he brushes up against me with his fully clothed body. I'm all hot and bothered, wondering what Keagan will do next.

He releases his hold and steps back.

"Beautiful," Keagan says as he unsnaps his jeans and toes off his boots.

I watch as his arm muscles bulge and shift when he removes his shirt, tugging it from behind his head. I'm mesmerized by his abs and muscular chest as he delivers the show, inch by glorious inch.

I've had enough and move to touch him. My

fingers skim over his heated skin. I stop as my finger finds one of the puckered scars. Keagan inhales a short breath. I kneel down, kissing each scar, hoping one day he'll tell me about them.

He gathers me up from off the floor. In a matter of seconds, he scoops behind my knees and I'm off my feet and into his arms. He heads into the bathroom.

"Time to clean you up, baby."

My shower is a double stall, walk-through style with no curtains or glass needed. Glorious. Once on the hand laid travertine floor, Keagan settles me back on my feet to turn on the water. He pushes a few of the buttons and the water spray begins. I'm impressed he knows which ones to use; it took me a while to figure it out.

As water cascades simultaneously down and around us, Keagan squirts a handful of my body wash into his hands.

"Turn around, angel."

He begins to massage his soapy hands over my shoulders, my back, my butt, then the backs of my legs. I'm lost in the pleasure. A moan escapes past my lips.

"Yeah. Relax, baby. I'm gonna take care of you."

Keagan continues with his ministrations as if he's committing to memory every inch, cleaning every single spot on my body, not one ounce of flesh forgotten. He even washes my hair. I'm going out of my mind from his affection when he moves to start cleaning himself.

"Oh, no you don't. My turn," I sound off in a husky whisper.

Keagan chuckles and relents. I begin my journey of mapping his body. I pay homage to each muscle, to each scar. The guy is loaded with both. I'm caught up in the sight of his magnificent form and rubbing him all over. I come to his penis and stop.

"Oh my goodness. That's such a big … thingy." The member in question stands tall and proud, ready for action, beckoning me further.

"Yeah, it's a dick, Jo. A cock. Your dick, your cock. Claim it," he says, taunting me, daring me to call it one or the other.

"My … dick. This is *my* dick." I like the way it sounds.

"Good girl."

He lets out a sharp hiss as I grip his cock in my hands and firmly pull up and down. Keagan places his hand over mine, aiding me for a few strokes. Then he moves his hand between my legs, plunging deep, and I'm in heaven. He captures my mouth with his as we duke it out with our tongues, licking and sucking as his finger plays the same game while I continue to pump his dick hard and fast.

"Gotta have you now, angel. Sorry, it's gonna be quick."

"I need you, too. Please," I beg.

Within a blink he's on me and I'm shoved up

against the wall, hanging in midair.

"Wrap your legs 'round me and hold on."

I do as I'm told, rewarded by his swollen dick sliding into my dripping pussy. He begins to pound into me frantically creating a rhythm so succulent, moving his hips around, hammering at different angles. He touches my sweet spot over and over. A shutter washes over me. Delicious tingles ripple up and down my spine. Keagan reaches between us and finds my clit, rubbing and tugging.

"Oh, oh, oh my god! Keagan!" My eyes close tightly, seeing stars as I shatter completely, squeezing and clenching his cock. He follows me.

"God, angel. Fuck!"

For years, I've lived a pretty anonymous life. Low key, simple, only doing what was necessary for work or visiting the View on occasion. My friends are scarce and that's the way I've always liked it—until now. I feel like my life is on the verge of change. Something big.

In the early morning sunlight, I gaze upon Keagan's restful face. The hurricane moved across to make landfall in Texas, creating massive storms heading northeast, fizzling out over the Appalachian Mountain Range. Thank goodness for that. Maybe things will dry out.

Last night, we went to bed right after the shower. In my bed. Keagan Fontneau was in my bed, all night long. I didn't ask him to stay; he just did. It was a weird experience, as if he needed to be with me for reasons he's keeping locked up tight.

He held me in his arms and it was wonderful, like coming in from the storm or in from the darkness. I keep getting glimpses of this amazing man. I yearn for more. I know I want more from this man. I'm not sure if he's ready to share more with me yet.

Looking at Keagan, he appears to be at peace right now, content with himself and the world. I struggle with trying to decide if I should interrupt his moment of peace to go for my morning jog or stay in bed. Keagan moves his head in my direction and the decision is made for me. He's awake.

"Good morning, sunshine," I joke.

"Good morning, angel. How'd you sleep?" Keagan tugs me closer and kisses my forehead.

"Real good, actually. How about you?" I pepper kisses all over his naked chest.

"Good."

I glance up and his face is perplexed. Is he debating on his good night's sleep? Got to leave that alone, for now.

"Alrighty then. I'm up. I've got a client coming into my office this morning for a session."

I move to get out of the bed and he snatches me back, burrowing his face in my hair.

"You sure ya wanna leave so soon, Boo," he mumbles.

"No can do, mister. Duty calls."

I bust out laughing when his fingers slide up my pajama top and tickle my sides, causing me to flip like a fish out of water on top of him.

"Oh … my … gosh, Keagan! I'll … get you … back, you!"

I reach around and find his stomach to begin my own assault. Before I can, Keagan grabs my arms in one huge hand, pulling them up over my head.

"Nuh-uh. No can do."

"You don't play very fair, Mr. Fontneau."

"Okay, baby. I get it. I gotta get back too. Missing persons to find and all."

And that's the end of it. Our magical time is over.

After finishing notes from the session that just ended, I snag my belongings and get ready to leave. Balancing the file and my things like a natural acrobat, I shut my office door.

"Here is Jillian's file, Angela. Can you please transcribe and leave it on my desk? I'll go over it in the morning."

"Yes, ma'am. Have a good afternoon."

"Thanks. You, too."

I exit the office building and I'm hit with the humid Florida air. I'm almost to the crosswalk when a stretch limo pulls up in front of me and the back window rolls down. I'm caught off guard when Desmond's face appears.

"Lovely day for a ride, wouldn't you say, Miss Blackwood? I need you to get in. Please don't make a scene. Think of the children."

I take a quick look around me and it's business as usual. No one notices what's happening. My insides are screaming *"NO! Stop!"* in light of everything I learned yesterday. Grayson and Addie flash in my head, and I carefully reach for the door handle and pull. Sliding into the seat facing Desmond, the door closes and the vehicle is moving. He's holding an open bottle of champagne.

"What do you want, Mr. Payne?" I respond in a condescending tone, composing myself and preparing for anything.

"Feisty today, are we? I have a proposal for you. One I believe you won't be able to refuse. Drink?"

He leans forward, offering a flute of the bubbly substance.

"No, thank you."

"Very well." He takes a sip. "Vintage. I'm a firm believer that a good glass of wine makes the most mundane tasks bearable."

"Please get to the point."

"You have information that I need and I have two very scared teenagers that you want to help find their way back home."

My throat tightens up. He's threatening Calista's children. "What information?"

"I want Paul Travers' location. He has information I need."

"I don't know a Paul Travers."

"You know him as Gunner."

"No. I still don't know him." What the heck?

"Tsk. Tsk. Tsk. We both know you do, lovely Jocelyn. It would be a terrible thing if something were to happen to the twins. Bad things happen all the time, you know. And I also know there is a certain preteen who lives in a place called Lakeview. It would be a pity, really."

My face heats to molten lava hot and I want to scream at this conniving snake sitting across from me, drinking his hoity-toity wine. Can I pluck his eyes out now? *No, think of the kids, Jo.* I close my eyes and take a deep breath.

"Why? Why are doing this?"

"Don't worry your pretty little self about the whys. Wrinkles on your forehead would distract from your beauty. You have twenty-four hours to decide."

"Or what?"

"First, I'll dispose of your precious Addie. Maybe sell her or end her. Either way works out for me. Then the two teens will be next."

The limo stops and the door opens.

"Until tomorrow, Miss Blackwood. Clock's ticking." He toasts.

What the heck just happened? I stand on the curb I've been dropped at and look around. I'm right across from the parking lot.

"That no good, yellow-bellied snake!" I holler out to the cars passing by on the street as I shuffle my feet at a piece of paper, stomping. "Of all the cockamamie things." I trample the paper on the ground a few more times for good measure.

I have to call Grandma. I have to tell Keagan. No, I can't mention this to Keagan. I trust him, but this isn't about the child he's looking for. My little sister. Holy cow, not good. I'll tell Grandma and she can make sure Addie's safe.

"Oh, God. This is so bad. Not good, nope."

I don't know what to do. I grab my head in my hands. Heading to my car, I unlock the door and slip inside, immediately locking the doors behind me. Either way, someone is going to get hurt. Either way, I'm going to lose Keagan or the kids. What would Keagan do? He'd go in barrels blazing and save the day; that's what he does. Will he understand if I do this? Will he forgive me? I hope so.

I push the button on my phone to call Grandma. It rings twice before I've pulled my car out onto the street. My grandma's affectionate voice answers.

"Jocelyn! Hello, baby girl."

"Hey, Grandma. We need to talk."

The conversation ends and I hang up the phone. Catherine Windsor's sobs replay in my head. Today's update was the same as yesterday's. We are getting closer and have more leads to follow, but the operation hasn't discovered little Trey's whereabouts. Thomas' inquiries sounded void of hope, dull of life. Both are aware that the more time that passes after a child goes missing, the less chance they have of gathering helpful intelligence.

"Hey, Keagan. Got a moment?"

"Sure thing, MacGyver."

"I really don't know why you call me that."

"You're just handy to have in a pinch."

"Thanks. I think. So, I went on a fishing expedition earlier."

"You don't say. Catch anything?"

"I think so. I've been looking for a trail using specific keywords and narrowing the parameters down to a manageable amount. The search looks for patterns based on the that input. Once the data collects from the hits, it's dumped into a file where the search is limited by relevance. There are several analyses running simultaneously. I've found a trend. One in particular caught my eye. I'm not sure if it's something that will help find the Windsors' child. I'm stilling those scenarios, but ..."

"You seem reluctant to tell me."

"He didn't want you throwing him out on his ass," Lukas voices, walking over and plopping down in a seat beside us.

"You're proving your worth, kid."

"Keagan, Ollie, and I talked about offering you a position with Trident, *if* things work out with this operation."

"I ... I really don't know what to say, Luc."

"Well, since this isn't an official offer, you can wait and answer when it is. Now. What don't you want to tell me?"

"The data I ran using the Blackwood name returned specific hits. Crossbreeding cattle, investment properties, bank accounts, and so on. When I added Rice into the search, more investment properties showed up all over the country. I went even further and checked the dates each property was acquired. Matilda's purchased a new residential home on a yearly basis for the last ten years. Some of those years, more than that."

"So, what? She's got the funds and probably needs the write off."

"That's exactly what I thought, too, but if you

connect the dots on a map, it's a zigzag pattern. And all of the houses are off the beaten path. Nowheresville, USA."

"Interesting. Anything else?"

"Ten years ago, she took a large sum of money out that was unaccounted for. Supposedly lost without a trace," Lukas quickly divulges.

"How much are we talking about?"

Gunner booms, "Five million buckaroos."

"Dayum. That's a smack load of Benjamins disappearing."

Lukas mumbles, "You're telling me. I didn't realize the Blackwoods were so well off."

"The little time I was around the entire family, Harold's children were the only ones that acted down to earth. Pop thought it was because of Matilda's influence on them. She didn't come from *old* money."

"I think she learned how to spend it," Lukas coughs, trying to hide his laugh.

"No kidding."

"One more thing my search found. Two days after her withdrawal, a deposit for the same amount was wired into an offshore account belonging to the Cabricci Family."

"Coincidence?"

"Doubtful. I'm still following the trail."

"Keep me posted on what you find."

"Roger that, boss man."

I'm trying hard not to smile when the cellphone

rings.

"Talk."

"Keagan, I'm running surveillance on Payne. He just pulled up in front of a downtown office building and Jocelyn got in."

"What the fuck are you talking about? She knows to stay clear of him."

"She's in his limo. Looks like the driver's been told to circle. We're almost back to where he picked her up."

"Don't lose sight of her. I'm gonna blister her ass for scaring me like this and kill that motherfucker when I get my hands on him."

"The limo stopped and she's getting out."

"Is she hurt?"

"Nope. The opposite. She looks pissed off. Hold on. She's yelling something and stomping her foot."

"Whew. That's good. I would rather have a pissed Jocelyn than an unhappy one."

"She's finished her tirade and now she's just standing there. Looks like she's in shock and she looks sad. She's moving in the direction of her car."

"Fuck. Keep your location hidden from her. You trail in stealth mode and ensure she gets home safely. I've got a beta team en route to intercept Payne."

"Affirmative. I'm in pursuit. I'll call if anything changes."

The phone line goes dead and I'm left deciding what my next move with Jo will be. Lukas and

Gunner discuss coverage of Payne.

"I'll be back later. Contact me if anything changes."

Opening the front door, Jocelyn's eyes seem to confess how she's going to play her earlier encounter with Payne. She's not going to mention her joyride to me. I'm disappointed initially because that means she doesn't trust me. The time we've shared, I felt connected to her, a bond forming between us. I make a quick decision not to push her for details. When she's ready to talk, I'll be there. Unlocking my arms, I extend them wide.

"C'mere, Boo. You look like ya need a hug."

She walks into my waiting, open arms. Her subtle body curves into the harder planes of mine. She fits perfectly. Rubbing her back, I shift and bend, cradling her close.

"What are you doing now?"

"We're going to put the rather large soaking tub you have to good use."

"Perfect. You can put me down. I can walk, you know."

"I wanna hold you close, angel. Amuse me and just go along with it, 'kay?"

"M'kay." She nuzzles closer, licking the column of my neck. "You're always trying to carry me, Keagan."

I deposit her on the bathroom counter and start the water. Steam slowly fills the room. When I turn around, she's naked. The clothes she was wearing, lying in a heap on the tile floor. Her hips sway provocatively from side to side and she walks closer to me. She stops and tugs the tail of the shirt I'm wearing. My fingers join hers and our gazes lock. She's radiates warmth and tenderness, something my battle weary soul hungers for, a healing balm only she can administer ... an intimacy between lovers.

She huskily whispers, "You have too many clothes on, baby."

I take over and swiftly discard my clothes alongside hers. She guides us into the steamy hot water, positioning herself between my thighs and trapping my throbbing cock against her smooth, round globes. Her head rests on my chest. A moment later, pulsing jets activate, massaging the muscles, and she exhales a deep breath. This angel in my arms is slowly changing me.

"You wanna tell me what's bothering you? I'm pretty good at reading your body like a book, but your mind's another thing."

"I've just ... well, been thinking about Fallyn."

She really isn't going to discuss Payne. Her life could be in danger. An ache emerges in the pit of my gut. Doesn't she know by now that I would move Heaven and Earth to help her? If she doesn't want me to know, then something serious is happening.

"You never did explain to me why she left."

She opens a conversation I need intel on. This

could help in the long run.

"I still don't understand what happened, Keagan. One minute, everything was perfect and the next, well, you remember. I never apologized for the way things went south. I'm really sorry about all that."

"Shhh, *cher*. Not necessary. We all have our demons to deal with, true?"

"Yeah, I guess that's true."

"Tell me, Jo. When was the last time you saw Fallyn?"

She pauses. I worry that I'm pushing too hard, too fast.

"I remember the last time I saw her like it was yesterday. It's one of those memories that stick with you, even in the stormy weather. And it was also the first and last time I ever met little Harper."

She stops and, for a second, I think she's finished. I place my hand on her belly and pull her closer, comforting her.

"I was pulling up to my grandma's house. I parked carefully in her driveway, a little bit of hope unfurling because I would get to see her: my sister Fallyn. I was hopeful. And, you know my grandma, she's a prickly woman, a dominant gal. The true monarch of the Blackwood family."

She looks over her shoulder at me and graces me with a smile.

"The woman's spunky and stubborn. She's never been one to let things slide in this family. She calls it like she sees it and takes care of everyone she loves."

"Sounds like someone else I know."

"Hmph. Your pretty words. Ha! Anyhow, when Fallyn first left, we didn't hear from her, only what was told to us through Grandma. She and my dad had so many arguments since the night Fallyn left. She won't ever let it go, not until the wrongs have been righted."

"I wouldn't want to cross that woman. Don't mess with the cubs, yeah?"

She giggles at my joke. I'm trying to ease her into reliving a hurtful piece from the past.

"No kidding. My baby sister, Sage, was with me in the car. Her eyes full and blooming with hope. I wondered if she saw the same in mine. But I knew it couldn't be. There was nothing there but sorrow. I remember Sage held excitement in her beautiful, large brown eyes. Along with unshed tears. We were gonna meet our niece, little Harper Blackwood."

I cup water in my palm and bring it over her chest, trickling slowly back into the tub. Her rosy nipples harden from the sensation. I continue the ministration.

"Faith Harper Blackwood was born a week before we actually met her. We weren't allowed to go to the hospital with Grandma and that stung so badly— another hole punched deep into my heart by my dear ol' dad. On top of everything that's happened, *he* was still the master puppeteer in our life. Pulling strings up and down, side to side, in the directions he deemed fit.

So Grandma set up this time for us to see the newest addition to the family without my dad's interference."

She pauses and rubs her chest gently like she's removing the ache from her heart. I replace hers for mine and stroke.

"Finish for me, Boo. Get it all out."

"Harper carries the Blackwood name, Keagan. Not many people know that. She's just as special as the rest of us, too. Fallyn didn't take David's last name. Well, they never got married. Fallyn said she wouldn't marry him just because they were having a baby. You know how she was. He was listed on the birth certificate, but Harper's last name was written as Blackwood. She is and will always be one of us."

"So Harper is a Blackwood? On paper?" I ask, a little puzzled by the revelation.

"Yep. So you know Grandma had already set up her trust and taken care of everything. Which leads me to believe that she helped Fallyn leave. For whatever reason, she helped them."

"Interesting." I'll get this little bit of info to Lukas and the kid, see what they can turn up. "So what did Harper look like?"

"Perfect. Absolutely beautiful. I was a hot mess that day, for sure. I've always been an emotional rollercoaster and that day was no exception. Fallyn was sitting in Grandma's rocking chair with a tiny bundle wrapped tightly in a pink and green blanket. The tuft of black hair was peeking out of the blanket and all to be seen from my vantage point. Baby Harper's little cheeks were rosy and flushed from a recent outburst. Her little nose and bow mouth were so perfect, I couldn't turn away even if I wanted to. And her big round eyes, the color was still indistinguishable, but she seemed to try and focus in on her surroundings … on me. I was immediately in love."

I'm deep in thought when she blows my mind.

"Tell me you love babies," she demands.

Laughter erupts from deep within. She makes me happy even with all the craziness going on. "Yeah. I love babies, Jo."

The jets stop. The water has cooled. I hit the stopper and the water slowly drains. She cranes her neck, offering those puffy red lips I can't resist. I can tell she's been gnawing on her lower lip from the pain of revisiting her past. Our mouths connect. I pour all of me into the searing kiss, trying to convey how much she means to me. She reacts by matching the intensity and passion with her own.

Jocelyn is collecting the scattered pieces of my soul, gluing them back together. She settles the restlessness, soothes the pain from the past, and calms the turbulence raging out of control inside. I'm happy again because of her, and I want her to find peace and make her whole. I will help her find Fallyn, and help her learn to trust me. I promise. Only then will we both be able to move on from what's holding us in the past and live in the present.

The vibration and light from the phone jars me from the twilight sleep. Jocelyn's leg is wrapped around my right thigh, her arm splayed across my chest. She fell asleep cuddled in the safety of my arms after we made love. I brace my left foot to get the phone and a prickling akin to needles shoots up my leg. The culprit releases a sleepy hiss; Miss Kitty is sleeping on me, too.

I read the message and know I have business to attend to that can't wait until the daylight. I'm not sure where we are going with this new connection forming between us, but one thing's for sure: I don't want to lose her. She's a light in the darkness, beaming a pathway home on the rocky waters.

I'm stuck. I can't move my feet. As I struggle to get out of whatever has a hold on me, I sink further in. Why can't I move? Somebody help me. The darkness is surrounding me, I'm drowning. *NO!*

I wake up screaming in bed as I hear my phone ringing insistently beside me. The feeling of being suffocated has my breathing labored, unsteady. My phone stops and I look around the dark room. My bedroom. Glancing over and reaching out to the place Keagan occupied earlier, it's empty. He's not here. He didn't stay.

I get up to splash water on my face and use the bathroom, darkness on the verge of taking me over again. Heading to the kitchen, I put the kettle of water on to boil. A steamy hot cup of Chamomile tea will soothe me. Hopefully in about thirty minutes, I'll be fast asleep again. I rub my temples, the beginning of headache in the works. The tea should help with that too.

My phone rings again. Looking at the clock on the wall, it reads 2:30 a.m. Dread consumes me and I run to get my phone.

"Hello!" I rush out in a puff of adrenaline and

worry.

"Miss Blackwood." The voice of the woman crying on the other end is broken and forlorn. I recognize her. Calista.

"Mrs. Payne? Is that you? Are you okay?"

I go into defense mode, ready to take action and help. After all, it has to be about her teens. She's married to a monster.

"It's ... Desmond. I—"

The line goes dead and a whole new fear grips ahold of my psyche. Oh my God! I didn't act quickly enough. He said I had twenty-four hours. I need to call and check on Addie.

My phone rings once more, startling me. I hit the answer button.

"Calista?"

"Yes. I'm here." She sniffs. "I'm outside and the service is not very good. It's my twins, Miss Blackwood. He's taken my children. You have to help me!" she cries out in pain, and I cringe.

"Alright, slow down and take some deep breaths. You have to calm down, Calista. You won't be any good to help your kids if you don't. Okay?"

"O-Okay."

"I'll count and you breathe. One, deep breath in. Two, exhale out. Three, deep breath in ..." I walk her through a few exercises until she's able to speak without crying.

"Thank you, Miss Blackwood. I feel more

composed."

"Good. And call me Jocelyn, please. Now start at the beginning. Tell me what happened and where are Cade and Crystal."

"Desmond came home earlier. He said the kids were fine as long as …" I hear her breath in and out. "As long as I did what he said. I don't understand any of this, Jocelyn. He said you had something he wanted. Information to be traded for my children. Please. Whatever it is, you must give it to him. Please!" She breaks out in an ear-splitting trill and I have to pull the phone away from my ear.

"Breathe, Calista. Everything's going to be fine." I pause at the irony in my statement. It's a sign that, at this particular moment, those words would comfort us both.

The whistle of my tea kettle goes off. I had forgotten about it. Walking over, I shut off the stove and pour the boiling water over the teabag waiting in my cup.

"You're right, Jocelyn. I'm breathing." I hear her deep inhales of air. Then she continues, "Will you help me? Will you help save my children?"

I release a long sigh. I pull the teabag up and down, watching the water slosh around in the mug. My mind's made up. It was yesterday after the horrible encounter with Desmond Payne. I will not let anything happen to those kids or any child for that matter.

"Yes, I will."

"Thank you. Thank you so much. You won't regret this, I promise." Her relief is palpable and I know it's the right thing to do. "He said to meet him at the library where the kids study first thing in the morning when it opens. Nine o'clock. He'll bring my children and you bring the information. For the exchange. No cops and no other witnesses. Do you understand? No one."

"Then nine o'clock it is. I'll meet you there. We'll take care of this together."

"Jocelyn, I don't know what to say. Words can never express my gratitude. I'm indebted to you, forever."

"Not necessary, Calista. I won't let you down. Nor will I let anything happen to your teens."

"I'll see you in a little while, then." Her voice is hopeful. "Thank you again, Jocelyn."

"Night."

I hang up the phone. The tension in my shoulders is exploding with pain. My tea finishes steeping and I sip carefully at the steamy brew, thinking about my decision.

The image of Keagan's crystal blue eyes haunt me and my heart spasms with guilt. He's going to be so mad at me. He has to understand, right? I hope he will forgive me for what I'm about to do and not leave me—this time for good.

The scars he carries on the outside mirror his turmoil on the inside. Even though I don't know the full story, those scars torture me too. I would never want him to gain another scar because of me. He already felt my sorrow tonight when he showed up. Keagan knew something was wrong. I didn't say a word about it. The disappointment was dripping off of him. Not trusting him with the truth was so difficult. It's something I'll have to live with for the rest of my life.

I need to give him something, though. Somehow, someway, he doesn't need to be there when all this goes down. My head starts to spin and I sit down at the bar.

Meow. Meow. Miss Kitty jumps up onto the counter and I reach over and pull her into my lap. I brush her fluffy fur with my hand as I scheme and plan. I come up with a brilliant idea. I'll text Keagan in the morning before I go to the library, asking him to meet me at the coffee shop around the corner from my office around ten or so. That's it. Perfect. At least I know he'll be away from the safe house and out of harm's way.

A fresh round of guilt pushes through. What about the other guys? Keagan's team? Do their lives mean so little that I would give them up to this monster?

Letting Miss Kitty go, I finish my tea and go back to bed. I need to figure out a way to save everyone. Not sure how yet, but I'm going to try.

It's a little past eight in the morning when I text the message to Keagan.

Me: Hey, u. Hated waking up alone :(

I wait patiently for his reply. A few minutes later my phone pings.

K: Had lots to do, Angel. Will make it up.

Whew, at least he doesn't hate me, yet.

Me: Ok. Wanna meet for coffee? At 10?
K: Sure. Could use the break. Where?
Me: At the coffee shop right by my office. Will text you address.
K: Good. See you then.
Me: ;) <3

I sent the last wink and heart hoping for something, but all I get is silence. Shoot. I send him the address to the coffee shop. At least I know he'll be out of the way by the time Desmond gets there with whatever he has planned. My guilt resurfaces and I stuff it back into the box. This has to work.

Driving to the library feels like walking death row. I've mentally prepared myself for what's to come. I already drew a map to the safe house, tucked away in my purse. I park at the front of the building and walk to the front doors and enter.

It's quiet. Too quiet, even for a library, and my

hackles flare up. I look around, glancing at the front desk, then the rows of bookshelves, and still I see nothing, not a soul around or in sight. As I turn to leave, I hear high-heeled footsteps echoing on the tiled floor coming towards me.

"I knew you'd come, Jocelyn. Like Old Faithful, dependable 'til the end. And right on time."

Calista is walking leisurely down a row of shelves in my direction, a snarky smile etched across her face. *What the—?*

"I told you I would. Is Desmond here yet? Is he with you? Did he bring Crystal and Cade?" I bombard her with my questions as I try to figure out what the heck is going on.

Bringing up the rear is a very tall and well-built man in a suit. I can't see his face in the dim light but I recognize immediately that it's not Desmond Payne.

"No, no, and no." Calista shakes her pointer finger as she sounds off with all her nos.

"Okay, so he's running behind, or coming soon? What in the world is…?"

My words fall short as the man following behind Calista comes into view. Things just got really strange, real quick.

"David? Is that you?"

The man reciprocates with a sinister smile and my blubbering continues.

"It *is* you. I remember you. Fallyn … Wait, what on Earth are you doing here? With Calista Payne? I don't understand."

My head is spinning with this new revelation. What the devil is going on? I believe I've stepped into it big time. My heart rate spikes from the anxiety coursing in my veins. This is not good. David just stares at me with that evil smile and the creeper factor rears its ugly head. His eyes are malicious and hateful. He was never my favorite or my choice for Fallyn. But I loved my sister and her happiness was most important to me.

"Oh, that's right. Ha. I forgot. Where are my manners? You know him as David, don't you, little JoJo? Let me introduce you to the boss of the Cabricci family. Roman David Cabricci. My cousin. And I'm his underboss, second in command."

I'm shocked at the news. I'm in the twilight zone. Quick, someone pinch me so I can wake up. My mind is muddled, but I have to keep it together. I keep my wits and don't give away anything on my face. I begin to do what I do best: talk while searching for answers.

"I'm ..." I play the dimwit blonde, a role I've excelled at over the years. "I don't understand. What's going on?"

I'm starting to get pissed at Calista's senseless ranting. JoJo, really? She's messing with the wrong girl. A Blackwood, to boot. Second in command of handbags, maybe. I play her game and bide my time. Why is David not talking?

"I'm so confused. Can someone please explain to

me what the heck is happening here?"

"It's rather simple, really. Something very precious was taken from our family, by *your* family, the Blackwoods, and we're going to get it back one way or another," Calista begins her tirade.

"My family? Is it possible you're mistaken, Calista? The Blackwoods are not in the business of stealing from anyone." Even my wayward dad wouldn't stoop that low. We have our own money, own belongings. No need to take from anyone else. We give to charities and help out as much as we can.

"Ha! You are just full of it. You can't even see the forest for the trees."

"Enough of the cryptic bull crap, Calista. What are you talking about?"

"And that would be too easy, JoJo." She sneers the pet name, laughs, and I'm ready to punch her in the face. Again, with the JoJo. No one calls me that except for my sisters and Grayson.

My face heats up and my body begins to shake. I remember the family Keagan and the guys were talking about. David—I mean Roman—is the head honcho. Oh. My. Goodness. When Keagan finds out … They were friends in high school. The same man who, ten years ago, ripped our family wide open when Fallyn got pregnant.

"Oh, you're so cute when you're angry."

"Shut up, Calista! Tell me what's going on. Where are your children?" I shout out at her.

"Oh yes, my beautiful, wonderful, crafty teens. Guess what, Miss Blackwood? You got played." She throws her head back in a wicked laugh and I look to Roman for help. He's chuckling under his breath with the same craziness in his eyes as Calista.

"They're okay then. Crystal and Cade were never in any danger?" I'm relieved and sickened at the thought. "This was all just a ploy to get me here, now? Was anything real? What about Desmond?" I spew forth question after question, although I'm sure nothing will be settled right now.

Then my mind turns even darker. Oh, no. What about my little sister?

"Are you seeing the bigger picture now? Desmond is just a capo in the family. An enforcer, if you will. Takes care of things so our hands don't get dirty. I married him after my husband was killed, God rest his soul. It's a marriage of convenience, really. Nothing more. He does what he's told. Just like you will, little JoJo."

I'm going geothermal here, ready to erupt molten magma at any moment. I've been had. On every front. Did she just say killed? Her husband died of cancer. It was all over the news, but she just said he was killed. I'll file that away to analyze later.

Calista's whiny voice catches my attention again. "He's got a thing for you, though. I just don't understand it. Doesn't matter. You will tell us where Gunner is and take Desmond to the location. He's waiting outside."

"No! I won't. You can't make me, Calista. You won't hurt your own kids. None of this was real."

"Yes, Jocelyn. You will."

She walks over and hands me her phone. On the screen is my grandma's house in Lakeview. It's streaming live as the person operating the camera zooms in on the window. Sitting in the parlor room is Addie and my grandma, unaware anyone is watching.

"Oh my God," I whisper. "You can't. You won't."

"I can and I will. All I have to do is give the order. So you see, you will take Desmond to the safe house to retrieve Gunner Travers. Or you can be the cause of the death of your precious Grandma and baby sister. Up to you." Calista shrugs and snatches the phone from my hand.

No choice. I want to throw up. Bile moves up my throat. I'm going to be sick. Clutching at my stomach, I lean over slightly and take deep breaths. I have to stay in control; my family members' lives depend on it.

"You've got me. I'll do it."

"Good girl. Now move."

I glance once more at the man I thought I knew a long time ago, shooting daggers his way, the man who singlehandedly destroyed my life along with my family. His face is a mask of insensitivity. I don't know what Fallyn ever saw in him. Maybe he fooled her too.

Walking out into the sunny Florida morning, my eyes squint as they adjust to the brightness. I check my watch for the time. Dread is consuming me. My watch reads 9:40 a.m. Keagan should be on his way to the coffeehouse. At least something is going right. The stretch limousine is parked at the entrance. The door open, waiting for me to get in.

I look around one more time, searching for what, I'm not sure. A way out? I'm not even sure if I'll make it out of this alive. And if I do, I will never be the same.

Glancing across the street, I notice a dark tinted car parked with the window barely cracked open. Something shiny glimmers in the open space. Hope unfurls. Is someone watching? Keagan has someone watching me. A little ambitious, but maybe. Or is my active imagination playing tricks on me? The window slides up in the next instant.

Once again, panic succeeds to drive me, causing the feeling of sharp pins and needles all over my skin.

"In you go, Miss Blackwood. Thank you for all your help. I would say 'see you later' but I won't. You won't be around for later. Or maybe you will. Who knows, really. Goodbye." Calista cackles again and turns around to Roman. "Time to go, boss." She doesn't even give me another look back.

Something hard pokes up against my spine.

"Get in," a voice I've never heard before pushes me forward.

"Alright. Jeez. Don't touch me."

I slide into the limo and Desmond Payne greets me.

"Hello, dear Jocelyn." He lifts up a glass of champagne and asks, "Would you care for a drink?" as he shoots me a menacing look filled with lust.

I'm in deep, deep trouble.

CHAPTER 24
KEAGAN

Alpha and delta teams await the signal. Instincts are a bitch. After I left Jocelyn, my gut reaction was to prepare for the unthinkable and maybe, just maybe, my overreaction won't come to fruition.

Then the unthinkable became a reality.

"The intel we've gathered leads us to believe she is helping Desmond," Lukas says.

Ollie nods. "The big question is whether it's voluntary or not. What is he blackmailing her with? I can't believe she would betray us. She's a good woman."

I'm partially listening. A feeling of dread surrounds me. She's in danger. I feel helpless and alone. All she had to do was confide in me. She didn't trust me with her secret. Just like all those years ago in high school. She didn't need me then. She didn't want my help. So, the only thing I can do at this point is prepare.

"You're sure the head of the Cabricci Family is en route?"

"Yes. The spotters have them on a private jet.

Flight plan is a direct route to Gainesville," Lukas reports.

"I don't like this. Something isn't right," Ollie mutters. "Do you think they would move the auction up a week?"

"At this point, I'm just not sure."

The phone rings and Lukas hits the speaker. "What's up, California?"

"I'm watching security feed from Matilda Blackwood's residence. We've got activity outside. Looks like someone is checking in on her. This dude's got some wicked surveillance equipment in his van. Cameras, satellite, the works. I assume he believes he's hidden by the trees on the back side of her property," he chuckles.

"Have you been able to identify who is he?"

"Not yet. Running his face through the database now."

"Whatever you do, do not allow any harm to come to anyone in that home. I hold you personally responsible for their safety, Cal."

"I'm on it. I'll let you know if anything changes," he answers and hangs up.

"Could be a coincidence, but I don't think so. Get ready. They're about to make a move."

Ollie gets up to leave. "I'm on Desmond. I'll keep you abreast as it unfolds."

I contacted General Fox requesting his assistance. The ATF, DEA, and local FBI agencies are all on alert waiting for the ambush to occur. They will provide backup, if necessary. I'm reeling at the realization that Jo is going to take on this entire situation without confiding in me. I know she's aware of the manner of business I conduct. It was a conscious decision on her part to alienate me once again. But, I will do whatever is required to get her out of this, unscathed and alive.

Grady and Rocky's teams are the best of the best, each consisting of former Army Special Forces members, handpicked by the team leaders to join Trident security firm. The lethal combination of skills form to create an elite force of highly specialized personnel that ensures accuracy and precision when called upon. Trident practices unconventional methods for a deteriorating society that is at war against the evil permeating our borders.

Several long hours later, shit's about to get real. I hear Ollie and what he says almost brings me to my knees.

"Operation storm chaser is a go," he reports through the comm-link attached at my ear. "She went into the library and returned ten minutes later outside. The driver forced her into the waiting vehicle at gunpoint."

The fear in my heart escalates. My angel is in the presence of evil and the danger is real. Why didn't she talk to me? I should have forced the issue. The what-ifs and should-haves don't matter now. I'm limited. I can only wait and pray the confrontation ahead ends without someone hurt or, worse, dead.

Grady reports, "Alpha team is in position."

"Delta team have eyes from the sky," Rocky supplies.

"Stay alert, men. We want this operation to go smooth and easy. No complications."

Lukas's warning is clear: no mistakes.

When this is over, I'm not sure if things can go back to the way they were. Trust is a huge factor in a relationship for me. Enough of this. I've got to get my mind right. I can deal with Jocelyn when this situation is over. Mentally prepared, I rise from where I was sitting, ensure my piece is ready, and replace it in the holder at my back. I whistle and Roxy appears at my side. She's ready for action.

"Let's roll."

"Just remember. We need him to talk, Keagan. He knows where those kids are," Ollie calmly reminds him.

"I know what my responsibilities are, Ollie. I've got this."

"We have activity. Four Phantom Prophets have joined the party," Rocky says.

"Make the call, Lukas."

"Roger that, Keagan. Agent Santiago is aware of the situation and moving into position."

"Show time."

The elevator opens and I walk into the open parking deck where the black limo and Phantom

Prophets silently wait. Roxy steadily keeps up with my stride. Damn, this could easily become complicated. I stop to wait. My loyal friend sits by my side.

The back door to the limousine opens and Jocelyn's curly blond head appears. Her emerald gaze searches and finds mine. I see uneasiness and fear lurching in that brief moment of time.

Buzz and the other biker from Perry flank them, weapons drawn.

Desmond appears from the inside. He is holding Jocelyn close to his body.

Rocky's voice filters over the comm. "He's using hostage as a human shield. There's a shot, but it would be iffy. Possible collateral damage."

I stiffen. I want to rip her away from the arms enclosed around her and place her in a secure place.

"No. Wait. Give Keagan a chance to talk him down," Ollie commands.

"Affirmative."

I brush my hand over Roxy and wait for his move.

In a smug voice, Desmond says, "I believe you have someone that belongs to the Cabricci Family. I'm here to collect him."

I continue to stare at him, allowing the pent-up anger from the hellish years to surface. The hate and revenge consuming every pore of my body. The pain of losing my friends and fellow soldiers. The nightmare I lived surfacing. The ache from the bullets penetration into my flesh. The months of recovery spent in hell. The betrayal of someone I cared for. I release all the anger, tunneling it towards Payne. He visibly flinches.

Jocelyn shifts and he securely wraps his hand firmer around her neck. Squeezing, he cuts off her airflow. She grabs his hand, trying to ease the hold, hitting him and wiggling to no avail. He laughs.

"She's a fighter. I look forward to taming the wildness in her." He laughs harder and strokes her cheek, removing a single tear that runs down it. "Don't cry, my beauty. We are almost done here and then we'll be on our way."

I remain stock still, dying inside at the situation unfolding before me.

"He's not here. Took off during the storm."

His smile fades and a sneer appears. "Do you really expect me to believe your bullshit? My sources informed me you are holding him and I'm here to collect Gunner."

"I don't give a fuck what you believe, asshole. He's *not* here. Haven't seen him."

"Well. Well. Well. I did try to do this the easy way. Didn't I, sweetheart?" He caresses her neck with his tongue. She winces. "I am a patient man, but you leave me no alternative. Buzz, you and your men know what to do."

Buzz signals and the parking deck floods with Phantom Prophets. Payne smiles triumphantly. His stance reeks confidence, an expression of victory displayed on his evil face. He believes he will retrieve Gunner and make it out of here alive.

"I count twenty hostiles," Rocky reports.

"We need a small diversion. Do ya think you can help us out, Grady?" Lukas requests with an ounce of humor laced in his voice. Grady is a demolition expert in the field and small is not in his vocabulary.

Grady doesn't hesitate to answer. "I think I can provide *small*. You ask for it, you got it. A *small* fuck-blast diversion, coming right up."

"Are you in position and ready, Ollie?" Lukas asks.

He whispers, "Let's do this."

The air is thick with anticipation. In the distance, a light drizzle of rain begins—the remnants of the storm. The symbolism is not lost on me. It falls on me. I sense the men. They are close.

"You and your friends need to go, Payne. This is private property and you're not welcome here. Jocelyn. Come. Here."

Her head jerks up and she struggles to move away from him.

"You're one cocky son of a bitch, Fontneau. She's coming with me," Desmond responds. "When I'm far enough away and finished with my beauty, I'll send her home, *if* she wants to come back."

"Last warning, Payne. Let her go. Then get the fuck outta here."

He glares at me. I know he won't budge. We are playing a dangerous game. I will send him straight to Hell for fucking with her. She's a weakness he wants to exploit. The conflict and uncontrollable anger inside of me begins and ends with her. His first mistake will be my last.

Fuck. Nothing's ever easy.

Scanning the area, I find Ollie. He's close enough to ensure her safety at the same time an explosion rocks the parking lot. Smoke encompasses the area. The diversion causes Payne to release the hold on Jocelyn and she's thrown to the ground. One second she is on the ground beside him and the next she's gone. Roxy attacks and Payne finds himself on the ground with the hundred-plus pound rotty snarling in his face. He thrashes, trying to roll away, but the grip she has on his arm constricts his motion.

The men stalking in the shadows waiting for the command make their presence known. The Phantom Prophets are surrounded by firepower and strength, strength they notice will bring their death unless they surrender. It's a choice they make quickly. Weapons lower, then arms lift in the air, surrendering to fight another day.

I walk up to Payne and gesture instructions to Roxy and she's by my side in a flash. He rolls and comes up on his knees, struggling to stand.

"I gave you a chance, motherfucker. I'm not the hangman. You brought the noose, put the fucker 'round your neck, stepped off the ledge, and hung yourself. All I did was watch."

I turn and walk away. Agent Santiago is there handcuffing the son of a bitch. Jocelyn shoves Ollie's hold on her and runs my way. I brace when her body collides with mine, wrapping her arms tightly around me.

"Keagan. I knew you would save me. I'm so sorry."

I hug and place a kiss on her brow following the path to her lips. Achingly slow, I relish the feel of them on me, the touch of her tongue with mine, the unique taste of my angel. Before the kiss deepens to the point of no return, I break away from her.

"Good luck, Jo. Take care of yourself."

"What? What are you talking about? Keagan?"

"See ya 'round, angel."

"Keagan?"

I lower my arms, rolling my shoulders, and walk inside the building listening to her call my name. I shut her out because dealing with the reasons behind her betrayal will only solidify my decision to walk away. I need an update on the take down. We need answers from Payne, a possible location to Windsor's baby. Time to work. Time to let her go. Time to move on.

"Whatta you mean he's dead?" MacGyver asks. "Guess his nine lives ran out, huh?"

The new member to the Trident team is up to his

normal antics. We returned to Lakeview a few weeks back. Paul "Gunner" Travers, now known to the team as MacGyver, accepted the formal proposal to join Trident. He's staying in the apartment above the garage attached to the old house we temporarily converted into Trident office space until we can find a new location. He's adjusting to the team. He is a well-needed asset especially with Lukas' struggle.

All personnel is present for Trident's monthly status report.

"Somehow he hung himself." Lukas absently shrugs.

"Payne was killed because the Cabricci Family didn't want any loose ends," Rocky speculates.

"Possible. At least we were able to get the information we needed out of him before that happened," Grady says.

Thomas and Catherine Windsor reuniting with their son will be a memory I won't ever forget. The look on their faces when the little boy was placed in Catherine's arms was priceless. Trey's retrieval is the reason we exist, uniting families and righting wrongs.

"Or that was the reason the hit was made," Moose considers.

"Either way, sounds like the world's a better place without that son of a bitch alive," Beauty's deep voice says over the phone line.

California inserts, "Agent Santiago's report gave us a new direction to pursue."

"You actually went to high school with Roman Cabricci, Keagan? That's some crazy shit," MacGyver concludes.

"I didn't know him as Roman. He fooled us all."

"Hmm. I wonder what the reasoning was behind sending Roman from California to Florida," Ollie mulls over.

"We all know the family doesn't act without reason," Beauty adds.

"There's a possibility we won't ever figure out their fucked-up logic. Our focus needs to be on locating Fallyn before they do."

"Matilda won't talk. I tried to explain the danger they were in if Cabricci finds them first, but she won't budge. Stubborn woman," Cal growls.

"She's always been that way. Nothing's going to change her. I've asked Ollie to run point on the search. I will be in and out."

"I'll hold down the fort." Ollie smiles.

"How's your current hunt going?"

"I don't want to give you false hope, but I have a few leads that look promising. I'm leaving soon to check on one."

"Good. There are still several unanswered questions that I believe, once we have them in custody, we can resolve."

"It's not going to be easy. The trail is old and she's gotten good at hiding."

"I don't care what it takes. We need to find them

first."

MacGyver interrupts, "I've narrowed it down for Ollie. Even after losing the trail, I'll find it again."

"Never doubted you wouldn't, brother."

The meeting wraps up. I finish some things that require my attention at the office and get ready for a visit with my folks. Momma's cooking is just what I need.

CHAPTER 25
Jocelyn

I'm in a living, breathing nightmare. My reality at this point in time sucks big time. I read the backs of jackets and shirts passing back and forth in the vast warehouse—ATF, FBI, DEA, and local Gainesville police. My mind is spinning so I go sit down on one of the chairs in the corner. I have to answer a few questions for one of the officers, an Agent Santiago.

A gray-haired man with a five o'clock shadow dusting his stoic face walks towards me. His polo shirt is embossed with the FBI logo with his name underneath.

"Miss Blackwood?" His baritone voice reaches out to me with warmth and concern.

"Y-Yes. I'm ... I'm Jocelyn B-Blackwood," I confirm as my voice shakes from the trauma the day has rendered.

I was held briefly against my will by a crazy man, a sadistic individual hell bent on making me his own all for his personal pleasure. For a few hours, I was unknowingly thrust into the clutches of Desmond Payne and the Cabricci family, a crime ring full of despicable treachery, the same family that has an undetermined vendetta against the Blackwoods.

When everything went down at the warehouse, the only hope I held on to tightly was that Keagan would save me. He stood proudly alone, fearless, a dominant force ready to take on evil. I was so thrilled at the man standing there, facing down the enemy with his best dog pal Roxy by his side. In that instant with the molten heat radiating from his piercing eyes, I felt we were on the same page. He would protect me and then make me his for all time. When Keagan called to me telling me to come to him, I wanted nothing more than to oblige, but my captor had other plans.

It all happened so quickly. One minute I was in the grasp of Desmond Payne and the next thing I knew, Ollie was hauling me through a darkened room telling me to duck and take cover, shielding me with his powerful body and protecting me with his life.

Afterwards, things got worse instead of better. Keagan kissed me tenderly and hugged me tightly, thankful we were together, unharmed. Then, he walked away from me. He told me, "See you around," and chose to leave me. My choice was too much for him to accept or understand. I stood there and watched him walk away. I couldn't stop him. I wouldn't. What could I possibly say that would change his mind? I betrayed his trust and I have to accept the outcome.

That's the thing about life: the choices we make define us. They're a reflection of our life, mirroring those selections. Sometimes those decisions are not always best for everyone involved, creating pivotal points, but at the same time offering an end result, whether it's good or bad. It is what it is.

I made a choice. To someone like Keagan, it was a choice of betrayal. To the others like my family, I'm the hero. Doesn't make it any easier to accept. I understood the consequences going in. I hashed them out thoroughly. And if I had to do it all again, I would save the children no doubt, my happiness be damned. It's who I am at the core.

Looking back at it now, I should've trusted Keagan. But you can't change the past. Just remember to never make the same mistake twice. If I ever get another chance...

"Miss Blackwood. Are you with me ma'am?" Agent Santiago interrupts my private thoughts.

"Yes, sir. M-M-My apologies. Please. Continue."

"I need you to tell me everything that went down, from the top. What is your connection with the Cabricci family?"

"Oh, y-yes ... I understand. Can I get a glass of ... of water, p-please?" I'm still shaking and cold from the aftermath.

Keagan walks through the open room. I track him with my whole body, silently praying for a quick glance, anything. I watch as he takes charge and answers questions, never looking my way and acting as if I never existed. It crushes me. Apparently Trident Securities partnered along with the other branches of government to take down the Cabricci family.

Off to my right, Ollie approaches and wraps a blanket around me, then hands me a bottle of water. I half smile up at him, saying thank you with my eyes. I notice immediately that his are full of sorrow and regret. I cringe and look away; I don't need his pity.

"What's all this about? Move out of my way, ya big oaf." I hear her voice before I see her.

Matilda Blackwood is storming into the warehouse full of government officials and demanding a response. "I'm looking for my granddaughter, Jocelyn Blackwood. Someone better show me where she is right this minute. Don't make me ask twice."

My legs are like jello and I can't stand to signal where I am.

"No need for any of that, Mrs. Blackwood." I'm relieved someone stepped up to calm her. "Right this way ma'am. Your granddaughter is over here."

A uniformed policeman comes into view, followed by Grandma. The moment she sees me, I'm encircled into her embrace and tears begin to stream down my face.

"Shh, baby girl. It's alright. I've gotcha. Shh."

Grandma consoles me. I'm a blubbering mess and I really don't care who sees it.

"It's okay, Jocelyn. Grandma's here. I'm gonna take care of everything. Mister...?"

"Agent Santiago, ma'am. Uh, Mrs. Blackwood, Jocelyn was just about to tell me, uh, about what happened." Agent Santiago seems to be stunned at what's happening in front of him. He gets all tongue-tied and misses a few words. If I didn't know any better, I'd be intimidated by Matilda Blackwood too. Although it seems like the nice agent man may have the hots for her, the way his eyes smolder.

"I see. Well, Jocelyn, honey, do you feel like telling this agent what happened?" Grandma asks like it's an option for me to cooperate or not. Black and white. And for a woman of her caliber, maybe it is. "If not, we'll get out of here now and you can deal with all this later."

"It's okay, Grandma. I can do this." My stuttering and shaking finally subsided.

I take a long drink from the water bottle Ollie provided and begin to tell my story, from my knowledge of David being Roman David Cabricci to the unsettling details of what it felt like to be in the grip of Desmond Payne. My tale was told, over, and done.

Grandma took me home to pack a few bags for an extended stay. She wouldn't take no for an answer, and honestly I was fine with it. She took charge and made arrangements. She even made sure Miss Kitty was nice and comfy in her carrier for the trip back to Lakeview. All I had to do was call my secretary Angela to take all my patients off the books for the next month and send them to a presiding doctor I've worked closely with in the past. I needed time off and

Grandma was going to take care of me like always.

Grandma and I chat during the quick flight from Gainesville to Lakeview. My mind is still a mess with all the events of the past few days. The continued soreness in my body worsens by the minute from the fall and tense standoff earlier. My head is hammering hard due to the goose egg on the side of my skull from the fall. But I have questions that need answering.

"Tell me about Fallyn, Grandma. I have to know what happened. I need to know the truth."

"Now, now, Jocelyn. You've been through a terrible ordeal. This is not the time to be stirring up more heartache. Besides, you know we can't talk about this. Some things are better left alone. You just have to trust me, baby girl."

"When I was at the library, David was there." I pause, looking in her eyes for a flicker of recognition. "Did you know his real name? Grandma, you have to tell me. Did you know that he's a part of the Cabricci family?"

Her silence tells me she's not budging on the issue, but knows more than she's letting on. Although when she nods her head in a yes, eagerness sparks and I continue.

"Keagan's men were looking into them. They wouldn't give me much, but your name came up, Grandma. A connection with that family. Why's that? Why would Matilda Blackwood or Matilda Rice have anything to do with a crime family?"

Grandma pales and tucks her head to her chin. She appears nauseous and upset. A feeling of unease and dread pound my heart as I shift uncomfortably in my seat.

"You just won't leave it alone, will you, sunshine?" Shaking her head, her eyes portray the immense pain she can't speak of. "Let me tell you this. You've got to understand a person will do anything to protect the people they hold dear. Absolutely anything. Walk through the fires of hell and greet the Devil himself, if necessary. Will go to great lengths to ensure lives are saved and not broken. I'm no exception, Jocelyn. I can't give you what you want, baby girl. Not today. Maybe one day in the future, but not today." Her eyes speak volumes. She's devastated and sad. "It will all come out in the wash, eventually. Then, I'll tell you everything you want to know. Alright?" She reaches out to touch my hands crossed in my lap. Affectionately, Grandma squeezes them and looks at me with anguish and a tinge of fear in her aging, wise grey eyes.

There's no use as I plead with her to give me something, like I've begged so many times before. And just like always, her answers are cryptic, never shedding light on Fallyn's whereabouts or what happened to her and Harper. So I have to table the discussion for another time.

When we arrive in Lakeview, I'm greeted by an overexcited tween Addie. She came to the private airport to meet us accompanied by a large, very muscled tan man around my age standing patiently beside her. His arms are crossed over his massive chest and a smile peeks out from behind his bearded face, a contradiction to his large frame. California, which is what Grandma calls him, is part of Trident Securities. He is assigned to watch over Addie and Grayson as needed.

"Jo. Oh my goodness. I'm so glad you're here."

She jumps into my awaiting arms as I reluctantly scoop her up. Pain radiates in my body but I cling to her anyway.

"Now, Adalyn Grace Blackwood, be careful. Jocelyn was in an accident earlier and she's hurt." Grandma brokers no argument without disclosing what really happened.

"Gosh, JoJo. I'm really sorry. I didn't mean to." She starts to wiggle and pull away.

"Nonsense. It's all good. So good to see you too, little squirt. I missed you, Addie. I'm relieved you're okay."

Addie grips me tightly in a bear hug. Well, a *cub* hug. I squeeze her hard too.

"Gosh you've grown since I last saw you. You're getting so tall, I might not be able to call you squirt much longer."

I squeeze her one more time before putting her feet back on the ground. I'm grateful she's alive and well. To know that she's out of danger and she's not aware of anything that went down in Gainesville aids to the weariness my soul is carrying around. My body is not very happy with me as I wince and smile. I don't want them to worry about me.

"You wouldn't like that too much, would ya?" Addie eyes me skeptically. "Well, I'm getting bigger every day. Grayson says that soon I'll be able to run as fast as him." She begins to run circles around me, proving her statement. "It's true. See? What do you think, JoJo?"

Grandma's heavenly laugh rings out loudly in the hanger along with mine.

"Wow, squirt. That's amazing! I'm sure you'll be passing Grayson up in no time."

Addie stops running and carefully snuggles up beside me. Wrapping her arms gently around my waist as I hug her shoulders, we continue walking to car where California is patiently waiting, Grandma hot on our heels.

"Happy you finally came home, sister," Sage's voice sings loudly in my ears and stops me short as she appears from behind the giant man.

All else forgotten, I run to Sage and tackle her in a huge hug because I'm so dang excited to see her, aching body out the window. Emotions wrap around us both, a torrential rainstorm finally feeding the parched crops.

"It's been too long, Buttercup," I whisper in her ear, tears leaking from my eyes as she hugs me tightly back. The love is tangible between us both.

"Agreed, JoJo. Don't let it happen again."

The moment is surreal. I've been thirsty for a drink for so very long and seeing my sisters aids to the discomfort and turmoil inside.

"How long will you be here sister?" Sage asks as we all pile into the SUV.

I gingerly sit onto the plush leather seat and lean back, wondering how much time I have until I can take another pain pill. Miss Kitty purrs loudly in Addie's lap. She's in heaven. I wish I felt like that.

"I'm not sure right now, Sage. I really don't have a clue."

"For an undetermined amount of time, baby girl. No time limits, and certainly no worries for a while. You've been through a lot," Grandma's stern, no-holds-barred expression tells us all: no arguing with her.

As if she can read my mind, Grandma gives me another white pill and a bottle of water. Amazing.

"Thanks," I utter to Grandma, then turn to regard Sage with a grin. "There you have it, Buttercup. The *word* has been spoken."

"So commanded, let it be done," Sage replies in a manly, aristocratic type voice and the car erupts in laughter.

I look out the window as the all-familiar streets pass me by. My body is aching from the top of my head to the bottom of my feet. I feel discomfort in places I didn't know existed. Numbness is setting up shop in my brain. The trauma caused by being used as a pawn in the Cabricci family's sick twisted game still wreaks havoc on me. In those brief moments, I didn't know if I would make it out … if I would survive.

We go through the drive-thru of the local ice cream shop. Grandma thought we all needed a little pick-me-up. Ice cream always does the trick. Tastie's Frozen Treats is a city hot spot and one we've frequented for years.

Addie's so excited about the chocolate-dipped cone she's currently devouring. I'm sucking on a straw and immensely enjoying my peanut butter chocolate milkshake.

"What kind did you order again? I know I didn't hear it correctly, Sage."

"Yep, you did. It's called an Elvis Presley. It has bananas, peanut butter, chocolate chunks, coconut, and walnuts all mixed together to make a hunka-hunka burnin' love, thank you very much." Sage offers us her best impression of the King and we all enjoy another bout of giggles.

My sides begin to implore me to put an end to the craziness, but it's taking my mind off of the horrible things that have happened to me. I endure the pain.

Later on, after we've all showered and gotten our PJs on, we lounge around in the TV room watching some comedy show that Grandma is all involved in. Sage and Addie decided to stay for a sleepover. I'm grateful for their love, but I'm tired and need to go to bed.

"Well, call me spent. I'm going to bed, ladies. We'll catch up more tomorrow."

Sage and Addie both stand and we share a group hug.

"Good night, JoJo," they both say.

Grandma puts her arms around me ever so softly and kisses my cheek.

"I love you, baby girl. Sleep well."

"You too. Thank you, Grandma. Thank you for … everything." My broken response is a reminder of all the hell I've been through. Tears begin to leak from the corners of my eyes.

"Nothing to it, sunshine." She lets go of me, staring into my tear-filled vision. "Ya know, tomorrow will be a better day. You're a strong woman, Jocelyn. I know it's gonna take a little time to fix this, but it'll all turn out. Even with that handsome young man who's stolen your heart."

What? How could she possibly know my feelings for Keagan, or anything that happened for that matter? I'm sure the look she receives is one of surprise laced with torment. I shake my head and close my eyes. I need to get it together.

"Okay, Grandma. I'm gonna get some sleep."

"That's good, baby girl. I left your pain pill on the bedside table. Make sure to take it before you go to sleep. Love you."

KEAGAN
(This Is Our Life #2)

She kisses my forehead and sends me on my way.

I wake up in a cold sweat a few hours later, tormented by his face … the mask of disappointment Keagan wore when he walked away along with the treacherous face of Desmond Payne. I shiver at the memory. Rolling over, I take a long drink of the water sitting on the bedside table. Gently, I lay back down and Keagan's beautiful eyes assault me. If he would only have listened to me or what I had to say, maybe he would've understood and not have been so quick to judge me. If he only would listen to the reasons behind the hard choice I made. Something in his past was driving his decision. The thought of how I hurt him sends a burning hot poker straight into my heart again and I can't catch my breath. I begin to inhale short, quick breaths. Before I know it, huge tears and ugly sobs are ripping from my mouth. My entire body is shaking from the onslaught of my sobs.

The bed dips beside me as strong, comforting female arms gather me up. Grandma strokes my hair away from my dripping wet face and hugs me to her.

"Shh, baby girl. I've got you." Grandma proceeds to rock me back and forth. "You're alright. I'm here. Shh."

The last thing I remember is her singing. "You are my sunshine, my only sunshine …"

Roxy's tail is hitting my leg. My girl is happy to be home. She wants to run. She's taken with MacGyver. He treats her like a princess. Somehow mystery bones keep appearing all over the place. He claims to know nothing about them, but I know differently. I pat her head as he shows up in my office.

"Let's go, Roxy girl. I need to stretch my legs."

She waits for my signal and then walks over to MacGyver, nudging his hand, seeking a pat of approval.

"I'm going to my parents for dinner tonight. Should be back later to get her. Thanks for taking her out."

"No prob. She's good company and I need the exercise after sitting in that meeting all day. Damn ass is gonna get big doing that kinda shit all the time," he says as he walks out the doorway with Roxy trailing behind him.

My thoughts turn to Jocelyn when I'm alone. She's back in the View staying at Matilda's place. I get random updates on her from California. I refuse to access the security feed, even knowing the relief that seeing her would provide my soul. The last few months have been a living hell. The nightmares returned, but instead of the soldiers' mutilated bodies that died on my watch, her face appears. Her green eyes, wide, agony painted on her angelic face. Reality check. She's alive and unharmed. And, the brutal truth is, I miss her. I miss holding her close. I miss her rants.

In the small amount of time we spent together, it was enough to change me forever. The expression on her face when she was questioned by Santiago shook me, but when fucking Ollie comforted her, I thought I would kill him until I saw the look he gave her. He was treating her like a sister, providing the comfort she desperately needed that I couldn't give. I'm so fucked up.

I'm so confused. It wasn't my decision to betray the one I cared about. It was hers. And she did it without thinking of the repercussions. She didn't trust me to take care of her or her family. But when it was all said and done, because of me, her family is intact. Unharmed.

I'm going to visit my parents. It's been awhile since I've had a good home-cooked meal. Maw called me last night reminding me of a promise I made a long time ago. No matter how fucked up work was, I would make time for family. She called me on it, and so here I am, pulling up to the ranch style house I spent my high school years in.

Pop is sitting on the front porch steps waiting for me. His embrace delivers the love and acceptance I've always received.

"Keagan, it's damn good to see you, son. Been too long," he greets me, patting me on the back while maneuvering me to the steps.

"Sorry, Pop. I've been out of town on business. Nice to be home for a bit."

"You're looking good on the outside, son. Rested and whole. But your eyes are all together another thing. What's botherin' ya? C'mon, have a seat and tell your pops." He gestures at the steps and sits down.

Even growing up, never could I get away from Pop when he noticed something bugging me. He'd be on me like a tick on the dog. Knowing this could take a while, I reluctantly join him on the steps.

"Where to start …"

"Start at the beginning. You need to get it out, K."

"I think I might've made a huge mistake."

"Hmm. Don't stop there. What kinda mistake?"

"I ran into Jocelyn Blackwood down south."

"Sweet little gal. I remember her well."

"She hasn't changed. Still the same. After all this time."

"You seemed sweet on her in high school. I recall she felt the same 'bout ya."

"Yep. I was her 'not-boyfriend' for a while … at least 'til her sister disappeared. She's a psychologist in

Gainesville. Seems really happy."

"Good for y'all. She's a pretty little thing."

"We had a chance to reconnect, spend time together. It felt … you know, so right."

"Then what's got ya so down, son?"

"A situation occurred and she chose to shut me out. Turned her back on me and put my entire operation in jeopardy. She didn't trust me to handle it. I really thought we had something going on, too."

"You got an idea in that thick noggin' of yours that she betrayed ya, didn't ya?"

"Yes, and for me, I'm not sure I can let it go. You know how I feel about it. That's unforgivable in my book, pop."

"Hell boy, if that was the way of it, you wouldn't be here today."

"You don't understand. She gave away a protected location to a …"

"Were ya able to handle the problem?"

"Yes, but …"

"Was anybody hurt?"

"No, but things coulda gone—"

"You handled the situation, right?"

"Yes, and we were able to find the child sooner than expected because we apprehended a major player in the crime ring, but …"

"Does she know about Afghanistan?"

"No. I haven't told her."

"Well now, then she wouldn't know that ya were

betrayed by someone close. That ya lost all those guys because of it, would she?"

"No. I guess not, but she still chose someone else over me again."

"What were her choices?"

"I'm sure she thought what she did was the better choice. I just wanted her to trust me and she didn't."

"So it's all or nothin' for ya?"

"Nah, Pop."

"Keagan, you can't keep walkin' away from the real problem. It's not just Jocelyn. You haven't forgiven yourself for what happened overseas. 'Til you do, you can't move on."

"Don't wanna talk about this anymore, Pop. Wanna go get supper?"

"I'm not done talkin' to ya. Sit back down and listen to me, son. You holdin' onto all that blame, doesn't make you stronger, just bitter and alone. She made a decision and knew you would be there to help pick up the pieces, right?"

"I don't know. Haven't talked to her."

"Well, I think ya oughta give her the chance to explain. Ain't no time before have I led ya in the wrong direction."

"I read the report. He threatened her Grandma and sister."

"Well, now. That's a little different. Family and all. Put yourself in her shoes, if it was you, what would've ya done?"

"I don't know."

"You've built these walls around ya to keep ya safe from the pain, but they're hurting ya more than you can imagine. Sometimes you've gotta face the facts. It wasn't your fault those men died and *you* lived. It was brutal, horrible, but ya aren't responsible for pullin' the trigger and living. Someone betrayed ya in the worst possible way. Let it go, son. It's eatin' ya up inside. It's time. *Past time*. Forgiving won't make ya weak, it'll set ya free. Then ya might be able to move on and really live. Give Jocelyn a chance. Talk to her. Listen to her. Your future is with that woman."

I'm not sure how I feel anymore other than the fact that I need Jocelyn. She quiets the storm, takes me back to the time when life was simple and easy. She lessens the painful memories. I think about all he's saying. In my heart, I know he's right.

"I'll try to talk to her, Pop. Think that is all I can give right now. Good?"

"Tryin' is half the battle, K. C'mon, I need some of that good grub ya maw was cookin' before ya got here."

Dinner is a chaotic event. Right before we sit down to eat, the rumble of bikes outside announce visitors. Ollie and Lukas show up with MacGyver in tow. Some things don't ever change, and Maw catering to her boys is one of those. Whether they are her sons by birth or choice, she makes everyone feel special. I watch her with MacGyver. Somehow, she knows the longing and acceptance he needs because she dotes on him most of the evening.

Later on, I'm sitting outside sipping a cold one when Maw approaches me. I can tell by the look on her face she's got something on her mind.

"You always were my stubborn child. The one I had to continually nudge when you got your hackles up."

"Where did that come from?" I chuckle. "I thought you said I take after you?"

She mumbles, "More than you know," while brushing away the lint from her pants.

"I'm pretty sure there's more to that statement than you're telling me, Maw. Where's Pop and the guys?"

"I left them playing cards. You know how your pop gets."

"Yeah. He's a little competitive."

"Little? Hmph. More of an obsessive compulsive thing. He won't quit until they do." She looks out over the peaceful hillside at the lightning bugs display.

"I was very surprised to see Jocelyn Blackwood in town the other day with her Grandma. It's been a long time. She was looking at the old Peterman's General Store. Isn't that the one you wanted for Trident offices?"

"Yeah, it was a possibility."

"There's talk about her staying here. Permanently."

"I heard."

"Are you going to see her?"

"I'm thinking about it."

"Take some advice from your mother, Keagan. Don't think too long. That's always been your problem. You just need to act." She pats my leg and returns inside.

I've been mulling her words over in my head for the last hour or so. Have I been thinking too much about why Jocelyn didn't trust me instead of what could've happened—if I wasn't able to lay eyes on her again? The idea of not touching her or seeing her smile overwhelms me. A familiar ache lodges in the pit of my stomach. What would my world be like without Jocelyn?

I *have* been thinking too much. Living in the past. Blaming her for surviving and outsmarting Payne. This isn't her fault. I need to trust my gut. My instinct is to go to her and find a way for us to be together. No more separation. No more guilt. It's time to put the past where it belongs: in the past. It's time to claim my angel. It's time to quit trying to fool myself into believing I can walk away from her, from us, and from what we share.

Fuck, I'm in love with Jocelyn.

CHAPTER 27
Jocelyn

Sitting on the front porch, my coffee cup in hand, I take a deep, calming breath. Miss Kitty is lounging around my feet, asleep and purring loudly. The landscape view is full of the gorgeous lake at the side of my grandma's. My nose is full of the sweet smells of gardenias and honeysuckle. I'm at peace. The birds are chirping their mating calls, along with the gentle sway of the water lapping at the lake shore. My senses are overwhelmed. I'm in awe of how this place swaddles me softly with serenity and peacefulness.

It's been a month since I came back here to Grandma's. I've had lots of time to enjoy this view and think. This is where I've spent most of my time, not wanting to have any run-ins with old friends or the one person who crushes me at the thought. I've become a hermit. My body has healed but my mind is still a mess.

I haven't heard a word from Keagan. I know he's home because his business and home is here in the View. My heart aches from the perpetual misery thoughts of him evoke. He's never far from my mind. But I recognize it's time to move forward.

When he walked away from me at the warehouse,

I shattered into millions of pieces. I fear I'll never be put back together. The coldness in his blue-eyed stare will torment my soul forever. I betrayed him. I didn't trust him enough to help me. I singlehandedly pushed him out of my life again. This time, I've lost him for good. I have no one to blame but me.

Over the past few weeks, I've realized I created the pain for both of us. Will he ever learn to forgive me? At this time, I just don't know the answer. However, I do know that he's hurting wherever he is, whatever he's doing. Keagan carries a burden within him from something in his past that I want to help him bear. It's not up to me, though. He ended what we started.

"You alright, precious girl?"

My grandma sits down in the rocking chair on the porch next to me, leaning over to put her hand on mine. The cool breeze coming off of the lake blows around us.

"Yes, ma'am. I'm good."

"Wonderful, because I've got some news. Want to hear it?"

Grandma waits until I nod my head. She seems really excited, so I try to smile for her.

"Ya know that place up on Main Street, right next to the courthouse? The historic one with the red brick and big beautiful windows across the front?"

"Yes, ma'am. I know the one. It was home to Peterman's General store for years, right? The one you'd take us to on the weekends?"

"The one and the same. Fantastic. You remembered. Of course you would." She beams across at me and her love surrounds us, creating an invisible barrier in which no one can penetrate or hurt us. "Well, the building has sat there vacant for a few years now and I decided it needs some love. So, I bought it."

It's that simple with my grandma. She's constantly ready to take on the world.

"Wow, that's great. It's such an amazing piece of history from this town and a work of art. I hope you're planning on resurrecting the historical elements, too."

"Absolutely, we are."

I know this building pretty well. How could I ever forget it? A red brick three-story structure. Arched glass windows line the first story front, complemented by the curved, vaulted entrance. It's an antiquity of the past when Lakeview was just beginning.

As a child we would frequent the general store with Grandma. She'd take us there because Mr. Peterman was one of the only places left in town that still carried all types of candy in big glass jars which lined one corner section of the store. A child's fantasy. I could take my pick of whatever I wanted. Even sample each one. Grandma would give us a bag to fill with whatever candy we liked. My sister's and I could eat on that candy for a month. But it took us only days. Fun times.

"We? What are you talking about, we?"

"Well, my dear. I've been thinking."

Oh boy, here it comes. Grandma has devised another plan. Taking the bull by its horns and fixing what she feels is broken. Gotta love her!

"Jocelyn. We've already discussed you coming back to Lakeview permanently. Right? We called and spoke with the realtor about selling your house just yesterday."

Grandma looks anxious and I need to calm her. I get the impression this is important to her.

"That's true. But I don't understand what that has to do with buying Peterman's General Store, Grandma."

"Okay, so don't say no until you hear me out. Deal?"

"Okaaaay," I say, the confusion apparent in my voice, but she's got me curious.

"I'm thinking it would be a perfect location to begin your new practice, Jocelyn. Right here in Lakeview. It's centrally located and needs the Jocelyn Blackwood touch to make it perfect." Grandma's face lights up with excitement. "You can gut it down to studs and make it however you like. Maybe rent out office spaces. The sky's the limit. What do you think, sunshine?"

"Grandma, oh my gosh. That's … well, that's incredible."

I pause for a few minutes to gather my thoughts,

overwhelmed by the possibility she's offering. It's just another unbelievable gift my grandma has bestowed upon me during my life—one more beautiful, selfless act from this extraordinary woman.

Is this the sign I've been looking for? Sage and I have had long discussions about me moving back to Lakeview. She's begged me to do it. It would mean so much to her. Mom has visited a few times without dad's supervision and it's been nice. I've also had the opportunity to spend more time with Addie and Grayson. Being around my siblings has stirred up emotions of belonging, like fitting the final pieces in a puzzle I've been working on for years. This would solidify the longing and need I've been feeling since my return, the need for my family that's been missing while I've been absent.

Well, all but one final piece to the family puzzle.

Although, I'm not sure if I can put the past behind me. It will be difficult to move forward in a place that caused tremendous anguish for me when I was younger, a place where Fallyn had to leave. But the past has nothing new to say, so I need to put it away and let it go so I can make my own future. After all, I'm the only one who can.

I've been in my comfort zone for too long. It's time for Jocelyn Blackwood to break out of her shell and do something positively spontaneous. That's exactly what Fallyn would want me to do. And I can do it. This feels right.

I glance back over to Grandma who is sitting quietly watching the ducks splash around on the shore, frolicking playfully. She is waiting patiently as my wheels turn. She understands the need for me to rationalize the decision on my own. I love her more and more every day I spend with her. This is a priceless gift I will treasure always.

"Alright. Let's do it. Why the heck not!"

"That's my girl."

We talk into the night about all the possibilities. Grandma's delightful behavior conveys a woman of passion and devotion for the people she loves. She's also very knowledgeable in the history of Lakeview, so that's a plus as we make plans for the building. For the first time in a long time, I'm stoked about the future. There's a change in the weather, a shift in the atmosphere. I'm finally ready. Jocelyn Blackwood is rising from the ashes as the Phoenix.

* * *

A few weeks later, I'm back on the porch sipping my coffee with Sage. Renovations are moving along smoother than I'd hoped. I just got home from meeting with the painters, floor installers, and the foreman. I picked out the most beautiful shades of green and blue, along with hardwood floors and antique fixtures. All of it has to be ordered. The estimated time of completion is a few more months.

It's good timing for me. I still have to go back to Gainesville and wrap a few things up before my move is final.

"It's all coming together. I love the open ceilings in the foyer between the first and second floor. Not exactly historical, but it adds a certain appeal." I'm animated as I explain all the cool features in my new office.

"I can't wait to see it again. Sounds really beautiful, JoJo."

"Truly. The fixtures they found for all the bathrooms are from the era when the building was first erected. I had to go modern with some things, but overall, I think it's going to be magnificent."

"Of course it is. It has the Jocelyn Blackwood stamp of approval on it."

"Ah, shucks, Buttercup," I say, using my best country twang and my nickname for Sage. "You're makin' me blush."

We giggle and laugh. I've been doing that a lot here lately: smiling at the world more and looking at life more like my cup's half full, not empty.

"So, Jo. You ever gonna talk about what happened? In Gainesville, I mean."

"Nope, little sister. Don't need to, really." My experience with Desmond Payne will always haunt me, but I can't let it rule my life. I still don't have all the answers about the connection with Fallyn and the Cabricci family, but I've laid that burden down for now. Change the things you can and all that jazz. And Keagan Fontneau … well, he's someone I'll always hold close to my heart, whether he's present in my life or not. He at least can't take that away from me. I keep that stuff locked up, though. I don't need any more worrying over me. "I'm turning over a new leaf. Letting the past stay in the past. No more need to drudge it all up when there's nothing I can do to change it."

"Hmph. Really?" She seems unconvinced. "Is something wrong with you, Jo?"

"Ha! I know. Crazy, right? But not at all, Sage." I laugh at her expression, which is one of confusion and humor combined. "It's as simple as a new start for me. A makeover. You know it's time I handled things in a better way than the past anyhow, Buttercup. It just took me a long time to figure that one out. Leaving here was just a Band-Aid."

"You're always so philosophical. Sometimes, I don't understand you." Sage shakes her head and giggles. "I'm proud of you, JoJo. I believe you've actually figured out how to be happy and without any help, no doubt."

My good mood stutters a little as I think about a certain someone.

"I had assistance from many people, Sage. So many who came into my life since I left here after high school and even before. Friends, family." I grab her hand and squeeze. "Even lovers."

As Sage squeezes back, a look of sadness crosses hers.

"What is it? What was that look for?"

"Nothing really." Sage appears confused and hopeful at the same time. "It's just this guy from work," she starts. "No, never mind, we were talking about you, JoJo. We can talk about that later, sister."

"Now you know better than to do that, Sage. There's nothing I'd rather do than discuss a boyfriend with you."

I smile in a dreamy fashion, batting my eyelashes and making kissy noises at her.

"You. Are. Not. Right. Jocelyn Blackwood."

We both burst out laughing and it feels so good to be home. Everything would be right as rain if a certain bald-headed-tattooed-beautifully-sculpted-hurt-by-me man was in my life. My thoughts, as always, turn to Keagan.

"What is it, Jo? We were just laughing our guts up and now you seem so sad. Distant. Where'd you go?"

"I don't know, Sage." I move my head back and forth.

"Come on, Jo. You need to get these things off of your chest. You've always been the one to encourage everyone else to talk about their feelings and blah, blah, blah." Joking, she smirks at me with those rich, amber-colored eyes, her straight coffee-colored hair falling gently off her shoulders.

I inhale deeply, giving in to Sage's request.

"Keagan came back into my life like a hurricane. Stormed in and laid waste. Literally, too. Right in the midst of Hurricane Georgia." I pause to compose my emotions. That's the way things go when I think about him.

"Really? How funny."

"Yeah. It is. But in the brief moments I shared with him, I really thought that Keagan and I had a chance of something more. There was an intense connection. We were creating the perfect storm. It always felt so different with him, ya know?" I glance at Sage and she nods in agreement. "He was my best friend at one time. The little time I got to know the man instead of the boy, I was addicted." *I'm in love with Keagan and always will be.* I leave those words unspoken. "Then I went and blew it all to heck by not trusting him. By not trusting in him."

I just barely catch a noise off in the distance. As if I'd blinked and nodded like Jeannie from *I Dream of Jeannie* to make my wish come true, I hear the noise again and recognize the rumbling of a motorcycle. I gasp for oxygen, drawing deep breaths into my lungs. I jerk my head up and lean my ear toward the sound. The memories of my first motorcycle ride with Keagan ambush me, piercing my heart. It's a fantastical notion or a vain hope to think he would come for me. All this time, he's stayed away. No contact. No response to my texts or phone calls. I just gave up hope. I'm sure Sage is looking at me, thinking

I've finally lost it.

The rumble of a motorcycle gets closer and I look to the bend in the road and wait. Can this really be happening? It's not long before I see him. Keagan smoothly glides around the corner on Black Beauty and my body tingles in anticipation.

He stops in the driveway and looks my way. I'm anchored to the rocker. I can't move or speak. My eyes drink him in as he sits there like he's waiting for someone.

Finally, my wait is over. Keagan addresses me, causing my insides to melt into a puddle.

"C'mere, *m'aingeal*. Don't keep me waiting."

CHAPTER 28
KEAGAN

For me, all paths led to Jocelyn Blackwood. I've known it all along. From the moment I laid eyes on her all those years ago, I've known we would somehow end up at this juncture in our lives. Even the times we went our separate ways, I knew. When my heart was cold, harden from life's trials, she broke the chains around my heart and replaced them with her light. The mission I'm on today is the most important one of my life: to secure a future with my angel.

Coming around the bend, the sight that greets me has my heart beating fast. I slow down in front of Matilda's house. She's standing only a few feet away. My eyes soak her in, from the wealth of curls on top of her head to the trademark boots on the bottom of her feet. The shock and uncertainty in her gaze undo me.

"C'mere, *m'aingeal*. Don't keep me waiting, Jocelyn."

I extend my hand towards her and wait for her to decide. She doesn't move or make a sound.

"Trust me."

She quirks her eyebrow, questioning. The next little while seems to be some of the longest minutes in my life, but I patiently stay where I'm at, allowing her to choose. There's a possibility she could turn around and walk out of my life, not give me a chance to explain, just wash her hands clean of me. Or, she could take a chance and place her hand in mine. Either way, it's her decision to make.

Seconds later, she takes my hand and climbs onto the back of the bike. I wait only long enough for her to secure the helmet on her head. When her arms wrap tightly around my middle, I accelerate and pull away, not giving her the chance to change her mind.

This feels so right. My angel. She's where she belongs.

We can't go back to my place. Too many people go in and out and there's no privacy. I'll have to do something about that soon, *if* things go the way I have planned. The bike picks up speed as we head out of the View towards the river and my pop's fishing cabin. We should have plenty of peace and quiet there. It's a little rustic, but the conveniences are covered.

We've been on the road for about fifteen minutes when I spot the dirt road that leads to the camp. Slowing down, I turn in and Jocelyn's head lifts from the middle of my back. The road winds for a stretch and then the cabin comes into view. It's not much, but it'll do for the privacy factor. I stop the bike and help her off. She's busy looking around.

"Where are we?"

"My pop's fishing camp."

"This is where you used to go?"

"Yep. His boat is around back."

"Why are we here?"

"We needed somewhere nobody would interrupt us. I share my place with the guys and I wanted to be alone with you."

"Hmmm."

"C'mon, let's get inside and we can talk."

I hold her hand and walk up the steps to the door. Bending down, I find the rock with the hidden key and unlock the door. Gesturing her inside, I replace the key and shut the door. The musty smell greets me, so I open a few windows. Jocelyn's walking around the one-room cabin taking in everything.

I walk up behind her and place my hands on her shoulders. She turns and I can't help myself from devouring her. I lower my lips, finding hers. Months of longing and need are exchanged in that moment.

"We gotta talk," I say, but I continue to kiss her.

"Yes, we need to talk ..." she murmurs, pulling me closer.

"Angel, we need ..."

"Shh ... Keagan, we need this more."

"But, angel ..."

Her tongue enters my mouth and nothing else matters. She's aggressive, taking what she wants from me. Her hands linger on the back of my neck before her nails slide down to my shoulders, scoring my flesh as she goes.

"Fuck, Jocelyn. What are you doing?" I ask in a husky voice, pressing my already hardening cock into the cradle of her hips.

She pushes her breasts into me and nips at the column of my neck. All the blood in my body rushes south. She's turning me on fast.

Jocelyn suddenly stops.

"Get your clothes off, Keagan. Undress. Now," she hastily demands while removing her top and throwing it on a nearby chair. "It's been months and I want you."

No better words have ever been said. I quickly strip off the t-shirt, toe the riding boots, and unbutton and push down my jeans. Her progress halts. She's watching me. Her eyes feast on my cock as I straighten up. It jerks in response to her attention. She saunters my way with a delicate smile gracing her beautiful face. Pink finger nails rake down my chest and pass my belly button to grab my throbbing member.

"*M'aingeal*," I murmur. "That feels heavenly."

She licks my nipple, sucks the pebbled flesh, and kisses a path to the other one waiting for her ministration. She works it into her mouth and it hardens in response.

"You're killing me, Boo."

"I've only just started," she says in a throaty tone

as she continues a downward path, stopping to kiss and bathe every scar with her moist lips and warm tongue once again. Healing me from the outside in. She nips my belly button teasing me before inching her body lower. Warm breath taunts the swelling crown of my cock, then seconds later her tongue rubs over it. Her fingers curl around the bottom of my shaft, pumping.

My knees weaken in reaction to her. Before I can respond, she takes all of me to the back of her throat. Groaning, I grab her hair, blocking my view from the sensual act, and concentrate on the desire building between us.

The urge to move overcomes me. I rock slowly into her. The sense for more of her surges through me.

"C'mere, Jocelyn. Need to hold you, Boo."

She doesn't resist. She recognizes the urgency in my voice. I gently wrap her body to mine. This precious gift she's unconditionally giving astounds me. The stone walls I built to protect me from pain, she is removing them one brick at a time. I'm stronger because of her. I'm alive because of her. I'm in love because of her.

The desire to become one with her drives me forward to the bed. Gently resting her body down, I remove the last of her clothing. Our eyes never waiver. They remain connected, igniting the passion we both feel.

"It's been weeks since I've felt you. Touched

you."

"Too long," she whispers.

I position myself above her. My eyes roam up and down her delectable body. Her perky breasts beckon for attention as they rise and fall with her accelerated breathing. I cup one in my hand and caress the pink tip with my thumb. A moan escapes her lips when my teeth connect with the other one. Delicious. Heaven.

My name escapes her lips when I suck the tiny morsel into my mouth.

"You taste so good, *cher*."

I tease and taunt her until the erect tip is red and swollen and the other is begging for the same. Adjusting, I give it all the consideration it needs. She squirms and pulls my head closer when my fingers find the treasure nestled at the apex of her thighs. Achingly slow, two digits enter her.

A piercing cry escapes her wet lips. "Oh, god!"

"That's it, angel. I wanna hear you scream."

My thumb circles her nub and she jerks, her hips lifting in motion, searching for relief from the building pleasure. Her pussy clamps down on my fingers. The feeling has me moving lower. Moisture collects on my fingers, sucking me in. My tongue connects briefly with her sweetness.

"Mmm. So good. So mine."

I lose myself in her. The pleasure intensifies as her knees bump against my head trying to close. I reposition my arms over her thighs and apply pressure. She's open and at the mercy of my tongue. I give her none. I devour every inch of her until she's screaming my name over and over again from the intense release coursing through her body. The muscle in her vagina squeezes my fingers as tremors continue to pulse from her.

My breathing is erratic as I crawl up her body and position myself in the middle of her thighs. I crave her. My throbbing cock aching, needing to feel her tightness wrapped around me.

She blinks and focuses her sparkling emeralds on me. I'm lost in her. Eyes locked. Time stands still.

"*M'aingeal.* From this moment on, I'm never letting you go. I need you, angel. Not gonna live without you."

I bare my heart and soul to her. She completes me and makes me whole. Her mouth forms into an O as understanding flickers in the depths of her eyes.

"I love you, Jocelyn. When I first met you, I honestly didn't know you were gonna be this important to me, but I think … I think somewhere deep inside of me, I've been in love with you from the moment I first saw you."

I seal my declaration with a scorching kiss and press into her welcoming warmth.

Heaven and Hell. Heaven surrounds my cock. *She's my angel.* Hell because my body's on fire and will soon succumb to the flames. I don't want this feeling to end. The intense ecstasy flowing through my body only increases when my hips slowly glide backwards and I drive into her hot, tight body.

Paradise. Bliss. The feeling of her fingers scoring my back as I thrust into her time and time again amps up the pleasure coursing through my veins. I'm an adrenaline junkie and she's the high I'm soaring on. I know I'm crazy and possibly blind, but I'm in love with an angel. She's demolished the walls around my heart, replacing them with a connection so complete and right.

She slightly adjusts her hips, taking me deeper. I slow down, drawing out the blissful feeling encompassing us. We are in our own world. The torture continues, and we cling to the drunken feeling, happy we are together.

The erotic display of her flushed cheeks and moans heighten my passion. I grip her leg and slide my thumb over her nub, drawing circles. Her pussy clenches and massages my thick girth. I lose all semblance of control, driving faster into her. Our bodies move in sync as we ride the high of pleasure.

I'm addicted to the sounds she makes as we climb towards bliss. Tremors swamp me as her climax hits. She screams my name as pleasure washes over her. I thrust once more and throw my head back, yelling her name, shaking from the intense pleasure of her muscle embracing me. The moment is already etched in my memory.

"I love you, angel. Forever."

"Forever. I love you, Keagan."

I kiss her brow. A smile escapes me. Little did I know, that night in the eye of the storm, that the precious woman I'm holding in my arms would heal the pain and save my soul. But she did. The course of true love never did run smooth. Many paths are stormy, turbulent. Highs and lows, just like the weather. But in the end, we are just blessed we found each other again.

CHAPTER 29
Jocelyn

I'm in the most perfect place on the planet: Keagan's strong, solid arms. Aside from the fish smell and small musty space, which isn't too bad, I couldn't be happier. I never thought I'd get this opportunity again, but here we are, wrapped up together on the small bed in the middle of the woods. And I'm not going to waste a moment of it.

Everything got a little out of hand earlier. One kiss led to another and in the end, it was epic. Keagan was tender and loved me as if I was his greatest treasure. I loved him back with every fiber of my being. Like every time before with this incredible man, it leaves me wanting more. My head was screaming for him to slow down. I knew we should discuss how things went in Gainesville first. We needed to figure out what was going to happen between us. I just couldn't seem to care the moment his lips touched mine. My body was demanding the satisfaction that only Keagan could fulfill. I'd missed him so desperately.

It was a homecoming, a mutual understanding of souls uniting, an intense forever kind of bond formed between two people madly in love with one another.

Yes, in love. Keagan Fontneau is in love with me. I'm walking on the clouds.

Unfortunately, now with the urgent need to be with each other sated, it's time for us to talk.

"Ready for our talk, angel? Yeah?"

I feel the deep vibrations of him speaking through his chest where my chin is resting. It causes a rush of excitement inside me. I want him again even after what we just shared. Will I ever get enough? Nope. I have to be a good girl, though, so I smile.

"Yes, I need to explain what happened." I take a deep inhale and continue. "I want you to understand why I made the choice, Keagan. I never wanted to hurt you." I gaze into his beautiful blue eyes as tears form in mine. "When Desmond approached me the day before all that happened at the warehouse, I was so sick, Keagan." I roll over on my back, grabbing his big hand with my smaller one and bringing it to my chest, clutching tightly and using it as an anchor to keep me grounded for what I'm about to say. This time, he won't walk away.

Keagan turns onto his side, using his other hand to prop his head up, watching me. "I'm listening, Boo. Go on."

"Whew, okay." My anxiety spikes, but I press on. "So, when Desmond mentioned hurting the teens— you know, the ones from the case I was working on? And his stepchildren, at that—I got so scared. Then he went and threatened Addie. I couldn't take the chance,

Keagan." I look over to see if he's paying attention, gaging his reaction. "I knew that you had an ongoing case and it somehow tied to Desmond, but I also knew it was centered around a baby. I just really felt it wasn't related." I pause to observe his expression. He's listening intently. His face portrays a man of resolution.

"I didn't give ya any reason to trust me with it, Jo. I get it. Your family's important. Besides, even though we had a history, this ..." He uses his pointer finger to wiggle between us because I'm clutching to his hand for dear life. "This was still new for both of us."

Nodding, I understand his meaning. We cared for each other, but the physical side of our relationship was just beginning. I continue with my story. "I received a call from Calista that night. You had already left. She was frantic about her kids. Well, I had to help her. You know how I feel about the kids, Keagan."

"I know, angel." He rubs his thumb against my fisted hands.

"At the library when Da—I mean *Roman*—walked out, and Calista was spouting her nonsense, I was so confused. I was set up. Somehow I'd been had. With all the knowledge and training, I didn't see it coming, all because of something they think my family took from them. I still don't understand that one."

"Yeah. Threw us all for a loop too, angel. Still

tryin' to figure that one out."

"At the warehouse when Desmond was holding me there, I wasn't sure if I was gonna make it or not. I saw you standing there. Like an avenging angel. You were majestic and all bad to the bone. And all I could think about was how you would feel if I didn't survive. I didn't want to cause you any more pain, Keagan."

Tears begin to spill and I roll into Keagan's neck to tuck my face away.

"It's okay, angel. Don't cry. I've gotcha."

I feel like I'm on a rollercoaster going one hundred miles an hour waiting for an end that never comes. I'm ready to get off this ride. I gaze up into his crystal blue eyes. The golden flecks play peek-a-boo with me. He caresses my cheek, his thumb stroking my bottom lip. Keagan leans in and nips said lip, then slides his tongue on top to soothe it. This man knows just how to redirect the situation.

"C'mere." He scoops me up on top of him. As he rubs circles with his nimble fingers, I calm down. "Ya know somethin', angel? I understand. You had a tough call to make. Either way, it wouldn't be easy."

I sigh in relief. He's going to forgive me, finally. Thank goodness. We're going to be okay. But that must mean …

"Keagan. Will you tell me?"

"Anything, Boo."

I slide halfway off him and reach down to his

stomach and stoke the scars that live there. His breath hitches and I worry I've gone too far. A few minutes pass until he speaks.

"At the very end of my last tour, we were ambushed." His voice carries just above a whisper, so I listen carefully so as not to miss anything. "Out in the middle of the desert with no backup, no way out." He closes his eyes, reliving a painful past that's the source of his anguish. "You see, Boo, I was the team leader. I led some of those men to their death that day. I was the last one standing and that wasn't for long."

Hugging him tightly in my grip, I pour all my love into him, hoping that he can feel it passing from me into him, trusting that he knows I'll carry this burden with him now.

"I'm so sorry, Keagan. That must've been awful. I can't even imagine."

"True. I hope you never have go through somethin' like that, Jocelyn. I won't ever let that happen to you. With my last breath." He kisses my forehead and sighs a heavy breath. "The worst part was, I couldn't do a fucking thing about it. Ollie and Lukas lay there badly wounded. And I wasn't sure if they were dead or alive. The other men who followed my order that day were scattered around us in parts and pieces. A sight I rarely go a day not thinkin' about."

I'm shocked by his admission. I knew it was bad, but the responsibility he carries around for those men who died … it's horrific.

"The kicker is, Jocelyn, the man who betrayed me is out there somewhere. Still breathin'. Takin' up space. We were betrayed by an unknown face in a godforsaken land." His voice is trembling, full of rage and emotion.

My throat clogs up. I'm humbled by his trust in me and I want him to know it.

"No one has ever really seen me, Keagan. Never really saw the real me, Jocelyn Blackwood … until you. Someone once told me true love is recognizing a person's faults and loving them even more for it. That's the way you make me feel. I love you, Keagan." I place a gentle kiss on his lips, sipping and tugging, hoping that he can taste my love. Lifting up again, I say, "Thank you for sharing your pain with me. Now I can help you carry it."

"*M'aingeal*. Love you so much."

He captures my lips as his hands delve into my hair, pulling me closer to him and back on top. We tangle up for a few more minutes.

He looks up at me. "You chase my demons, angel. Can't live without you." He dives in for more and I respond in kind.

"Keagan," his name utters across my lips as he kisses my neck and ear, paying special attention to the sweet spot there. I squirm and wiggle on top of his hard body as his cock hardens between my legs. Want and need pursue my thoughts, making my body sing and tingle in its wake. But there is still so much I have to say.

"I want ya to know, angel, I will never again let you fall behind. I will always come for you. Even if I have to carry you the rest of the way. We're a team, you and me. And I know I can't make it without ya. You're everything to me. I won't live another day, another moment without you in it."

I'm conquered by his words, this beautiful man whose rough and tough exterior has completely captured my heart and soul.

"Say you'll be mine forever, Keagan. I want you to be mine for always. No more take backs, no more second guesses." I stare deeply into his eyes. "You are mine and I am yours, forever."

"Let me show you somethin', angel." Keagan gets up and fishes something from his jean pocket he was wearing earlier. "Here."

He hands me a small gold coin embossed with the letter K. It looks worn and tarnished, but as I flip it over I can still make out the words. "Never give up. Always believe" is inscribed on the back.

"Oh my gosh, Keagan, you kept it. All these years."

In this moment, I'm humbled even more by the truth of what Keagan's showing me. After all this time, he was thinking of me. He carried a piece of me with him everywhere he went after he left Lakeview all those years ago. Tears fall freely and unashamed.

This powerful man is sentimental and now I know: I'm his treasure.

"Yeah. I did. Many a night, it kept me sane. Thinkin' about you. What ya might be doin'. I never gave up hope that I'd see you again one day, angel. Even if it was for a moment."

He lies back down with me on the bed, nestling his arms around me and placing me against his chest as I look upon the coin I gifted him long ago.

"I kept your earrings, too, ya know. You've always had a special place in my heart, Keagan."

"I'm never ever letting you go, Jocelyn."

"Good, because you're stuck with me, forever."

EPILOGUE
Jocelyn

They say you can only fall in love once, but that can't be true, because every time I look at Keagan Fontneau, I fall in love over and over again.

True love is handing someone the power to destroy you, but trusting them not to. I trust Keagan with my life.

Another hurricane season has come and gone since Keagan and I worked things out. A year of blissful happiness. Shortly after we got back together, I decided to give Keagan the top two floors of my new office building for Trident Securities. I certainly didn't need the whole building to myself, and it was nice knowing he'd be right above me, watching over me. My life couldn't be more perfect.

Currently, I'm on the back of Black Beauty. My new favorite place. Keagan is speeding down old ninety-eight. He's taking me to the beach. A quick trip, but one we do weekly. One of our favorite spots. A secluded beach where we've spent many afternoons and evenings enjoying the surf and each other.

The wind is whipping around us, cocooning the both of us in its salty sweetness. The sun is making its way to the horizon. Another day will be closing in a few hours. This is my new cherished time of the day.

The view of the ocean unearths memories of a past that shaped my future. I recognize a storm is brewing. Dark ominous clouds are scattered over the water. The waves are crashing violently on the shore giving way to a disturbance in the Gulf.

Keagan pulls up to Paradise Beach and I notice more cars are parked than usual. I glance over by the water and that's when I see them.

Grandma, Sage, and Katrina are beaming rays towards me. What's going on? Keagan's Mom and Pop are standing next to them. I also see MacGyver and Lukas waiting.

The engine cuts off and I tug on Keagan's leather jacket.

"Why is everyone here at our beach, Keagan? What's going on?"

He gets down on one knee and my whole world explodes into fireworks. My dreams come true as he speaks the most beautiful words.

"Need you in my life, angel. Forever."

Today is the beginning of a new life. My life with Jocelyn. The salty air from the Gulf of Mexico permeates through my senses. My Boo is on the back of Black Beauty securely wrapped around me with her body pressing against my back. I have a surprise for her. Let's hope she doesn't do bodily harm. Ollie and Lukas think she might protest, but they don't know her like I do.

We arrive at Paradise Beach. Matilda, Sage, and my parents are waiting. I cut the engine and get off. Jocelyn turns as I go down on a knee and hold her hand. She gasps.

"Need you in my life, angel. Forever."

I remove the ring from my pocket and hold it out for her to take.

"Today, I want the world to know you are mine. Wanna make it official. Just you and me. Marry me?"

"Oh, Keagan. I … I don't know what to think … Today? Really?"

"A wise woman told me once to stop overthinking and just act. I think you should take her advice, angel, and marry me."

She smiles. "Yes, Keagan. I'll marry you!"

I lift her into my arms and twirl her around, kissing her.

"You've made me the happiest man in the world. Let's do this."

Her eyebrow quirks. "Let's do this? Um. Not exactly the right way to say it, do you think?"

I chuckle. "Knew I would get ya riled. Just don't want you changing your mind."

Later that afternoon, I'm staring into the eyes of my wife, Jocelyn Blackwood Fontneau. It's official. I captured an angel.

My cell phone vibrates in my pocket. Seeing the number, I answer.

"Talk to me. Okay. Hmm … Yeah. Keep me posted … Thanks."

Hanging up, Jocelyn's gaze is plastered to mine.

Leaning over to her ear, I whisper, "He found them. He found Fallyn and Harper."

EPILOGUE
Jocelyn

Several Years Later.

Today, we're all going fishing at Grandma's house. Keagan's going to teach some of us how to fish. Should be lots of fun. Grandma's cooking a big spread of all our favorite country foods. Momma's bringing her famous strawberry shortcake. Can't wait for a bite of that.

Right now, I'm gifted with the most beautiful sight on the planet: Fallyn and Harper laughing and having fun, carefree and home.

"Harper, honeypot. Don't get too close to the water, ya hear?" Grandma's voice is laced with concern. I know because I feel it too. We don't want to take any chances since we found them; we don't want to lose them ever again.

"Yes ma'am, Grandma. I'll be careful," Harper replies.

The breeze is light today and I catch a smell that makes me all warm inside, an all-familiar scent that captured me long, long ago. It's one of home, love, and ultimate satisfaction.

My husband.

KEAGAN
(This Is Our Life #2)

I glance over and coming towards me is the most beautiful man I've ever laid eyes on. He's carrying two cups and heading my way. His handsome suntanned head glistens off the majestic water encompassing our surroundings. He has on his old holey jeans and biker boots with a snug baby blue t-shirt that makes his aquamarine eyes pop, eyes that I have personally gotten lost in countless times. My Keagan.

Leaning into me, he places a gentle kiss on my lips. "Hey, angel. I brought you some tea. You feelin' alright?"

He's smirking as he hands me my cup. Not the sexy Keagan smile, but a smile that says "I'm the man and my world is awesome". Since I found out I was pregnant, he's doted all over me. I love it. Would never have believed I could love him more, but I do each and every day.

He sits down on the chair right beside me, grabbing my hand in his. We sit in silence for a spell, just enjoying the beauty of the lake and watching everyone laugh and carry on. Our family is happy. All is right in our little world.

"Hey, JoJo. You gonna sit there all day or are we gonna fish? Keagan, you're supposed to be the master fisherman, am I right?"

The beautiful sounds of my sister Fallyn laughing and making jokes sends a bolt of love straight to my heart. Fallyn and Harper are back home where they belong.

"Yeah, Uncle K. What's the deal? I thought you were gonna show me how to fish!" Harper's angelic voice sings loudly around the lakeside and I smile up at my husband.

"That's right, big brother, you're supposed to show us what to do," Addie's singsong voice sounds off, full of laughter and joy.

"I need you to show me a thing or two bro, come on. Let's catch some fish. I'm hungry," Grayson chimes in.

"You better get going, Mr. Fontneau. The masses are waiting." I laugh and he nips at my lips before he makes his way to the water.

"Love you, Boo," he hollers behind him.

I smile with my whole body. This is what life is all about.

Fallyn walks over and sits down in the seat Keagan vacated. "Keagan Fontneau ... I knew there was something about him when we first met him in school. Ya did good, JoJo."

"Thanks, Care Bear. I did." She grips my hand and our eyes collide. "I'm glad you're home where you belong, Fallyn."

"Me too. Thanks for never giving up. I told you everything was gonna be fine." She squeezes my hand just as Harper lands a huge fish on her line.

"Oh my gosh, oh my gosh. Momma, come here quick," Harper calls out.

I watch Fallyn take off to be with Harper. I look over to see Keagan watching me again, his eyes boring holes into my soul.

Keagan and I made it. We survived the storm. I can't even imagine my life without this man. It didn't come easy for us. Life has not always been so kind. However, through it all, we weathered the rough tempest together. It just goes to show that anything is possible. On our journey, there were so many bumps in the road. Some of them, I thought we would never recover from. But I'm a believer in the power of love and soul mates. Keagan is my soul mate, the Yin to my Yang, the one person in the world who sees me.

This is our story. This is our life, our love, and how we got to this moment in time. Beside my best friend, my lover, my everything.

THE END

Other books by F.G. Adams

This is Our Life series:
Grayson: Book 1

And coming soon...
Oliver: Book 3
Lukas: Book 4
Styx: Book 4.5

The Enchanted Immortals Trilogy:
Book 1: Aldin's Wish

And coming soon...
Book 2: Fox's Awakening
Book 3: Marcus' Vengeance

About The Author

F.G. Adams writes contemporary and paranormal romance about sexy alpha heroes and feisty-mouthed heroines. The wonder twin sisters forming F.G. enjoy a healthy obsession of reading that started at a young age. Their books reflect an avid imagination that was cultivated by their grandmother who taught them the mind has no limits and to use both hands when reaching for the stars. Partners in writing, they both thrive on creating unique storylines for you, the reader, to enjoy.

When not writing, you can find them on a beach with their significant other enjoying the waves or riding a Harley on a country road somewhere in the USA.

Tell Us What You Think. Please leave a review. We enjoy hearing reader opinions about our books.

You can find us at...

Website:	www.authorfgadams.com
Facebook:	www.facebook.com/AuthorFGAdams
Goodreads:	www.goodreads.com/FGAdams
Twitter:	twitter.com/authorfgadams
Newsletter:	http://eepurl.com/bRThVb
Pinterest:	www.pinterest.com/authorfgadams

ACKNOWLEDGEMENTS

First, we would like to thank our husbands for their never-give-up attitudes. For understanding the endless days of take-out, dirty laundry and short-answer conversations while we write. Your ideas, suggestions, and never-ending support goes to show that happily-ever-after happens outside of a book. Thanks for being awesome!

Our Street Team full of fabulous ladies and Erin our right-hand gal, thank you so much for everything. We use those words because we wouldn't be writing another book without all that you do for us. Chance brought you ladies into our life and we so grateful to be able to call you our friends.

Feisty Flock...you ladies are awesome. Your support is truly appreciated and we love you, all! Thank you for your endless dedication in helping to share and support our books.

KEAGAN
(This Is Our Life #2)

Thank you Daryl Banner for your editing and formatting expertise and taking on the dynamic duo. Twice the edits ... twice the fun. Your endless patience and dedication to our cause contributed to making Keagan not just a good book, but a great one. We love you.

Thanks to Mayhem Cover Creations for bringing our vision to life and creating a badass cover. You listened and created a beautiful work of art.

To our cover model, Alfie Gordillo, you are the perfect Keagan. Also, Reggie Deanching and his beautiful skill for creating stunning photographs. Thank you both.

Our new found friends from PCB, thank you for sharing your wisdom and words…and your home with us. You rock!

Thank you to our dear friend, the amazing Stephanie. Lady, you are the boss. We love you and appreciate everything you've done and continue to do to help us.

To all the bloggers and readers: Thanks for taking a chance and reading our book. After all, we wouldn't be here without you!

This story was truly a labor of love. It was a transformation for both of us, in the fact that we grew so much while writing this book. Putting Keagan and Jocelyn's story into words was therapeutic. The undercurrents of abuse, forever love, and people who are lost to us, brings to light that anything is possible, if we just believe. We hope you enjoy it.

xoxo
F.G. Adams